Two Moon Bay

A two moon bay mystery

Book One

Alyssa Johnson

ISBN: 1542303990
ISBN 13: 9781542303996
Library of Congress Control Number: 2017900028
CreateSpace Independent Publishing Platform
North Charleston, South Carolina

For Mom and Dad

Table of Contents

1

Pity Party for One

I lifted my head above the fish bowl-sized margarita in which I attempted to drown my sorrows and glared at my best friend. "What do you *mean* I can't move there?" I wailed, slurring a little. My voice was rising to levels that only dogs could hear.

As if on cue, my golden retriever, Raegan, who was sprawled, unconsciously, of course, before the fireplace, woke just long enough to give me an inquisitive look. He apparently decided it wasn't worth the effort, though, for he promptly closed his eyes and returned to his nap.

Sipping from my pink bendy straw, I groaned. This was, without a doubt, the worst day of my life; my marriage had ended, my fortieth birthday loomed like certain death, and I seemed to be making a host of bad choices when it came to planning my new and uncertain future.

Regrettable decision number one: Quitting the job I'd held (and loved) for the past thirteen years. The logic behind this one? Since my marriage was over, I figured I needed to do something different with my life, something more "meaningful."

Regrettable decision number two: Buying a beach house on the southern Gulf Coast of Florida — in a town I'd never even heard of! Reasoning? The house was a great deal, a real don't-pass-this-up kind of opportunity. I further justified this decision by convincing myself I would fix it up while finishing the manuscript I'd shut away in a drawer ten years ago. Mmm-hmm.

And then there was regrettable decision number three: Thinking that the first two decisions were *actually* good ideas!

The more I thought about it, the more worked up I got. A trail of uncertainties ran through my mind like headlines on a news ticker. What if I'd been *wrong*? What if leaving my home and job to start a new life was a big mistake? What if the money from my divorce settlement wasn't *actually* enough to live on while I worked on my novel? *And*, when it was finished, what if no one wanted to publish it?

Anxiety welled up inside me as a swarm of ugly doubts pitched a tent in my mind and made camp for a while. To top it all off, I had a thirty-year mortgage-sized case of buyer's remorse. Gazing into my glass, I swallowed the lump of dread that clogged my throat.

I stared at Britlee, my hang-dog eyes seeking her clever counsel. Brit gave the *best* advice. I just knew she would make me feel better; she *had* to. It was her sworn duty as my best friend. "Brit," I began, pausing to calm my racing heart. "Please tell me I made the right decision. I mean — I already made an offer." I paused as the gravity of my situation sank in. "And it was *accepted!*"

Omigod, I thought wildly, hearing how terrifying it sounded, even to me. I *had* made a huge mistake! Letting out a mournful moan, I resolved that there was only one thing to do — keep drinking. Fumbling for my straw, I wondered if there was a faster way to speed the liquid solace into my system.

Britlee's sugar-sweet Southern accent broke into my thoughts as I slurped up my fate. "Now, wait a minute, wait just a minute," she replied, looking over her shoulder at me. She was seated at my writing desk, facing the massive window with a view of the mountain beyond. "I didn't say you *can't* move there. I said I can't *believe* you're movin' there!"

I groaned, taking a gulp without lifting my head. The sticky beverage dribbled down my chin. Not one of my proudest moments. "Oh, but that's even worse!" I managed to cry out, carelessly swiping at my mouth with the back of my hand.

Who was I kidding anyway? My life was over. I could walk around with a permanent margarita mustache if I wanted to and no one would complain. Certainly not Raegan, I thought, eyeing my sleeping retriever. Well, maybe Brit would. She was kind of particular about things like that.

Then, snapping back to reality, I realized with renewed alarm that I was in the middle of bemoaning my huge mistake. "Oh, Brit," I slurred. "What have I done?"

But rather than launching into the reassuring diatribe I was expecting, Brit was oddly silent.

"Um, hello?" I muttered to myself, taking a nice big gulp of booze. What could she possibly be *doing*, I wondered, baffled that she wasn't leaping at the chance to indulge me and join my pity party. Being silent in *any* situation was highly unlike her. Slurping up the last of my drink, I gazed around the room, seeking both the pitcher of refills and my friend's much-needed cheer. "Brit?"

Blinking to clear the haze, my eyes settled on the carafe we'd mixed just moments ago — or maybe it was hours — who could tell? I vaguely remembered pouring my first drink after my morning coffee, when the mail lady had brought the piece of paper that meant my life was changing whether I wanted it to or not. Now it was official — I was *actually* that which I feared most — a single woman on the verge of her fortieth birthday. Oh, my freaking . . .

"Brit?" I pushed myself back from the old crate coffee table, retrieved my glass, and hobbled across the room to my desk.

Peering over her shoulder, I could see Britlee's reflection in the window. Her face was keen with interest as she stared at the computer screen, lounging in my favorite chair. Much to my annoyance, she was completely absorbed in whatever she was reading. How dare she not commiserate with me!

Determined to get her attention, I put on what turned out to be a completely pitiful spectacle. "Yo — Brit," I mumbled, sloshing a refill into my glass. "Over here," I drawled, snapping my fingers. My feet somehow weren't as in sync with my balance as I would have hoped, and I stumbled around, more concerned with not spilling my drink than with falling. Deciding that maybe I should sit, I made my way over to the bar stools. I half-sat, half-fell into one, trying to look like I'd planned it that way.

Suddenly, Britlee slid to her right, crying out, "Hey, watch it!"

Wondering what I could possibly have done, I put down my glass. "Huh?"

She leaped from the chair, tossing her cocktail napkin on the edge of the desk as a river of liquid spilled onto the floor. "Hand me those towels over there." She pointed to the dish cloths that lay atop the pine bar behind me.

Fumbling for the towels, I handed them to her, somehow managing to spill more of my drink on the floor.

Cleaning up the messes, Britlee shot me one of her disapproving looks. She reached wordlessly for my cup, grasping it with both hands. She didn't say anything, but with those eyes, she didn't need to.

"Sorry, Mom," I muttered sarcastically, not even bothering to fight for my drink. I was drunk, not stupid. I needed that drink like I needed another pair of Jimmy Choos in my shoe addiction — er, collection.

Going back to my desk, Britlee unplugged the battery cable from the back of my laptop and spun around to face me. Carting the computer over to the coffee table, she plunked down, faced me, and began to read aloud: "'The legend of Two Moon Bay, the safest inlet on Florida's southern Gulf Coast . . .'" She paused, arching her eyebrows, her brown eyes intrigued. "This place sounds just positively *adorable*! I might have to retract my earlier statement."

Rolling my eyes, I realized that leaning back against the bar took way more coordination than I currently possessed, so I shuffled my way back to the couch. I flopped into the deep cushions as she continued, "'Blackheart Bellacroix, the most ruthless pirate of the 1700s, pillaged ships and plundered the seas off the Florida coast for many years. Known for his cruelty, the notorious captain's life was forever changed, however, upon sailing into Two Moon Bay. On Christmas Eve, 1745, it is told that the ruthless pirate's 'black heart' began to beat with love as his eyes fell upon the ethereal image of the town's most coveted young woman, Destina Delgado.

"'The daughter of a wealthy merchant, Destina had a willful, rebellious spirit. Angry at her father's insistence on marrying her into a powerful Spanish family, she fled his mansion atop the bluff that overlooked the bay, outran the angry guards, and disappeared into the night. So determined to flee her father's control and her impending wedding, the beautiful maiden disappeared, it is claimed, like a phantom into the darkness. Seeking the freedom she knew she would never have, Destina was rumored to have combed the beach alone, singing beneath the moon's cool light . . .'"

I interjected, if for no other reason than I was miserable and wanted Brit to stop poring over the stupid story to give me some gosh-darned attention, "Moon-schmoon."

She looked up at me and hissed, "Riley, not now; I'm *readin'*."

Hah! I thought, with embittered irony. As if reading the town's pirate legend was more important than *my* sob-worthy story! I grimaced, making a face as she turned back to the screen.

". . .'No one, it seems, could have predicted the young maiden's fate, not even Destina herself. For as Blackheart's ships sailed into the bay that night, the light of the bewitching moon cast its double on the surface of the quiet inlet, creating the illusion of two moons lighting the night sky. Blackheart's watchful crew took this to be a bad omen, and insisted they turn back.

"'But at the same moment, Blackheart's ears discerned the singing of a hauntingly beautiful voice. As he glimpsed the beautiful Destina, he was overcome with the desire to make her his own. Ordering his crew to run aground immediately, he ignored their protests, threatening to execute anyone who defied his orders. The reluctant crew obeyed, and followed the still waters into the bay. But just as they'd feared, the inlet was well-guarded by the townsfolk, who surprised the pirates with a vicious land and sea attack. The battle was long and bloody. Blackheart's entire crew was overtaken and killed, while the captain himself was captured, tortured, and executed. His head was staked on the mast of a ship that guarded the bay, a signal for other pirates to avoid the peaceful inlet, lest they be cursed by the light of the two moons and meet a similar fate.'" Britlee paused, staring at me. Her eyes were alight with excitement.

I groaned. "Ugh, don't remind me," I murmured, slumping over to bury my face in the cushions. That charming legend had sucked me in, too; heck, it was the only reason I had ventured to check out real estate in the quaint little beach town in the first place!

Ignoring me, she continued, "'Ironically, the maiden Delgado was never seen or heard from again. Some surmised that she had been captured by Blackheart's men and was killed aboard the ship. The vessel, under heavy fire, had taken on water and sunk to the ocean floor. Others assumed that as she walked the shore that night, she was killed in the crossfire that filled the beach with smoke. Still others claimed that Destina had thrown herself into the ocean in one final defiant act against her father, choosing death over marrying a man she didn't love.'"

"That's what I'll do," I interjected. "Find myself an ocean . . ."

Glaring at me, Brit finished, "'On nights when the moon is full, Destina's voice can still be heard, echoing across the rippling water, beneath which lie the ghosts of the infamous Blackheart Bellacroix and his ill-fated crew.'" Taking a breath, she looked over at me, an animated expression on her face.

"Lord help us," I grumbled. "I know that look." Peering from between my fingers, I waited for the inevitable explanation. I glanced around anxiously, searching for a place to hide.

But when Britlee Matlin was excited about something, there was nowhere to run. The volume cranked up a couple of decibels on her already-fills-the-room voice, her grin got even bigger, and her eyes sparkled like stars in the night sky. "Oh. My. Gosh. I *love* that story!" she exclaimed, sipping daintily from my ludicrously-large glass.

I glared at her. That was my drink.

"Riley, you have *got* to move there!" she cried, getting up to set my laptop back on the desk. Making her way back over to me, she perched once again on the crate table and placed a reassuring hand on my knee. "I know you don't want to hear this right now, Riley Larkin, but I'm gonna say somethin' you *really* need to hear." A pregnant pause widened between us, the kind I hated most. They were the kind from which you just couldn't hide.

I sighed, sitting up. Suddenly feeling much more coordinated and far less drunk, I wished I wasn't so stinking clear-headed at the moment. Although only five years older than me, Britlee sure had a way of sounding exactly like the mother I had never known. Maybe that's one of the many things we needed most about each other; I needed her guidance like she needed my devotion. Although we had met only a decade before, it felt like we'd known each other our whole lives. As close as two friends could be, we fought like sisters and loved each other like family. No matter what was said, I knew that in her mind, an insult to me was an insult to Britlee herself. And I felt exactly the same way.

Leaning back, she raised a questioning eyebrow at me. Was I ready?

I nodded, answering her unspoken question. "Go ahead."

She closed her eyes dramatically for a second, the way she always did when preparing for a speech — or just a really important point that I needed to hear. "*Now*," she began, which meant she was going for the in-between: an anecdote. "Riley E-lizabeth Larkin . . ."

"Avery," I corrected.

She gave me an incredulous look. "Ex-*cuse* me?" Brit had a way of sounding indignant, even when she didn't mean to. Sometimes it made me want to throw something at her.

Now was not one of those times, however. Instead, I grabbed a pillow and held it up defensively. I felt like *I* needed a weapon. "Avery," I clarified. "My middle name is Avery."

She rolled her eyes, waving a perfectly-manicured hand in my direction. "Well, *I* know that," she retorted. "I just like your name better as Riley *E*-lizabeth Larkin."

I nodded, considering her point. It did have a nice ring. Lowering the pillow, I prepared for the longer version, the one she'd intended from the start.

"*Anyway*," she intoned, closing her eyes to begin again. "I know that all you want to do right now is jump into this aquarium you call a margarita glass . . ."

Well, *duh*. I nodded, rolling my eyes. It was delicious.

"But," she continued, taking another swig of my cocktail. "That's not what you need right now. Right *now*, you need to come to the realization that your marriage endin' is the best thing that could have happened to you." She pointed a square-tipped burgundy fingernail at me for emphasis before tipping the glass back again. I think Brit had just realized how good it was. "Jason's stupidity is what got him into this mess, and, ultimately, it's what drove you away."

I stared bleakly at her, refusing to believe that it wasn't my fault.

Britlee's eyes narrowed. She recognized my expression. "And before you go tellin' yourself that it's *your* fault, you need to listen to me . . ." Her eyes twinkled as she said this next part. "Even though I'm your *much younger* and better-lookin' sister, you know that I give the best advice."

Despite my resolution to not get sucked in to her charming mood and incredibly accurate, just-what-I-needed-to-hear guidance, the corners of my mouth cracked into a smile.

Grinning, her white teeth shone against her olive complexion. "There! Ya see? You know I'm right, Riley E-lizabeth Larkin." She nodded, affirming her own truth. "What you need to do now is tell yourself that the choice you made to buy that beautiful beach house and move to that charmin' little town to live out your dreams is not only the best thing for you, but the *right* thing for you."

Although I knew she was right, something deep inside tore at me, nagged me into thinking that if I gave in and faced the truth, all the lies I had built around me like comfortable, protective walls would come crumbling down. And then I'd *really* have to change.

But, I reasoned, looking out the window, my eyes fastened somewhere beyond the glass, my life *was* changing, whether I wanted it to or not. Snow was coming down on the mountains that surrounded my cabin like a fortress, blanketing the already-covered ground in yet another layer of white. Despite the roaring fire and coziness of the cabin that had become my primary residence since the separation, I felt a chill from somewhere deep within.

"Riley?" Brit's eyes lured me out of my brooding thoughts. "Riley, look at me."

Reluctantly, I met her gaze.

"Tell me I'm wrong. Tell me that I'm tellin' you lies." Her eyes bored dark spears of truth into my soul, making it impossible to look away.

I shook my head. "No," I started meekly, but then something snapped inside me. All those years of doubt and suspicion, of stomping on my intuition and telling it to just be quiet, to shut up and not tell me what was so painfully obvious boiled inside me. But instead of feeling like anger and hurt — I'd already been infected by those poisons, had felt them slide through my veins for far too long - now it just felt like acceptance. Resolution. And yes — clarity! *And*, I was amazed to admit, it felt *really good*.

The liberating feeling bubbled over into laughter, which somehow came out sounding a little maniacal.

Britlee looked worriedly at me. "Riley, you ok?"

Feeling empowered, I snatched the glass off the table where she'd set it, and took a defiant gulp. Daring her to yank the drink from my hands, all my favorite Oprah-isms ran through my mind: *I* am the writer of my own life script, *I* am in charge of my own destiny, *I* am going to chase my dreams. Someone that powerful wouldn't be bullied into *not* drinking herself into oblivion if she wanted to!

My voice was firm as I declared, "Brit, you're right. You're absolutely right." I looked squarely at her, my own dark eyes staring back into hers. "I've been cowering in fear and doubt for far too long." I closed my eyes for a second, thrusting the drink toward her. It suddenly didn't taste as good anymore. Opening them, I continued, "And even though I'm kind of terrified, I've got to do it. I've got to move on."

She squinted at me, cocking her head to the side. Her perfectly-coifed shoulder-length brown hair shifted, echoing her inquisitive expression.

The moment didn't need any words. Heck, we could probably have this whole entire conversation through facial expressions alone, but the silence made me uncomfortable, so I continued, "You're *right* that it's Jason's fault our marriage broke up. I mean - I've been blaming myself for the past year, wondering why *I* wasn't good enough, but it wasn't me; it was him."

She nodded silently, her eyes sparkling as she caught my energy, urging me to go on.

Emboldened, and finally articulating that which I had come to realize but had been too afraid to say aloud before, I proclaimed, "And you're *right* about it being a good thing that it's over. All those years, I'd thought that we were *blissfully* happy," I said with sardonic air quotes. "I realize that what I'd *mistaken* for happiness was just plain ignorance; I'd *chosen* to ignore that he was unfaithful, even though I'd known it all along."

I shook my head, amazed by how obvious it now was. And how stupid I'd been. But I was free of all that now. None of it mattered anymore. "And now," I paused as it all sank in. "I don't have to do that anymore!" My voice rose as I looked defiantly around the room, feeling like I was shouting my truths to a captive audience.

My lone spectator rose to her feet, clapping slowly. "I applaud you, Riley *E*-lizabeth Larkin. You are darin' to do what so many of us refuse to. You are provin' that you *can* live happily on your own, that you *can* embrace a change that you may not have chosen, but you're makin' the best of it and goin' after your dreams." She took a deep breath. "I am *so* happy for you."

Feeling intoxicated by the optimism that flowed through me, I rose to my feet. Grasping her hands, I shouted victoriously, "I can do this, Brit — I'm really going to be ok!"

We jumped and giggled, as giddy as schoolgirls. Despite the fact that I was terrified of dying alone, a pitiful old woman with some rescue dogs and a house full of plants, I knew I would be ok. Growing up in foster care had taught me how to survive. I had gotten through that, which meant I could get through this.

Brit's phone dinged, announcing an incoming text. "Oh, let me check that," she said, retrieving her phone from the desk. "It might be Savannah." Her daughter was a senior in high school, and despite the fact that it was Thanksgiving break, it was a Friday night, and Savannah was popular. A mother's work is never done, I thought, smiling.

Walking around my desk, I peered through the massive window, searching the falling snow for the secrets of the night. How is it that everything looked so different in the dark, when the world was white and pure? In that moment, as I stared into the darkness, at the mountains I had loved for nearly half my adult life, instead of feeling lonely, I felt full, complete. I think what I felt was *hope*. Yes, I would miss these mountains, and, yes, I would even miss the snow. But I was ready. It was time to move on, time to embrace the change that had, in retrospect, been unfolding for years. It was time.

Taking a deep breath, I turned around and faced my friend. Throwing my arms out to the sides, I caught her off-guard as she typed a reply into her phone. Shouting at the top of my lungs, I declared, "Two Moon Bay, Florida - here I come!"

2

Homebound

I inhaled deeply of the humid air, feeling Florida with every one of my senses.

"Ah, Rae," I said to my copilot, whose head had been stuck outside the passenger window since we crossed the Georgia/Florida line. "We're home."

Despite the fact that it was December — just a week before Christmas - the sun shone in golden splendor in the baby-blue sky. At this time of year in the mountains, the sun made rare appearances, but even on its best days, didn't come close to the brilliance of this amazing morning.

Anxious to get to the beach house, I glanced at the GPS. Five miles to go; approximately twelve minutes, the Jeep's software thought. Good, we were close. Drinking in another lungful of the dewy air, which tasted vaguely of salt, a slight breeze ruffled my hair. "Almost there, Rae-Rae," I promised.

My golden looked over at me when he heard his name. He opened his mouth to begin a light pant, his red lashes blinking lazily over soulful topaz eyes. As always, Raegan was content in the moment — a trait that I resolved to mimic. He blinked at me, then slowly turned back to his window.

"Good idea, buddy," I told him, returning my gaze to the amazing scenery. The sides of the narrow road were heavily forested and verdantly green — tall pines, low-lying palms, ferns, and other species of flora whose names I had yet to learn grew from the rust-colored earth. The faded road was straight and flat, and sparsely trafficked - a welcome change from the busy-ness of the snow-covered mountains. No more winter for me!

Suddenly, the forest opened up to reveal marshy swamps on either side of the road. On the right were tall, craggy dunes and the white-sand coastline. The ocean sparkled in aquamarine splendor, looking like an open treasure chest of jewels.

"There it is, Rae-Rae! The beach!" My hands pounded excitedly on the steering wheel as I caught sight of the ocean. I couldn't wait to wake up every morning and go for a jog on my very own stretch of beach.

As if he had been thinking the same thing, Raegan woofed happily.

The blue-green water lapped against the shore as white-capped waves curled into peaks that I would love to create in my lemon meringue pie.

I'd never lived in a beach town before, and had always fantasized about having an actual palm tree in my yard. Ready to embrace the coastal life, I was dressed the part, despite what was probably a cool morning for the locals. Not even nine o'clock and it was already fifty-six degrees! For me, that was positively beach-worthy. The high today was expected to be near eighty, which, in my mind, meant shorts, flip flops, a tank top, and, of course, a beach hat. Just for good measure, I had thrown on a long sweater, light enough for when it warmed up, but warm enough that I could roll down the highway with the windows and sun roof open. "Home sweet home, right, Rae-Rae?" I said aloud, grinning at my pup.

He turned to look at me, barking twice in agreement. This was a new start for both of us.

The town's welcome sign came into view just then, surrounded on both sides by water. To the left, the marsh continued, little eddies of brackish water weaving like veins toward the beating heart of the town. We whizzed past the white sign whose curly-cue font announced in airy shades of yellow, pink, and blue, 'Welcome to Two Moon Bay, where life's a little brighter.'

"You can say that again!" I exclaimed, smiling. Then, "Wow. Population: Six thousand?" I looked to my companion, whose head was stuck outside the window again, snuffling lungsful of the Florida air. "That's even less than I read on the Internet," I murmured in surprise. In a town that small, everybody must know everything about everyone else! Always having lived in fairly decent-sized cities, the thought was a little daunting.

Coming into town, the quaint buildings boasted an island-like feel. Most places were painted in warm, beachy colors — golden yellow, sky blue, grass green, and my favorite, although not a beach color — rosy pink. The blue and yellow Little Country Grocery was on the left, next to a bakery/café, photography and art studio, and some adorable-looking gift shops. The post office was a little further up on the left, smack dab across from the stately stone library. All along the right was a smattering of mom-and-pop restaurants, a hardware store, an old-fashioned ice cream parlor, craft store, and, to my delight — a N.Y. deli. I had grown up in New York State, and let me tell you - we Yankees take our delis as seriously as Southerners do their sweet tea. Hoping an actual New York native owned the place, I made a mental note to have lunch there soon.

As we continued down the bustling street, I noted the people who were out and about at this early hour on a Friday. Several joggers - a couple of men who looked to be in their sixties, a thirty-ish-looking couple, and two girls who appeared to be in their mid-twenties, both pushing baby carriages - were exercising along the main street, happy looks on their faces. A diverse crowd of all ages and races was dining al fresco at Huey's House of Pancakes, and another bunch could be seen getting their fix inside the pink café.

Marshy streams flowed behind the buildings on both sides of the street, which probably meant that every place had a water view. As the rest of the downtown came into view, I guessed that the water met at the back part of the main street, where the Two Moon Bay Inn was located.

"Whoa," I said aloud, studying the bleached-wooden boards of what appeared to be an old hotel and saloon. It looked remarkably different from the cheeriness of the other businesses. "Creepy." Although the building had a certain sort of charm, there was something a little . . . *off* about it, I realized, trying to put my finger on it. I looked at Raegan. "I'll bet there are some serious ghosts in there."

Just then, my cell phone rang. The smiling face of my realtor, Dixie Patton, popped up on the screen. Her short, curly, red hair peeked out from beneath a yellow hat, her rosy cheeks glowing. "Hey, Dixie," I said brightly. "I'm almost there!" I glanced at the navigation screen on my dash. "Three more miles."

Dixie's Savannah accent responded, "Well, hey there, sug! I'm real happy to hear that. I'm almost to your place; I'll wait in the driveway 'til you get here."

"Ok, — I'll see you soon!"

She started to hang up, then said in a rush, "Oh, and sug — the floor guy will be callin' you to arrange a time to come out, and the yard crew will start first thing tomorrow mornin', just like you asked."

I nodded, impressed. "That's great, Dixie. Thank you."

As I hung up, I turned right out of the downtown and cruised down a lovely residential street that looked like it was straight out of Mayberry. Here the houses were colonial and ranch styles, many with chimneys and white picket fences. All had impeccably-manicured lawns. The local school was on the left, consisting of three stately brick buildings that were all connected. According to the signs, each building was its own school, so the elementary, middle, and high schools were all in one place. The entrances were united by a large bus circle and landscaped facade. Wow, how great would it be to go to school with palm trees and an open courtyard? Again with the palm trees! I was beginning to think I had a problem. But, then again, always having lived in colder climates, I was eager for any sign of the tropics.

The GPS lady barked at me in her robot voice, "Turn right in three-tenths of a mile onto Beach . . . Boulevard."

I nodded, signaling. Approaching the stop sign, I scanned the hand-made signpost, painted in the same font and colors as the town's welcome sign. Gazing around, I sought to get my bearings. It looked like the left turn would take me to more residential condos and beach houses, while the right, where I was headed, consisted of much of the same. Several blocks must have been between Main Street and Beach Boulevard, I was figuring, trying to envision a map in my head.

Completing the turn, I said aloud in my own computer voice, "Now turning onto . . . Beach . . . Boulevard."

Apparently tired of the scenery on his side of the street, Raegan looked over my shoulder, his eyes fastened on the ocean. I followed his gaze. The waves crashed against the shore, their sounds lulling and rhythmic. Much of the beach here was untouched by houses, and no hotels adorned its banks; from what I had read online, the town council had decided long ago to preserve the area's natural beauty, free of the commercial giants. The vibe here was surfer-chill, country-casual, and all-around relaxed.

Counting the house numbers aloud, I clapped my hands together and let out a little squeal as mine came into view. "Twenty-four Beach Boulevard!" I cried, switching off the GPS and signaling left.

Turning into the circular drive, I parked in front of the palms that were smack-dab in the center of my yard. The shrubs and walkway were slightly overgrown, but with a little love, this place would be spectacular before you knew it. Parking so I was facing Dixie's white BMW coupe, I unhooked my seatbelt and hopped out, shutting the door after Raegan's feet hit the ground running. He barked a greeting at the skinny real estate agent, who, as usual, looked like she should be shopping on Fifth Avenue, rather than selling real estate in a small beach town on the southern tip of Florida's Gulf Coast.

Taking off her designer sunglasses, Dixie's blue eyes sparkled as she gave me a hug. "Well, hello there, sug! Aren't you lookin' lovely this mornin'?" She gave me a casual once-over, but I knew in that one sweep she took in everything about me.

Feeling somehow underdressed in her presence, I wrapped my long, light-pink, open sweater around my middle. "Thank you, same to you!" I returned, pointing to her outfit. Then, seeing Raegan cantering toward her with a determined look in his eye, I hollered, "Raegan, no! Down!" But it was too late.

Letting out a shriek, Dixie's stick-thin body was pushed back beneath the force of Raegan's eighty pounds of enthusiasm. As I watched in horrified slow-motion, the immaculately-dressed woman landed butt-first on the brick paver drive, her expensive hot-pink jumpsuit taking the brunt of the fall. Her floral-printed Dooney and Bourke shopper bounced open, spilling makeup, car keys, and two prescription bottles across the walk.

Scrambling to help her up, I apologized profusely. "Dixie, I'm so sorry," I told her, sending chastising remarks after the offending creature who bounded gaily toward the back yard, completely unaware of the destruction he'd caused. "Are you alright? Oh, my gosh; I'm so, so sorry," I muttered, making a worried face as I assessed the damage. The back of her jumpsuit was torn and dirty — ruined. "Dixie, I'll pay you for your outfit," I said quickly, fumbling for the contents of her bag.

Ever the Southern belle, Dixie masked her frustration impeccably. Dusting herself off, she accepted the keys and makeup from my hand; I let her get the prescription bottles so I would feel like less of a voyeur. "Aww, don't be silly, sug," she told me with a mega-watt smile. "This old thing was ready for the rummage sale, anyway," she assured me, indicating her brand-new-looking jumpsuit. Snapping her purse shut, she waved grandly toward the front of the tan stucco beach house that was my new home. "Shall we?"

I beamed, accepting her hand. "We shall."

But as we started up the brick walk, the sound of a speeding car caught our attention. Expecting someone to come tearing up the drive, we stopped, looking over our shoulders in surprise. A shiny, silver Mercedes convertible, the top down, zoomed into the drive and came to an abrupt halt just inches from my back bumper.

Stunned, I muttered, "O-*kay*," as an extremely tan, well-dressed man who appeared to be in his early fifties stepped out of his little sports car. He was dressed to the nines in what I presumed to be very expensive golf gear. The deep purple-and-white outfit contrasted smartly with the vibrancy of his golden tan and ultra-white smile. Everything about this guy screamed 'over the top'; looking at him, you just knew that when he entered a room, *everyone* noticed. I had no idea who he was, but Dixie sure lit up at the sight of him.

"Well, hey there, Cal!" she cooed, waving. "What brings you by?"

Cal grinned in response, and all I could think was that he should be doing ads for cosmetic dentists everywhere. Removing his designer shades with a practiced, casual air, his sky-blue eyes twinkled as he looked me up and down, blatantly checking me out. "Hello there, Dixie," he greeted my agent, somehow managing to rip his eyes away from my chest long enough to respond. "I was just on my way to the club when I saw your car."

His eyes slid back to mine, though he was still answering Dixie. "Seein' you walkin' up the drive with this lovely young lady, I thought I'd stop by and introduce myself, and welcome our new neighbor."

I nodded and smiled, sensing that he was about to continue. The man was incredibly charismatic, I had to admit; Dixie was obviously smitten, and even I felt engaged by his larger-than-life presence.

Although his eyes were unabashedly direct, Cal's grin was somehow mischievous in a harmless sort of way. "Hello, little lady," he said warmly to me. "My name is Calhoun Foxworth the Third, but all my friends call me Cal." He kissed my hand ever so gently, maintaining eye contact the entire time. "It's my pleasure to make your acquaintance."

Thinking I had stepped outside my life and into a 1950s version of an absurd parody on the Old South, I managed what felt like a smile, but probably looked more like a grimace. "Hi, Cal," I said, somewhat lamely; compared to his well-groomed manners, I sounded a smidge dull, even to my ears. I cleared my throat. "Nice to meet you." Hoping he would let go of my hand soon, I shook it as if we were business acquaintances.

Dixie, who had gotten fidgety since his approach, giggled nervously as she ran a hand through her curls. "Riley, Cal here is a very important person in our town," she informed me, smiling a little too widely at him. "In addition to ownin' the most popular restaurant in town, he owns several other businesses, and is our very own claim to fame; he's a professional golfer." She smiled bashfully at him, but, with his eyes riveted on me, Cal didn't seem to notice.

I paused, connecting the dots. "Ohhh," I nodded, recognition dawning. "*Now* I know why your name is familiar."

His face brightened. "Oh, you play?"

I shrugged, managing to slip my hand discreetly from his grip. "You know — a little here, a little there."

"Well," he said, his eyes twinkling. "I do hope you will do me the honor of joinin' me at the club sometime soon." He produced a card, his eyes never leaving mine.

I accepted it, nodding politely. "Thank you, that's very generous of you." I had absolutely no intention of doing anything that would give him the wrong idea, but didn't want to be rude.

Don't get me wrong: I'm sure Cal was a perfectly nice guy — once you got to know him, and, er, once he stopped staring at your chest. He was just a little too direct for my taste.

"Isn't the club the other way, though?" I asked, pointing to the right, which was south. If I remembered correctly, the world-famous golf club here in Two Moon Bay was located at the southernmost point, where the coastline jutted out into the Gulf atop a high, craggy bluff. It was one of "the Bay's" most-famous and -photographed spots.

Cal's brow furrowed for a moment. Then, remembering, he said quickly, "Oh, well, yes — I was on my way to pick up a buddy of mine; we have a tee time in . . ." He looked down at his gold Rolex. "Oh, my goodness — five minutes!" He looked at Dixie, laughing.

Dixie giggled girlishly, patting her hair again self-consciously. "Oh, well, Cal," she fawned. "Everyone at the club knows you — you can be as late as you please!"

Thumbing the bill of his Kangol cap at us, Cal took his leave. "Well, I don't like to take advantage. Or delay anyone else's time. After all," he said, looking meaningfully at me, "as every golfer knows, a good day on the greens starts in the mind." He finished by tapping the side of his head for emphasis. He kissed my hand again before reaching for Dixie's. "Ladies," he crooned with enough swag to make Rico Suave blush. He held our eyes for a moment before striding back to his convertible.

Dixie tee-heed bashfully, staring after him as his tires spun onto the road.

Surprised that my poised realtor was so easily ruffled by the flashy golfer, I thought how appearances can be so deceiving. She seemed like the type of woman who never lost her cool. But, crushes have a way of turning even the strongest woman into a giggling schoolgirl, I reminded myself.

Hearing a series of petulant-sounding barks from the back yard, I gave Dixie a worried look. "Uh oh," I muttered. "That sounds like trouble."

Regaining her composure, Dixie snapped back into business mode. "Oh — right, well, let's get out the keys," she said, rifling through her purse. "And get you inside your brand-new beach house!"

I accepted the keys with a sense of pride, and we hot-footed it up the path to the front. The wide veranda was painted white, but I had visions of a golden mustard or rust-colored trim. Same for the plantation shutters that lined the four large windows along the porch. Forming a mental checklist in my mind, I realized it wouldn't take much to get the entrance up to snuff. Hearing Raegan's barks abate to only an occasional woof, I figured he was fine. "You ready?" I asked Dixie, keys poised over the lock.

She grinned. "Well, of course, sug — let's go!"

Inserting the old-fashioned key into the lock, I pushed open the double doors. Sunlight dazzled through the glass-lined back of the house, which opened onto yet another veranda. From the entryway, I could see straight through the open great room, past the eat-in kitchen and family room, through the back porch, over the in-ground pool, all the way to the dunes and beach beyond.

My heart skipped a beat. Feeling unexpected tears spring to my eyes, I stared around me.

Seeing my emotion, Dixie pretended not to notice, and busied herself with a task. "I'll just let you look around while I check on this door back here."

Her heels clipped daintily across the hardwood floor. As she fumbled with the lock on the sliding deck door that opened along the back wall of the great room, I closed my eyes, feeling the warmth of the sun on my face. The moment was surreal. Feeling like my life was just beginning, I opened my eyes — only to see another pair looking right back at me!

"Oh!" I gasped. Stepping back toward the open front door, I gazed at the powerfully-built overalled man before me.

His freckled face broke into a huge grin as he said quickly, "Well, I don't mean to scare you, little lady!" He stuck out a hand. "I'm Stump. Miss Dixie asked me to git ahold of you today to see 'bout gettin' some work done on yer place."

Still recovering, I shook his hand slowly. The name confused me. "Stump, is it?"

He nodded enthusiastically.

"Right, hi — I'm Riley." Realizing I was still pumping his hand, I stopped. "It's nice to meet you."

Finished faux-fixing the perfectly-working door, Dixie came over to us. "Oh, well, hello there, Stump!" she greeted the powerhouse redheaded man with a graceful hug. "I thought you would be callin' Riley here about her floors, but how nice of you to stop by!"

He looked around the great room, his eyes combing the floors. "Yep, well — I was on my way to another job when I seen yer car out front here an' decided to stop by." He stepped over to the kitchen, where the wood floor met the tile. "Some a them boards is a little messed up here," he said, following the floor through the great room and down the hall to the right, where it led to one wing of bedrooms and bathrooms.

We followed behind, listening as he surveyed the place.

"An' a couple o' the bedrooms need some work — moldin' included." He trod back the length of the wing. "I kin help you with that," he said with certainty, his eyebrows furrowed together, deep in thought.

As he passed Dixie and me where we stood in the great room, across from the open dining room, she told me, "Stump here is the best handyman in all of Two Moon Bay. He does it all — floors, woodwork, sheetrock, paint - you name it." She nodded emphatically. "Yep - he's the best around, sug. In all of the southern Gulf, really!" She gushed as he disappeared down the left wing, where two other bedrooms with a Jack-and-Jill bath resided, along with a spare room that I thought would make an excellent craft room.

I stepped forward, stopping at the corner of the great room, where the office and half bath lived on opposite walls. "Hey, Stump," I called, thinking how awkward that sounded to my ears. He poked his head out of the craft room. "Do you think we could add a wall of built-ins there — along the back wall?" I moved inside the white-walled room, noting some spots that would need to be repaired before painting. I explained my vision to him, drawing a hasty map on his clipboard.

He eyed the drawing, then the wall, contemplating. "Yes, ma'am — I do b'lieve that's possible." He looked at me. "I could git my crew on it first thing in the mornin', if yer ready to start."

I nodded eagerly, impressed. "Sure — that'd be great!" I agreed. I wondered how big his crew was, but didn't ask. The sooner the work was finished, the sooner this place would be home.

Dixie smiled graciously as Stump and I walked down the hall, meeting her in the foyer. The front doors were closed now, but light cascaded through the glass panels on either side, forming a yellow haze about her tiny form. "Well, it sounds like you're set for a big day tomorrow, Riley!" She gazed from Stump to me. "I'll come by tomorrow to say hello, see how you're doin'."

We shook hands, then embraced. "Thanks, Dixie. For everything. You're welcome to come by *anytime*." I smiled warmly at her as she turned to leave. Then, catching sight of the tiny hole in the back of her pants, I called after her. "Say, Dixie — how about I take you out sometime soon for a nice dinner — you know — since Raegan ruined your outfit and all." I looked guiltily at Stump, who stood beside me in the door. He quickly averted his gaze as he caught sight of the frilly lace peeking out from the tiny gash.

Turning around, Dixie smiled reassuringly at me. For a middle-aged woman, she was remarkably youthful, I noted. "Aww, sug." She waved a hand as if Raegan's destructive antics were no big deal. "You don't need to worry about this ole outfit! But, since it's botherin' you, how about we grab some cocktails at The Real Macaw? It's a great local hangout. And I'd love to introduce you to some folks."

I nodded, thinking she meant sometime next week, or maybe after the holidays. "Sure, any time — drinks are on me."

She beamed. "Well, then, it's settled: Macaw's at eight. Now there's no parkin' lot, sug, so dress warm enough for a walk on the beach. From your house, it's about a mile that-a-way," she said, pointing to my left, back near town.

Caught off-guard, I stammered, "Uh, ok!" It's not like I had anything else to do besides compulsively clean tonight, anyway. And a night out with Dixie was sure to be a good time.

She beamed, getting into her car.

"See you then," I said, waving.

Returning the gesture with a dainty finger-wave, Dixie called, "Bah-bye!" as she pulled out of the driveway.

Stump cleared his throat, stepping toward the door. "Miss Riley — ma'am." He stuck his hand out to shake mine. "Thank you for allowin' me to work on yer home," he said politely. "I look forward to workin' with ya."

Taken aback, I marveled at everyone's politeness. It was as though they all were graduates of the same refinement school. While I was used to the civility of the mountain folk in North Carolina, this was altogether a different scale of decorum that I had not been expecting.

Closing the door behind me, Raegan's insistent barking reminded me that I needed to track him down. Trudging through the great room and onto the back veranda, I followed the sound to the backyard. Bordered on both sides by privacy shrubs that had grown to about six feet, the lot had an oval-shaped pool that looked a little worse for wear, patches of grass interspersed with sand, a scattering of palm trees — yay! — and shrubs that lined the back porch of the house.

My fingers were just itching to dig in and start weeding. With a little effort, this backyard would be ready for entertaining! Well, as soon as I made some friends, that is.

Raegan's woofs stopped for a moment. Sometimes it's when your kids are quietest that you need worry the most, I thought grimly. "Raegan?" I called warily, scanning the yard. Then, as he resumed his barking - this time more forcefully - I charted the sound around the left side of my home.

There, before the shrubs, stood my golden. His tongue hung out of his mouth in an excited pant, as he stared down at a yellow lab, who lay between the house and the bushes, surrounded by tiny newborn pups. Her big gold eyes looked up at me in wonder.

"Oh, my gosh!" I exclaimed. Taking a step back, I didn't want to overwhelm the new mother, didn't want her to think I was a threat to her and her babies.

As the little ones scrambled to stay close to her body, her tail thumped in friendly greeting.

"Raegan, get back," I commanded, pointing by my foot. He cast her a grudging look, then reluctantly did as he was told, sitting resolutely at my feet.

I surveyed the scene. The pups looked no more than a few days old — a week, at most. "Where did you come from, girl?" I asked the mom, who thumped her tail in response. I looked at the house to my left, a stately colonial style that was well-kept, but appeared to be unoccupied. Maybe she was someone's pet? Dixie had said that both of my next-door neighbors had primary residences in other states, so I would likely only see them a few times a year. "Well, we'll put up some signs around town," I told her. "See if anyone is missing you." I hoped she wasn't a stray, but given the fact that she had chosen to have her babies outside a house that had been vacant for the better part of a year, I guessed she was homeless.

Determined to help the poor girl out, I looked down at my own pet. "Come on, Raegan," I said, patting my leg. "Let's go get our new friend something to eat. And then we've got some work to do!" I told him, clapping my hands together. I couldn't wait to start cleaning.

Excited about the prospect of another new adventure, Raegan wagged his tail as he trotted ahead of me, back into the house.

Adding to the mental shopping list I'd been forming since we drove up, I decided that another couple of dog bowls would be needed for the new mother. And a decent-sized bed for her; I hated to see a dog lying in the dirt. Maybe once she trusted me, we could even move her into the back veranda, keep her and the puppies comfortable and out of the elements.

As I started to shut the door behind me, I decided to leave it open. "Let's get a little fresh air in here, Rae-Rae," I told him.

First thing to do: change into some work clothes. My cute 'Florida, here I come!' outfit might do well for a future lunch at the N.Y. deli, or maybe a jaunt to the bakery/café, but would *not* work for the cleaning marathon I was about to begin. That's what I would do, I decided, hopping into jean cut-offs and a tank top — tomorrow I would start the day by exploring the adorable town. A coffeehouse that cute must have some good brew, I told myself.

Carting in containers of cleaning supplies, I sanitized the white marble kitchen counter, appreciating the grayish-blue veins that ran artfully through the rock. "Thank you, buyer's market," I said aloud, marveling once again at the amazing deal I got on this house. Easily a million-dollar home in a stable market, the stagnant economy had made it possible for me to get this modest yet beautiful beach house for a steal. Of course I *never* would have been able to afford this home on my meager teacher's salary, so I guess I should also say that I had "divorced-up." Not *married*-up, since Jason turned out to be a big, fat *jerk*, but, he was a big, fat jerk who was a brilliant businessman and computer whiz. So . . . really it was Jason I should be thanking!

There, clean as a whistle. Wiping my hands on my shorts, I set up my docking station in the corner where the counter met the wall, and turned on my 'Cleaning' playlist. Yes, I am that anal. And, yes, I have a playlist for everything. It's just one of my many . . . *qualities*, shall we say.

Filling Raegan's bowls with food and water, I cleaned the kitchen floor near the corner nook so I could set up a space for him. "Is this good for you, boy?" I asked, watching as he immediately plopped onto his pillow. "Guess that's a yes!" I told him, smiling. Grabbing his extra bowls, I filled them for our newfound friend and started out the back door. "Unh-unh," I told him in a firm voice as he started to get up. "You need to stay here; we need to give the new mom some space while she eats. I'll be right back."

Watching me with curious eyes, I knew he was wondering where I was headed with his bowls.

"That's a good boy. And thank you for sharing with our houseguest." Compliments are always appreciated, I told myself, hoping to inspire Raegan to observe reasonable boundaries when it came to the new mother and her pups. A naturally-inquisitive soul, I knew he was just dying to get outside so he could keep an eye on the lab. His curiosity sometimes got him into trouble, God love him.

Coming back into the house, I was surprised to see a shadow in the front doors' windows. The next thing I knew, the doorbell rang.

Always eager to make a new friend, Raegan launched into an animated bark, running to the foyer. Seeing the tall figure outside, he leaped up, slapping his paws against the glass.

"Who could that be?" I wondered, thinking that maybe Dixie had returned. But she wouldn't ring the bell, I wouldn't think. And she wasn't that tall. "Raegan, back," I commanded, pointing to the edge of the foyer, where I wanted him to sit.

Letting out one last whine, he grudgingly obliged, sitting on his haunches as I approached.

"Oh," I muttered unthinkingly, startled as I threw open the door. There before me stood a very good-looking, very fit guy whose muscular body filled out his delivery uniform all too perfectly. The whites of his dark-brown eyes smiled against his light-brown skin as he held out the clipboard to me. "Mrs. Larkin?"

"Ms." I corrected him, smiling politely. "I'm Riley Larkin."

His eyebrows raised at the correction. "Well, Ms. Larkin," he replied, handing me the clipboard. "I have some boxes for you. Please sign here."

Dutifully scrawling my name, I looked up to find him subtly checking me out. Catching my gaze, he made a swift recovery. Accepting the clipboard with a smile, he slid the pen into its little holder. "Thank you, Ms. Larkin," he said, stepping back from the doorway. "I'll just go get your packages."

Unable to stand it any longer, Raegan let out a single bark from where he sat inside the foyer, then charged forward before I could get the door closed. His eyes were fastened on the brown shorts and well-muscled legs that strode athletically down the driveway.

Feeling like it was Groundhog Day, I hollered out, "Raegan, no! Down! Down, Raegan!"

Hearing my pleas and the clicking of toenails against the brick walk, the delivery guy turned at just the right second. As Raegan went sailing through the air with his curly red ears flapping in the breeze, the man gracefully avoided a run-in with the overly-zealous welcome committee. "Whoa there, buddy!" he said in surprise, laughing.

As Raegan landed, he turned abruptly and trotted over to the man, who had knelt in the walk, offering an outstretched hand for sniffing.

Figuring I should try to apologize once again for my unruly child, I closed the heavy wooden door and skittered down the walk. "I'm sorry about Raegan," I told him as I approached. "He's a little . . . enthusiastic," I finished, at the same time he offered, "Intense?"

We both laughed.

Nodding, I agreed, "Yeah, he's enthusiastically intense."

He smiled down at me from a height of about six-two, I was guessing. I was five-nine, but he had a few inches on me. "I'm Ryan," he said, offering his hand.

"Riley," I repeated with a laugh, since I'd already introduced myself. "Nice to meet you."

He nodded in silent agreement, not saying anything for a moment. His eyes, though, said it all. They had a way of looking so closely at you that you felt seen, appreciated. It was a different feeling, I realized, being the center of his attention. "The pleasure is mine," he said after a moment.

Feeling the need to break the spell, I interjected, "So . . ." I cleared my throat. "Do you live here in Two Moon Bay?"

Ryan nodded, pointing vaguely over his shoulder, toward the village. "Yeah, uh, near town. I'm from Jacksonville, originally. My sister's lived here for about eight years — her husband's a professor over at the college." He chuckled good-naturedly. "I'm a city boy born and bred, but, after just one visit, I kind of fell in love with the place."

I smiled in understanding, nodding.

He trained his eyes on me, his gaze warm and sweet, like milk chocolate. Little golden flecks danced around his irises as he continued. "Anyway, I moved here about six months ago to start my own business." He pointed to the van. The logo, I'd just noticed, was one I didn't recognize — I took that to mean the truck and the name on the side belonged to him. "This guy my sister knew was selling his delivery service — time to retire, he said. She encouraged me to go for it. So I just figured, 'Why not?' And . . . the rest is history." He paused, giving a self-conscious laugh. "*Anyway*, I guess that was a lengthy way of telling you that I'm a newbie here, too." He smiled, gesturing over my shoulder at my fixer-upper.

"Oh — yeah," I agreed. "Well," I quipped with a posh British accent, "It's nice to meet one of my own kind." He laughed as I continued, "I can't wait to get settled in here. Two Moon Bay seems like a great place."

"It is," he assured me. "Coming from a bigger city, I thought I'd hate it, but it's actually been pretty enjoyable. But," he paused, studying me. "There are still some places I'd like to explore."

Feeling like I knew what was coming, I waited expectantly. Sort of wanting him to ask me out, but also kind of hoping that he wouldn't, I held my breath. Then, wondering what the heck was wrong with me, I exhaled, chastising myself. Brit would tell you to mellow out, I thought in annoyance.

"Maybe you'd like to do some exploring with me sometime?" he asked, studying my face with those eyes again.

"Uh, sure," I answered, wondering why I felt so uncertain. A nice, cute guy was asking me out and I felt . . . what did I feel? *Weird*? Like

I was doing something *wrong*? Darnit, it was *guilt*! I realized with frustration. For some unfathomable reason, I felt as if I were cheating on Jason. Well, you need to get over that quick, honey! I told myself firmly. "That'd be great," I told him casually, betraying none of the mental illness that was going on inside my head.

He smiled once more before turning back to the truck. "Let me just get those packages," he said again, this time opening the back.

Inside was a collection of boxes, all different sizes. The ones closest to the back I presumed to be mine. "Mind if I help?" I asked him. I couldn't stand watching other people do something for me without offering to help. Especially when it came to physical labor; I absolutely *lived* for that stuff. Instead of being a dusty old paper-ridden English teacher, I should have been a free-roaming park ranger or a landscape architect — or *some* occupation that was physically engaging. I had totally missed my outdoor calling.

Stepping back from the truck with a large box held over his head, Ryan sounded surprised as he answered, "Uh, yeah — sure. Just don't get hurt," he laughed. "Maybe take one of the . . ." His voice broke off as I reached in and grabbed a box the same size as the one he'd picked up. ". . . *smaller* ones," he finished lamely.

I smirked, passing in front of him. "What was that you were saying?" I said flippantly, tossing my partially-pinned up hair over my shoulder.

He grinned as I flitted by.

Raegan cantered joyfully around, delighted with his new bountiful yard.

Then, seeing him bounding around the right side of the house, where the lab was, I hollered out, "Raegan, no!" My inquisitive baby just couldn't stay away.

Hearing the no-nonsense tone in my voice, he stopped, satisfying himself with smelling around the nearby shrubs as Ryan and I hauled box after box inside the house.

As we deposited the last of the load into the sanitized kitchen area, he asked, "So, did you plan to have all this stuff delivered on the same day?" He pointed at the spread. "I mean — they're all from different stores. I would think that would be kind of difficult to coordinate, what with different shipping rules and all."

Surveying the various brands, I nodded slowly. "Yeah, it took a little planning," I agreed, taking my handy-dandy multi-tool out of my pocket and cutting into a box from Target.

While most of the packages were bedding and bath items, I had a few bigger pieces for the living room that would be coming tomorrow. We'd just carted in a lovely porch set that I had slated for the back veranda, but other than that, I figured I'd pick up most of the furnishings in the months to come.

Britlee had encouraged me to bring some of the gorgeous furniture with me from the home I'd decorated and shared with Jason for the past nine years, but I hadn't exactly felt attached to anything in that house since the day I'd seen those pictures. And while the mountain home had some great furniture, it was all super cabiny, and wouldn't do in a beach house. Plus, the mountain home was the one thing I had asked for in the divorce settlement, and I wanted to keep it just as it was. It would be a great vacation home for me and the girls, and was an excellent source of rental income. I planned on picking up the major home furnishings — actual furniture for the bedrooms and office - over the course of the next few months. Between the modern box stores in nearby Naples, and the antique stores I knew I could find along the neighboring highways and towns, I felt confident that my beach bungalow would be shabby chic-sleek in no time flat. Decorating was kind of my passion. And, call me crazy, but I felt that bringing each room to life with a personality and style of its own was part of my healing process.

Realizing that Ryan had been staring at me, waiting for me to go on, I added, "But it wasn't too bad. Most places have next-day delivery, and I already had my wish lists in place, so it was actually pretty simple."

He didn't say anything, just watched me quietly.

Feeling like I needed to fill the silence, I added, "So, the big stuff gets here tomorrow!" I smiled, pulling out a pretty new runner that would go before the sliding deck door. "Hey, would you like something to drink?" I asked, going over to the refrigerator. I had brought some beverages and healthy snacks for the car ride, so there was at least *some* food in the house.

"No, thanks — I'm fine," he answered. "Actually, I have a few more stops to make, so I've got to run."

I walked him to the door.

He turned in the threshold, gazing at me with those soulful brown eyes. "Here's my card," he said, pulling a brown leather case out of his back pocket. "My cell's on there, along with my work number. Give me a call sometime when you'd like to go exploring."

I accepted the card, this time thinking that I just might use it. "Sure," I replied. "See ya." I waved as he hopped in the truck. "And thank you!" I hollered as he started up the engine.

Putting the truck into gear, he laughed. "I should be thanking *you*! You made my job a lot easier." He waited to pull forward, watching as Raegan bounced across the driveway, barking blissfully as he chased a bird. "Don't forget to call me," Ryan added, starting to circle around the drive.

I held up his card in answer, waving goodbye.

As he pulled onto the road, I wondered if I actually *would* call. Probably, I told myself, smiling.

After rounding up Raegan, I went back into the house to get some work done. The microwave said it was one o'clock, which meant I had a whole seven hours to clean the master bedroom and bath, set up the air mattress and TV in my room, start organizing my closet, and get ready to meet Dixie at the bar.

"Ok," I said to Raegan, who had immediately sought his bed and was already preparing for a nap. "I've got to get some work done, buddy. Keep an eye on the place for me, will you?"

His eyes already closed, Raegan responded with a contented sigh.

Not wasting a second, I gathered my cleaning supplies and headed to the master suite. Located at the end of the right wing — with a view of the beach! — was what could only be described as the boss of all bed-rooms. I'm not an extravagant kind of girl, and I try to buy everything on sale, but I *do* appreciate good quality. And this suite — the whole house, really — screamed of refinement and good taste. The master ensemble was a total indulgence for me; it was spacious, open, airy, and furnished with the finest materials - without being all braggy about it, which was probably the thing I liked best of all.

As you turned left out of the hallway, you stepped down slightly onto dark wood floors. Approaching the sleeping quarters, you passed two of my favorite things - the closets. On either side of the corridor were walk-in his-and-hers closets, each one adorned with cream-colored, antique-finished, wooden organizers, matching homemade shelves, and built-in shoe racks. It was literally a dream come true for me. I had fantasized about having an impeccably-organized closet all my adult life, and now — unexpectedly — it was a reality for me. Even better? Since I was single, I got *both* closets all to myself. A definite upside to my divorce.

I smiled appreciatively as I turned right and stepped into the bathroom. The same white marble from the kitchen had been used for the countertop in here, which ran along the left wall. Above it was a wide rectangular mirror — it had to be seven feet long, I guessed. The edges were squared-off and painted antiqued-cream, the same as the closets' shelves, but through the streaks, I could see hints of the original dark wood. At the end of the double-sink counter was the walk-in shower, complete with see-through glass, very contemporary. I loved that the bath was a mixture of old and new — while the fixtures were brushed nickel and very modern, the style of the room was somehow classic. The floor was a gleaming white tile with just the tiniest flecks of silver in each sixteen-by-sixteen diamond. The color palette in here would be much the same that I had planned for the kitchen — a beach motif of blue-green sea, cream, and a hint of tan. I had visions of a grand, upright chair sitting at the end of the shower and opposite the amazing spa tub, which was just below the ginormous double windows. Along the right wall was a smaller vanity, complete with a tinier version of the mirror on the opposite wall. My faux sheepskin rugs and sisal bath mats would be placed in here very shortly, just as soon as I scrubbed it all down.

Looking around, I was once again grateful for Dixie's help in getting my place in such good condition. When I'd bought it via live-auction webcast nearly two months ago, the rooms had been dirty and unkempt, with damaged walls and leftover broken furniture everywhere. Fortunately, Dixie had paid a maintenance crew to clear out the debris and patch up the walls, so all I really had to do was sanitize everything to make it livable. Gazing around the airy room, I vowed to take a bath later on tonight in that gorgeous tub. I was thinking wine, candles, relaxing music, and a good book. For now, though, it was time to get down to business.

Making a right into the bedroom, I stood in the heart of the space, my eyes focused on the two large windows whose expansive view perfectly showcased the gently-crashing sea. My bed will go there, I thought, studying the wall that abutted the bathroom, which conveniently faced the ocean. It was large enough to house a king, I thought — maybe even a California king - without overtaking the space. I wanted this room to be simple, anyway — a beautiful bed, a reading chair that would face the water — I'd probably put that near the patio doors, I thought, sizing up the space. That would work well, especially since the builders had been generous with the canister lights, placing one in just the right spot for my reading nook. And, I noticed, the back wall would be perfect for some built-ins; a long window bench with storage underneath would be just right, I thought. I made a mental note to talk to Stump about that tomorrow.

Setting to work, I gave the master bed and bath a good scrub down. Meghan Trainor's "All About That Bass" came on my playlist, which totally renewed my energy as I sang and danced myself into the laundry room to get a new bucket of water. Although I hadn't been planning to, I sanitized the hall bathroom for good measure; you never know when company might arrive, so it's best to be ready. Besides, Dixie had said she'd stop by tomorrow, and in case the workers needed a restroom, I wanted them to have a clean space.

Next, I gave the laundry machines a thorough scrubbing, unloaded the bath and kitchen towels from their boxes, and stuck them in the washer. I swept the cobwebs off the front and back porches, and hung a wreath Brit had made me on the front door — one of her craftsy Pinterest endeavors. Beneath the front door, I placed the welcome mat the girls had given me as a going-away present, smiling as I thought of them. By then, the towels were clean, so after tossing them into the dryer, I ran a mop through the master bedroom and bath.

As the afternoon dwindled away, I needed a break. I helped myself to a protein bar and was just finishing a bottled water when the doorbell rang. Raegan, who'd been in a self-induced coma for the past three hours, leaped from his bed. He rushed to the door, jumping up to greet the surprised mail lady.

"Raegan — back," I ordered him, pointing to the spot where he'd earlier waited to welcome Ryan. Opening the door, I took the letters and a couple of smaller packages from the smiling blonde-haired mail carrier. Her blue eyes were warm and friendly as she welcomed me to Two Moon Bay.

"I'm Ginny," she told me, shaking my hand. "Me and another guy, Pearce, split this route. We been wonderin' if anyone was ever gonna snap this place up," she said, gazing around at my porch. "It's so beautiful. Looks like you've already got a good start on fixin' it up!"

I laughed. "Oh, thanks. Yeah, it's coming along. Still has a good ways to go, though," I added, smiling. "Ginny, would you like something to drink?" I asked her. The sun was out, shining brightly into the yard. Even though the afternoon was waning, I figured it was still in the mid-seventies.

"Oh," Ginny replied, declining with a wave. "Thank you, but I'm good. I've just got the rest of your street to finish, and I'll be headin' home. Another time, though, I may just take you up on that!"

I smiled, waving to her as she started down the steps. "Thanks, Ginny!" I had just barely gotten the door closed when Raegan decided to make a break for it. His toenails braced for a quick stop, which reminded me to put out the entry rug and runners. This place was a virtual race track without them.

Finishing up the afternoon's chores, I set up the bathrooms, pumped up the air mattress in my room, slapped some sheets on it, and hung the TV. Wow.

Unable to believe how much time had passed, I entered the kitchen, surprised to see the sun lowering in the sky. 5:20, the clocks said. My work for the day was done.

"You hungry, boy?" I asked Rae-Rae, who was standing over his food bowls, pondering their empty state.

His eyebrows moved independently of one another as he gazed back at me. "Well, duh," he seemed to be saying, but then commenced a relaxed pant.

"Alright. Feeding time it is." I filled up his bowls and then carted out another meal for the new mom. She was polite as I approached, greeting me with the customary tail wag I had come to expect. I gave her an ear rub and stepped back to let her eat in peace. "There you go, mama - *bon appétit!*" I told her as I started to turn away.

Heading back to the house, I caught sight of the colors in the late-afternoon sky. "Wow," I breathed, stopping to stare. Deciding that I just had to experience my first sunset in Two Moon Bay firsthand, I hurried inside to uncork a bottle of wine. I poured a glass and carted myself out to the edge of my property, where a little concrete bench had been set up near the dunes.

From there, I could see over the hump of grasses that sloped gently down the white-sand beach, several hundred yards to the darkening ocean. The sky was an amazing panorama of fiery colors — pinks and purples of all shades, even some reds and oranges mixed in. Although the day had been sunny and clear, clouds had settled as night approached, bringing with them an accompanying breeze. The air had a suddenly-cooler tinge to it, and I wondered vaguely if we were in for some showers.

Staring off to the left, down the empty stretch of beach, a gentle voice caressed my ears as it drifted along the breeze. Soft and sweet, it was definitely female, and definitely sad. Searching for the sound, I got up from the bench and crossed to the wooden steps that led to the beach. I stood there, at the threshold where my lot met the sand, looking left, then right. Although the sun hovered just above the horizon, there was still enough light to see. No one walked along the lonely shore - in fact,

I could see for miles, it seemed, in both directions. As I stared about, wondering where the song was coming from, it suddenly disappeared.

Thinking I must be losing my mind, I turned back around, facing my property, my hands on my hips. What the . . .?

And there it was again! Subtle, as before - subtle, sweet, and sad. 'Mournful' was the word that came to mind. Like someone was singing for something lost. Or maybe for something she feared she would never find.

Wondering if perhaps a neighbor was playing music nearby, I sipped from my glass, my eyes sweeping the darkened homes. While most appeared unoccupied, three houses to the right someone was home — every room was lit up, including the back veranda, which showcased a glowing Christmas tree. Inside, I could see a woman cooking at the stove, a couple of kids seated at the bar. Maybe the music was coming from there, I thought, searching for an open window or door. But their back porch door was closed, and the windows appeared to be, as well, so the sound was definitely *not* coming from there.

Looking left, four houses up from mine, there was a cook-out going on; beneath the colorful strings of lights, several groups of people gathered in various places throughout the yard. Music blared from a large speaker, but it was a festive, contemporary song - an altogether different sound than the plaintive tune I'd heard.

"Whatever," I said aloud, shaking my head. I could drive myself crazy carrying on like this. Someone was singing from somewhere nearby, I decided. Mystery solved.

It was time for a shower. I would head down to the bar a little early, I decided.

Closing the deck door behind me, I stared out into the night, thinking once again what an unexpected turn of events this was. Not even a month ago, I had thought my life was ending. But now, looking out at the incredible view that was my backyard, I felt alive with anticipation.

Something amazing was going to happen for me here in Two Moon Bay.

I could feel it.

3

An Unexpected Surprise

So it turned out that the mile walk Dixie had described was actually more like two. One point seven three, that is, from my house to The Real Macaw. I was no math major, but when I mapped the distance online, I was a little surprised. Smirking, I grabbed a pair of silver thong sandals from my closet, and chose a long open sweater. It would shield me from the cold on the walk back, I thought, admiring the pretty lavender color. The temperature was still above sixty, so I really wasn't worried about being chilly on the walk there.

"Well, Rae-Rae," I said to my dog, who was sitting up in his bed, watching me. His head cocked to the side at his name. "Hold it down for me, will you? I'll just be gone a couple of hours." Bending to pet his head, I made sure the volume on the TV in my room was loud enough to be heard in the kitchen. Call me an overly-protective pet parent, but I didn't like to leave him alone in a silent house. The rescue shelter he'd come from had played classical music to keep the dogs calm, so I always tried to have relaxing music on for him while I was gone. He'd be zonked out before I reached the beach, anyway, but still.

Closing the door, I walked over to the shrubs where the lab had camped out, but she was gone. Her pups squirmed blindly around, searching for warmth. Maybe she had gotten up to go to the bathroom, I thought, hoping I could move them all into the back porch soon.

The beach at night was a completely different experience than during the day, I realized, inhaling a lungful of the cool, crisp air. The sky was deep and black, a perfect backdrop for the sprinkling of stars that glittered like diamonds in a treasure chest of darkness.

A contented sigh escaped my lips as I walked along the shore. I shivered in delight as the tide lapped its cold tongue against my feet. "Amazing," I said aloud, studying the homes that lined the beach, most of them dark. If I didn't know how safe Two Moon Bay was, I might find the emptiness a little disquieting, but, instead, all I felt was comfortable. And grateful. That thrill of anticipation continued to burn inside me, and I couldn't help but think that something incredible was happening.

Lost in my thoughts, I was startled by the sudden vibrating inside my clutch. Pulling out my phone, I saw Britlee staring expectantly back at me. Accepting the call, I giggled at her grinning face. "Hey, Brit!"

Her eyes lit up as she caught sight of me. "Well, hey there, Riley *E*-lizabeth Larkin!" Her voice and familiar smile washed over me like welcome rain. "How was your first day in that adorable little town I just can't wait to see?"

I smiled, panning the phone around so she could see the beach and starry sky for herself. "Omigosh — it's amazing. Indescribable, really."

Her brows furrowed as she surveyed the view. "Now what exactly was I just lookin' at, honey? I saw nothin' but darkness. Are you in a cave of some sort?" Her face grew worried. "Omigod, Riley — are you lost? You know how you are with directions."

I laughed, then said defensively, "Uh — hello, that was *one* time, and the navigation thing-a-ma-jig was outdated. Not my fault."

Britlee's eyes got that indignant look as she said flatly, "Honey, you know that was one time out of about *fifty* others when you've been lost in a familiar area. And I do believe you just said 'navigation thing-a-ma-jig.'" She paused dramatically. "I rest my case."

Chuckling despite myself, I relented. "Alright, alright, you got me." Then, thinking someone was coming up behind me, I whipped my head around.

But no one was there.

"Riley?" Brit questioned, sounding concerned. "What's wrong?"

Meeting her gaze, I hesitated before answering. I could have sworn I'd heard something — someone talking, or singing, maybe? A woman, I thought, just one voice. But it'd been so faint, and was gone before I knew it. "Uh," I murmured, trying to shake the disconcerted feeling that had suddenly come over me. "Nothing, I just thought I heard something."

Britlee's eyes grew worried. "Honey, what are you *doin'*? You never did say. It looks like you're outside or somethin'."

"I am," I answered, dropping my voice. I thought I heard it again, whatever it was. "I'm on the beach. That's what I was trying to show you a second ago — it's so pretty here, so peaceful."

Britlee's eyes grew as round as saucers as she repeated, alarmed, "Walkin' on the beach! At almost eight o'clock at night? Honey, you could get mugged!"

I giggled at her flair for the dramatic. "Brit — this place has like no crime. They don't even have a jail, for heaven's sake — the last documented crime occurred in 1867." I paused. "I think I'm pretty safe."

Getting that disapproving tone in her voice, Britlee replied, "Sure — the last *documented* crime. I'll bet there's plenty that goes on around there that doesn't get documented, as well. It is, after all, the twenty-first century. Stuff happens, whether we like it or not."

She *did* have a point, though I hated to admit it. I was just about to open my mouth to reply, when I heard it again. That sugar-soft voice was back, singing. The words were indistinguishable, but the sound was unequivocally sad.

Britlee reacted before I did. "Omigod!" she cried. "Riley — is that singin' I hear?"

I gaped at her. "You can hear that?" I whispered, afraid that talking too loudly would somehow make it go away.

"Well, of course I hear it, honey — am I hard o' hearin'?"

We both fell silent, listening.

And then, just as abruptly as it had started, it suddenly stopped. The voice was gone.

We stared at each other for a moment.

Britlee was the first to break the silence. "I cannot *believe* we just heard that," she said incredulously.

I shook my head in annoyance. "Me either," I said, misunderstanding. "I heard that same song earlier, down by my house, but I couldn't figure out where it was coming from." I looked around at the houses here — only one in a swath of about ten had lights on. It was near enough, though, that the sound could be coming from there. "I just can't believe how far their music traveled — my house is a least a mile away!" I exclaimed, noting the time on my watch.

Britlee looked at me like I had just missed the ginormous elephant on the beach. Then, she said snootily, "Riley *E*-lizabeth Larkin, have you lost your mind?"

I gawked at her. "What are you talking about?"

She rolled her eyes. "That wasn't a *neighbor's* music, silly! I don't care how far an ocean breeze can travel. That was *Destina Delgado*! Singin' her sad song along the lonely beach at night."

Now it was my turn to roll my eyes. "Oh, right. The ghost of a long-dead woman who snuck out of her house and was 'never seen or heard from again'? Three *centuries* ago?" I guffawed. "Pah-leez."

Britlee abruptly put her hand over the mouthpiece as she hollered to her son in the background, "Caleb, I need you to set the table for me! Dinner will be ready in ten minutes." She faced me again, and uncovered the microphone to continue our conversation. Then, as Caleb argued with her from the other room, she bellowed, "*Now!*" over her shoulder, in her no-nonsense voice. "Sorry," she apologized. "I didn't mean to shout in your ear. That chile needs to get his back-talkin' behind in gear," she told me. "He's about ready to work my last nerve."

Suppressing a smile, I thought it was business as usual at Britlee's house. Suddenly, I missed her more than I would have thought possible after only two days.

She continued, "Anyway," as she closed her eyes, preparing to deliver a lecture. Judging by the look on her face, I had a feeling I wasn't going to agree.

Trudging through the sand, I told myself that I'd entertain her theory, but I didn't have to believe it.

She explained, "You know the legend as well as I do, Riley E-lizabeth Larkin; Destina Delgado combs the shore alone, singing a mournful tune as she longs for the freedom she knew she would never have . . ."

'Mournful,' I thought, recalling that that was the *exact* word I had used to describe the voice to myself just a few hours ago. I didn't think I had read that descriptor anywhere, so I wondered where Brit had gotten it.

She continued the tale: "Her tune can sometimes be heard on quiet nights, for those who long to hear it . . ." Brit's voice faded into the night as she watched for my reaction. "I think that you, Riley E-lizabeth Larkin, are one of those people who longs to hear it. And so she sings to you." She raised an eyebrow at me. "Well, tell me, honey; am I right or am I *right*?"

I looked speechlessly at the phone, feeling an unexpected chill. What if Brit *was* right? What if the legend *were* true, and the spirit of the lonely Destina really did sing for those willing to hear her song? Could it *be*? I wondered to myself.

Brit mistook my silence for disagreement. "Anyway, you can think what you like," she said, waving a dismissive hand in the air. "But I know what I believe: The voice we just heard was Destina Delgado's."

As I mulled over Brit's theory, Caleb suddenly came into view behind her. He opened the cabinet doors to retrieve a stack of dishes.

Glancing over her shoulder at her son, Britlee said casually, "Well, Riley, honey, I'm gonna leave you with your ghost so I can get dinner on the table." She smiled breezily at me. "You be careful now. And call me soon!"

"I will," I promised. "Love ya."

"Love you, too, honey. Bah!"

As she clicked off, I was left to face the sudden silence. Pondering what she had said, I found myself considering Brit's theory. She *did* have a point — the legend did say that on certain nights, the young woman's song was able to be heard by certain people — usually women — who walked the beach alone.

Still, though, I had a hard time believing in that stuff. I mean — just because someone *claimed* they heard something — even multiple someones over multiple years, all alleging that the same mysterious occurrences happened to them — didn't exactly mean that what they said was true.

Chalking it up to my own particular belief — that a neighbor was playing, or even singing a song that had been transported along the breeze — I studied the sky once more. A crescent moon glowed silverly above the steadily-crashing surf, reflecting off the dark water and white-tipped waves. As if to further convince myself that Brit's theory *wasn't* plausible, I recalled that on one of the websites I'd consulted, the legend had mentioned the song was heard on nights when the moon was full; well, if that notion was correct, this crescent meant that the legend was off by several weeks. Not exactly proof positive, I'd say.

Feeling somewhat reassured, I steered my mind away from thoughts of supernatural songs, and tuned back in to my immediate surroundings. Just ahead, the elegant beach homes ended at the mangroves that separated the residential section of Beach Boulevard from the business part. That meant I was almost to my destination.

As the swampy water trailed eastward toward the center of town, and the coastline curved into the bay, I studied the businesses' piers and handmade signs that were rimmed with festive Christmas lights.

The gloomy sound of a blues tune spilled out from the partially-open doors of Blackheart's Blues Café, a crowded bar whose dim lights glowed in cool blue neon as I passed. The words of a Langston Hughes poem leaped immediately to mind, as I listened to the sorrowful melody, "In a deep song voice with a melancholy tone/I heard that . . . old piano moan—'Ain't got nobody in all this world/Ain't got nobody but ma self. I's gwine to quit ma frownin'/And put ma troubles on the shelf.'" I wondered, vaguely, if the speaker in that poem didn't have something in common with the lonely Destina Delgado. And me.

Even if I didn't believe that her ghost *actually* walked the beach at night, singing for those who 'longed' to hear it, I did know what it felt like to be completely alone in the world. As soon as I'd been born, my mother had signed me over to the state, where I'd disappeared into the foster care system. Yes, I *knew* loneliness. But, I knew how to rise above it, too. And, like the singer in "The Weary Blues," I had put my "troubles on the shelf" and dared to feel a different emotion — the most dangerous one of all, hope. Maybe that's what Destina had felt as she sang her song, with only the moon for company.

I wondered, as I stepped onto The Real Macaw's deck, shaking the sand from my feet, what had *actually* happened to the mournful maiden from the town's most famous story? Had she ever made it out of Two Moon Bay? Had she managed to escape her father's control and find the freedom she so desired? Or had she done the unthinkable and boarded the pirate ship that night, as it glided into the bay? I couldn't help but wonder, as she'd walked the shore alone that night, dreaming of adventure, had she met some crueler, darker fate?

Thinking that I would probably never know, I glanced around the crowded bar, which opened out onto the expansive back deck. Upright heaters had been set out along the boards for the locals, although, to me, the temperature was positively spring-like. Spotting Dixie's red hair at a table on the inside of the bar, beneath the glowing Christmas lights, all thoughts of Destina Delgado and her sweet, sad song disappeared from my mind.

The bar broke into a raucous cheer as the performers bowed a final time. It was Karaoke night at The Real Macaw, and from what I could tell, this crowd took the whole thing pretty seriously. So close to Christmas, the entire place was decked out in holiday lights and gaudy decorations. A festive vibe and competitive flair permeated the beachy air.

Dixie, two of her girlfriends, and I were seated inside the bar, which happened to be built over the mangrove I had spotted on my way up the beach. The inside of the room had floor-to-ceiling windows that rolled up like big garage doors. When it was warm enough, Dixie had explained, the doors were put up so that the patrons and birds for which the place was named could enjoy the outdoors. Several large gilded cages had been custom-built for the beautiful macaws the owners had rescued. At the moment, the well-trained creatures seemed content in their fancy palaces, all of which included a play gym and a bounty of toys.

Startling me out of my musings, Dixie laid a hand on my arm and pointed toward the back entrance. "Oh, look, sug!" she cried, her voice excited. "There's Cal!"

Sure enough, the good-looking older man was standing at the edge of the bar, talking with the bartender and a small woman with a dark pixie haircut. She had an edgy, contemporary look, complete with a Marilyn piercing, black zippered leggings, Doc Martens, and a long flannel shirt.

"He's talkin' with Apple Cassidy," Dixie informed me, "who owns the health-food store. Word has it, she's thinkin' of runnin' for mayor next term!" She looked around at our tablemates, who seemed intrigued by that piece of news.

Spotting us, Cal put up a hand and waved. I couldn't tell if his teeth or watch sparkled more, but in the murkiness of the dimly-lit room, I thought that between the two, someone could go blind.

We all waved as Apple turned to greet us, as well.

"And that's Abby Gellis," Dixie continued, pointing to another patron. "Owner of the bakery/café. That man standin' next to her? That's her husband, Darrell. He's the current mayor."

I nodded, taking in the pleasantly-plump blonde woman who was probably in her mid-forties, but looked much younger. Her round face and jovial smile were warm and inviting, even from a distance. Abby's husband was tall and tanned, with that year-round Florida glow that comes from living in a tropical climate.

Dixie added, "They're talkin' to Cherry Moore. She's the town's librarian."

As I raised my glass to my lips, I choked back an incredulous laugh. Wow, really? Apple and Cherry? I was about to ask where Blueberry was, but held my tongue.

Dixie gazed at me, concerned. "Sug, are you alright?"

I coughed, gaining control of my voice. "Yep — I'm ok. Just went down the wrong way."

She nodded understandingly, swaying to the house music that started to fade out as the DJ's voice shouted excitedly into the microphone, "Mayor Darrell!"

The friendly-faced mayor looked over at the stage in surprise, his sandy blonde hair shining as the spotlight hit him.

"It's time for you and your lovely wife to come on up here and sing your special tune for us!"

Abby's face lit up, as her husband laughed heartily. Must be some sort of inside joke, I figured, noting how the audience laughed and clapped in appreciation. Mayor Gellis — er, Darrell - waved a bashful hand in the air, politely declining. His wife, on the other hand, ran gleefully toward the stage, clapping in excitement. Spotting a striking bi-racial woman who was standing to the side of the bar, Abby grabbed her by the arm, pulling her along.

The DJ announced in surprise, "Oh, there you have it, folks!" He paused as people cheered when the spotlight caught the woman's pretty face. "It looks like Bébé Beauchamps will be joinin' Abby Gellis on stage instead of Mayor Darrell. This is a real treat, y'all! Come on up here, ladies!"

The crowd whistled and cat-called as the smiling women hopped onto the stage. Since our table abutted the north wall and the stage was set up along the south wall, despite the many tables between us, we had a perfect view.

Much to the crowd's delight, Abby and Bébé performed a raucous rendition of Andy Grammer's "Honey, I'm Good." Both could sing, and they harmonized perfectly in just the right places. As the crowd clapped and sang along with the chorus, people sprang to their feet, really getting into the show. Both women were natural entertainers, I thought, wondering if they did local theater.

As they took their bows, hurrying excitedly from the stage, Dixie's eyes were fastened across the bar, staring out toward the back deck. "Oh, my goodness gracious," she murmured, patting her hair self-consciously. "Don't look now, girls, but it's Brooks McKay."

Dixie, sitting at the end of our table and to my left, and her friend, Calista, who was directly across from me, glanced over their shoulders with barely-suppressed excitement on their faces. Cathy, who sat next to Calista, just plain freaked out. All three uttered various exclamations of alarm, fidgeting nervously and whipping out little handheld mirrors to check their lipstick.

I watched their flustered movements in mild amusement, wondering what the big deal was. "Who's Brooks McKay?" I asked, shrugging as they stopped primping to stare at me.

Returning her lipstick to her clutch, Dixie told me, "Why, he's only Two Moon Bay's most eligible bachelor, sug. Good-lookin', kind, and *rich*, he's the one that got away — from us all!" She laughed, looking to her friends for agreement.

Casting anxious looks behind them, the women agreed. "Oh, yeah, honey," the mocha-skinned Calista said. "Despite all o' us throwin' ourselves at him, he still manages to elude us all." She shook her head in wonder.

I raised my eyebrows. What made this guy so desirable, I wondered. There were lots of men who met Dixie's description. Maybe in Two Moon Bay they're harder to come by, but I kind of doubted that. Attempting to catch a glimpse of the wanted man, I gave up as a Paul Bunyan-sized guy standing in front of our table pretty much eclipsed the entire bar.

While Dixie and the girls whispered nervously amongst themselves, I excused myself to go to the restroom. Waiting until the cocktail waitress skittered around the lumberjack, I started past him, not noticing as an incredibly good-looking guy made a break for it from the opposite direction. Our eyes met at the same moment. He looked as surprised as I felt. We crashed into each other, our arms clasping for an awkward second in order to avoid falling.

As we righted ourselves, I stared up into the softest, bluest eyes I had ever seen.

The tall, dark-haired stranger broke out into easy laughter, his voice sounding musical and somehow familiar. "Oh, man, I'm so sorry!" he cried, looking down at me. "Are you ok?" he asked in concern.

Feeling out of breath for some unknown reason, I responded, "I'm fine — thanks."

We held each other's eyes for a moment. Then, at the same time, realizing that we were still grasping each other's arms, we let go, taking a step back. Staring up into those enigmatic eyes, I felt an overpowering sense of déjà vu, like I had met him before — even *known* this man I had never seen. How was it possible, I mused, to feel that way when you've never *actually* met? I shook my head in an attempt to clear the thought. Meeting him was somehow . . . un-nerving. And also more exhilarating than any first-encounter I'd ever experienced in my entire life.

His eyebrows furrowed as he asked, "Have we met before?"

I shook my head slowly. "I don't think so," I answered. Although you do seem *very* familiar, I thought to myself.

"Huh," he said, looking unconvinced. "You seem so familiar to me."

Omigod! I was screaming inside. He's reading my mind! "I'm Riley," I said, offering my hand. How could someone whose heart was beating so fast sound so calm, I marveled, impressed with myself.

His hand was warm and strong as it clasped mine. Let's just say I was *not* expecting the firestorm of chemistry that erupted suddenly between us. Little waves of electricity tingled through me as he held my gaze, brushing his lips across my fingers in a chivalrous, and somehow *not* cheesy, greeting.

I almost died right there in the bar, but still I managed to keep my cool.

"It's nice to meet you, Riley. I'm . . ." he started, as the booming voice of Calhoun Foxworth the Third bombed the moment like a vocal cannon.

Cal sauntered over, beaming. His teeth gleamed like perfect diamonds. Hugging me hello, he exclaimed, "Well, hello there, Miss Riley!

I see you've met ole Brooks here." He chuckled good-naturedly, clapping my prince on the shoulder.

Brooks and I exchanged an amused look as I answered, "Hey, Cal." I could see that Brooks was trying to hold back a grin. It surprised me that I could so easily read this sexy man to whom I was so unbelievably, incredibly attracted. "I was just in the process of meeting him when you came over."

Cal's smile flashed again in the darkened bar.

I chastised myself for leaving my sunglasses in my purse at home. Had I known he'd be here, I would have brought them with me.

His voice thundered, "Oh, well, hey - don't let me interrupt y'all!" He clapped Brooks once more on the back. "It's good to see ya there, buddy."

Struggling to right his drink, Brooks agreed, "Yeah — yeah, nice to see you, Cal."

As the golfer started toward our table, I thought I might actually make it out of a meeting with him without being checked out or hit on. But as he passed by, he glanced down at my butt. Darnit! I thought, disappointed. So close.

"Oh, and Riley," he added, turning back to face us. "Remember our tee time tomorrow — nine a.m. at the club."

Brooks looked questioningly at me.

I shook my head at him before turning to Cal. "Uh — Cal?" I asked with a smile. "You and I don't *have* a tee time tomorrow. Remember? You gave me your card, and I said we *might* play together sometime?" Might, maybe, never, I thought with a smirk.

Cal's tanned face registered surprise. Then, he let out a hearty laugh, his flawless teeth sending beacons of light across the bar. If he stood on the shore, I mused, he could serve as a lighthouse. Keep the boats safe from harm.

"Well, that's right, now, ain't it?" he asked, chuckling. Holding up his highball glass, he said, "Maybe I've had one too many o' these." He winked at Brooks. "Or maybe I was just dreamin'." Then, catching my eye, he promised, "You'll say yes eventually, darlin' — you'll see."

I couldn't help but smile as he walked away. Despite his appreciative, wandering eye, one thing Cal sure had going for him was his charm.

Brooks and I looked at each other, then burst out laughing.

"Wow, seems like you've made a friend," he said, gazing after Cal.

"Yeah," I agreed. "I guess you could say that. I mean - he seems like a nice guy." I glanced over my shoulder as Cal greeted Dixie and her friends with a hug and a drool. I guess every girl got that kind of treatment from him, which was actually quite comforting.

"Oh, he is," Brooks assured me. "Real nice guy. He has kind of a reputation, but he's actually pretty harmless."

I raised my eyebrows. "Reputation, huh?"

He smiled, taking a gulp of his drink. "Yeah, as being a ladies' man." He pointed back to the table, to where Cal led a blushing Dixie out onto the dance floor. "My guess? He started it himself."

I giggled. "You're kidding!" I cried, watching as they boogie-oogie-oogied to The Beatles' "Twist and Shout." Karaoke was temporarily suspended during the DJ's bathroom break.

Brooks shook his head. "Wish I were, Riley. Wish I were."

Thinking how easy it was to be in Brooks' company, I was surprised when a light-brown hand reached out of the crowd and grabbed my arm.

I looked over in surprise to find the shockingly-pretty Bébé Beauchamps standing next to me. Her dark-brown eyes stared at me. "You need to come with me," she said, her speaking voice as sultry as her singing one. I thought I detected the unmistakable lilt of a Louisiana accent. She was Creole, I was guessing.

I looked dumbly at her. "Pardon?"

She glanced at Brooks, then laughed. "I'm up next," she explained slowly, as if I might not understand. "And I need a partner. You look like a girl who would know the words to every Bangles song ever written." She peered at Brooks for agreement.

He shrugged. "Ya gotta give her that," he said, grinning.

"Seriously?" I gaped first at him, then her. "Hi, I'm Riley," I said, sticking out my hand. "And sure, I'm a Bangles fan; thank you both very much for stereotyping me," I quipped, eyeing them suspiciously.

Bébé stared skeptically at my hand — and didn't bother shaking it. Not rudely, I observed, letting it fall to my side. She just seemed to have her own unique way of doing things. "Uh huh," she continued, anxious to get on with it. "And I'm your new best friend. Now let's git goin', shorty, and sing the heck outta this song."

As the enigmatic woman shoved me toward the stage, I shot a pleading look over my shoulder at Brooks. He shrugged, holding up his drink as though he were completely powerless to stop her. I couldn't help but note the grin on his amused face.

"So," I asked, making conversation with my abductor. "What are we singing?"

Arriving at the foot of the stage, she looked at me like I was some kind of moron. "Duh. 'Eternal Flame'."

I nodded. That *was* a pretty awesome choice. When I did Karaoke with the girls back home, I personally liked Roxette's "It Must Have Been Love," but "Eternal Flame" was a solid selection.

DJ Way Too Cool, or whatever his name was, came over the mic, ushering us to the stage. "Awww, ladies and gents!" he cried, giving us both the once-over as we grabbed our microphones. "We have a newbie in our midst." He gave me a questioning look as I told him my name. "Bébé Beauchamps and Riley Larkin are gonna bring down the house with this one — a real tear-jerker: the Bangles' 'Eternal Flame'! Give it up!"

The crowd threw up a cheer as the lights went down. A hush fell over the audience as the spotlight hit us and the instrumental intro began. Although we hadn't talked about it, both Bébé and I had somehow agreed that she would lead. She took a deep breath and delivered the first breathy words. Her voice was luscious and velvety, wrapping around you and holding you tight.

The audience swayed to the music, completely under her spell. I tapped the beat on my leg, closing my eyes as I listened to the syrupy sound of her voice.

I stepped forward as the chord changed. The spotlight morphed into a pale purple as I sang, staring out into the darkened room, wondering vaguely if anyone was listening. The light in my eyes prevented me from seeing the audience, but I knew I would continue anyway. That's how it was when I was singing, completely at the mercy of the music.

My voice crescendoed as Bébé joined in at the chorus. And then, the next thing I knew, the song was over. The red and green lights were spotlighting us once again. DJ Whatever hopped onstage as the crowd went nuts. "Oh. My. God. Ladies and Gentlemen! That was *insane!*" He shook his head in wonder as we returned our mics to the set. "I can see why their flame is eternal - am I right, fellas?"

As we scooted down the steps, I fanned myself with my hands. I had forgotten how hot it can get onstage. Bébé was looking at me, I realized. Her dark eyes were raw and real, like they saw everything and hid nothing. "What?" I asked, wondering with a sense of panic if I'd just performed to a packed house with something stuck to my face.

She shook her head. "Nothing. You're just — you're good," she answered, cocking one hip. Though she was a couple of inches shorter than I was, Bébé was long and lean. Her pale-sienna skin looked soft and shimmery in the shadows of the bar. She had springy brownish/blonde curls that framed her features - cheekbones that would make Gisele green with envy, and a perfectly-crafted nose. Her no-nonsense attitude was as direct as her gaze, and her dark eyes didn't miss a trick.

I nodded, taking her in. Although I didn't know her, I felt like I did. And I instinctively knew that we would be great friends. "So are you," I said simply.

Just then, Dixie ran up, with Cal hot on her heels. Both were flushed and giddy with excitement - or drink, perhaps. "Omigosh, sug," my realtor gushed, grabbing my arm. "Y'all were *amazin'*!"

Cal nodded enthusiastically. "Y'all really were," he agreed, staring at my chest. "What a number! I thought Dixie here was goin' to start bawlin' any second!"

She swatted him. "Oh, you hush," she told him. Then, to me and Bébé, she whispered, "I actually *did*! Y'all made me cry."

At that moment, Apple and Cherry hurried over, and a little crowd formed, all offering their praises. Before long, their attention became overwhelming, and I found myself craving some air. I smiled my thanks at everyone, squeezing through the bodies. Pushing past Paul Bunyan, I made a break for it when I caught sight of the back deck.

Standing at the railing, overlooking the marsh below, I took in a deep breath. The air was cool and crisp, refreshing against my hot skin. Realizing I had left my sweater and clutch inside, I rubbed my arms, turning around to head back inside.

To my surprise, there before me stood Brooks McKay. Holding my clutch in one hand, and my sweater in the other, he looked at me with an unabashed smile on his lips.

Getting over my initial shock, I laughed in relief. "Oh," I murmured, clutching my heart. "You scared me." I stepped forward to retrieve my items. "How did you know?"

Helping me into my sweater, Brooks explained, "I saw the mob. You got totally squeamish as they swarmed in, so I grabbed your stuff, thinking you'd make a break for it."

I smiled at him, thinking there were so many things I was feeling at that moment that terrified the crap out of me. "Thank you," I said quietly, feeling like he somehow knew everything I *wasn't* saying.

He stared back at me for a moment, and I swear I heard little sparks of electricity sizzling on the Florida air. Finally, he shrugged, his demeanor lightening. "Hey, it was no big deal. I mean — I thought, this way, I'd have an excuse to walk you home." He smiled at me, wriggling his brows and offering his elbow.

Grinning back at him, I linked my arm through his as we trudged down the steps and onto the beach. "Slick," I told him, as we walked along, our arms dropping so that our fingers found each other's, tentatively at first, yet eager and searching. We walked along that way for what seemed like hours, a comfortable silence stretching around us like a warm, familiar hug.

Gazing up at the moon, I found it hard to believe that this was only the first night of my life here in Two Moon Bay. Everyone I'd met so far was so real, so open - it was like we were instant friends. Especially the enigmatic Bébé Beauchamps, with her silky voice and 'screw you' attitude. I felt like we had known each other our whole lives.

And this man, I thought, studying his profile as we walked. This man whose eyes and voice and touch were as familiar as my own, but spoke to me a thousand words without uttering a sound. How was it possible that we had just met, I wondered, staring out at the ocean. How was it possible I had not walked this shore before, even a thousand times?

A sudden breeze stirred the dunes just then, startling me from my thoughts. In the same moment, a gentle touch grazed my left arm. I stopped, glancing down, only to realize it wasn't Brooks at all.

On my right side, he peered down at me, a curious expression on his face. "You ok?"

I waited before responding, for that lonely song started up again, capturing my attention. This time, it was closer! And *this* time, I could almost make out the words. "Do you hear that?" I asked, pointing to my left.

Brooks listened, then shook his head. "I don't hear anything, Riley. Just the waves."

My eyes grew wide. "Seriously?" I asked dubiously. "You really don't . . .?" But my voice trailed off as he shook his head again, his face answering for him.

"Never mind," I said, not wanting him to think I was crazy. But then again, I argued with myself, I *must* be crazy! Hearing phantom voices and sweet sad songs? What's next? Would I glimpse Blackheart Bellacroix's ship on the horizon, too?

"Uh, Riley," he said gently, pointing. "I think we're here."

Surprised, I followed his finger toward the glowing yellow light inside my house.

"Oh," I muttered, wondering, at first, how he knew where I lived.

As if reading my unspoken question, Brooks quickly explained, "It's a small town. We all knew 'Riley Larkin' was moving in, like, a *day* after you bought this place." He grinned.

"Right," I said, remembering the welcome sign — population six thousand. "The rumor mill works over-time in a small town."

He chuckled. "Yep, it's pretty much an around-the-clock gossip factory."

"Well," I started, feeling like that awkward part of a first date had descended upon us. Even though this *wasn't* an actual date, I reminded myself. Mounting the wooden walkway, I asked, "Would you like to come in? I can make you some coffee. Offer you a protein bar," I said with a smile.

He laughed, shaking his head no. "As hard as that is to turn down, I'm going to have to say no," he said. "I've got the girls, who will be getting ready for bed, and a babysitter who needs to get home."

I nodded, wondering how old his daughters were, and where his wife was. Oh, God, I thought frantically, is he *married*? But then I remembered Dixie had said he was single, so I relaxed. I really *am* going crazy, I told myself, hoping my face didn't betray any of the turmoil that was going on inside my head.

"But," he continued, stepping onto the deck, so close that our toes were touching. He placed a gentle finger beneath my chin. "I do hope you'll agree to have dinner with me sometime soon. My place, my treat." Tilting my chin up, he gazed into my eyes as he whispered, "What do you say?"

Feeling that undeniable energy drawing me in, I nodded. "I'd like that."

As his lips met mine, I melted into his chest, his body, the solid feel of him. His arms encircled my waist as we lost ourselves in the moment. Whether it was seconds or hours when our lips parted, I couldn't say. All I knew was, I would never be the same.

I hadn't gone looking for this. Hadn't asked for, nor expected it. To be honest, I hadn't even been *wanting* any kind of relationship — to say nothing of a full-blown love affair! Oh, God, I wondered, panicking. Is that was this was? *Love*? Naw, couldn't be. It doesn't happen like that, does it? Just find you when you're least expecting it?

As I turned away, my mind reeling with so many questions, I could feel Brooks' eyes on my back. I could feel them boring into me like a thousand exclamation points of emotion. And suddenly, it hit me like a lightning bolt. I knew one thing for sure.

Whatever *this* was — whatever you'd call it - it was unstoppable, real and true. It had found me, surprised me, caught me unaware.

And even more terrifying?

I was ready to embrace it.

4

New Beginnings

$\mathcal{I}$t was a *long* night.

In a totally good, romantic, and swoony kind of way. As the wee hours of the morning ticked closer to the dawn, I replayed all of the heart-stopping moments I'd shared with Brooks. Translation: sleep was *totally* out of the question. I mean - every time I tried to close my eyes, all I could see was Brooks McKay's handsome face.

And those eyes — wow, those eyes. The softness of his gaze, the way I felt so . . . *seen* when he looked at me. Like he knew me completely, despite the fact that we'd just met. It was amazing, yet terrifying, the more I thought about it - especially since I felt like I knew him already, too. I marveled again and again that when our eyes met, it felt as if the whole world stopped, and it was just . . . *us*. In a word: it was breathtaking. The man literally took my breath away.

As if *that* wasn't enough to keep me up, there was also the matter of his lips — and that *kiss*, which I just couldn't get out of my mind. Honestly, I couldn't remember *ever* feeling that way with Jason. Crazy as it was, although Brooks and I had just met, I'd felt more of a connection with him in the few minutes we'd spent together than in all my years with Jason.

And that, I suspected, was the source of the *other* thing that had kept me awake: the guilt. I guess after six — technically, seven — years of marriage, I was conditioned to feel guilty when someone other than my husband expressed an interest in me. And since I was so incredibly drawn to Brooks, I think *that* pushed my guilty conscience over the top. Silly, I know, but I was new to all this - and quite frankly, surprised by it all. I mean, I hadn't exactly been *looking* for a relationship.

But, I reasoned, staring at the ceiling, waiting for sleep to come, whether or not I'd been looking for . . . whatever this was, it didn't change the fact that I had undeniable feelings for Brooks. And he seemed to have them for me, too.

So rather than flipping through the channels to distract my racing thoughts, I decided to embrace my insomnia and tackle my growing to-do list. What does that mean in sleep-deprived Riley-speak? It means I ditched my PJs for my work clothes, turned on my 'Cleaning' playlist, and took to the house like a woman possessed. Every room got a thorough scrub-down. That included the bedrooms on the left wing - which I kind of thought of as the girls' rooms - the office and craft room, great room, bedrooms on the right wing — even the back veranda. Raegan seemed flustered by my constant sweeping and vacuuming, and finally got up from his bed, just as the sun was coming up. He stood by deck door, staring out into the yard, whining faintly.

"What is it, boy?" I asked. Then, realizing it was probably time for a bathroom break, I held open the door for him. "Time to go out?"

But instead of running out into the yard, he sat back on his haunches, staring fixedly ahead. It was like he was looking at something. Something I couldn't see.

"Rae-Rae?" I questioned, then stopped, thinking I had heard something. Listening, I strained against the silence.

But nothing was there, save for the wind that felt a little heavy, like it carried with it the threat of rain.

Still staring toward the dunes, Raegan let out an unexpected bark before darting out the open door. As the sky started to lighten, I saw his wagging tail disappear behind the mound of grasses near the beach.

"Huh," I said aloud, thinking it seemed like he was answering someone's call. Shrugging, I brewed a pot of coffee and relaxed on my newly set-up back porch. One definite plus to being awake so early in the morning was experiencing the magnificent sunrise. As I polished off the last of the coffee, listening to the sounds of the ocean and the birds, I drank in the panorama of colors that lit the sky. What a way to start the day!

Deciding it was time to feed Rae-Rae, I figured the mama dog must be hungry, too. Since she'd had her babies here, I felt confident that she wouldn't be moving them any time soon. So after the canines were fed, I got my day started, too. After a steamy shower in my showroom-worthy bathroom, I brewed a fresh pot of coffee (it's an addiction, I know) and made my to-do list for rest of the day. I had just sat down with my java when a man rounded the left corner of my house. He was young — probably in his mid-twenties, dressed in tan cargo shorts, combat boots, and a plain white T-shirt. As he made his way to the center of my yard, he carefully inspected the flower beds that lined my house.

Figuring he must be with the lawn crew, I got up from my seat and met him on the pool deck. "Hello!" I called, closing the screened door behind me.

Hearing my voice, Raegan, who had returned just in time for breakfast, let loose with a succession of excited barks as he ran toward our guest.

The gardener smiled, his perfect teeth contrasting nicely with his copper skin. "Hi, there! You must be Miss Riley."

I nodded, smiling.

"I'm Chuy," he told me, pumping my hand warmly. He handed me a business card.

'Juan Carlos Lopez - Owner,' it read, with the name 'Chuy' beneath it. Owner, I thought, impressed. He seemed so young.

"I hope it's not too early," he said, looking around. "I'd like to get an early start if that's ok with you. Looks like we have a good bit of work to do around here."

"Yeah, definitely," I agreed. "And it's not too early at all," I assured him. "So, tell me," I said, eager to hear about his ideas. "What do you have in mind?"

We walked around the front of the house to look at some plans he'd drawn up. I was inspired by his vision, which was perfectly in sync with the tasteful, elegant concept I had in mind. "This looks great, Chuy," I told him. "You drew this up yourself?

He nodded, humbly averting his eyes. "Thanks. Yeah — I've always thought this was a beautiful piece of property, so it was kind of easy. Say," he said, his eyes brightening, "you ready to see what I'm thinking of for the pool area?"

I stared at him. "You do pool stuff, too?"

He shrugged. "Well, yeah — lots of lawn guys here do. Usually, people want landscaping and pool work done at the same time, so we provide that service. Unless you don't want that," he said quickly, trying to get a read on my wants. "It's just that Dixie had mentioned . . ." he began, but I interrupted, "No, that's perfect!" He looked relieved.

I explained, "I was going to have to call someone for that, anyway, so if you can do it, that saves me the trouble. Let's see what you came up with!"

As we finalized our plans, I knew that, with Chuy, my yard and pool were in good, capable hands. "Thanks, Chuy," I told him gratefully. I shook his hand to officially seal the deal. "Ok — you're hired!"

He grinned, rolling up the plans and sticking them back in his truck. He signaled to his crew, waiting patiently inside their vehicles. As they sprang into motion, I told Chuy that he and the boys were free to use the entryway bathroom. He politely declined with a shake of his head. "Oh, thanks, Miss Riley, but we'll try not to enter the house. With our dirty work boots and all, we don't want to track inside. My men will alternate their breaks every few hours, though, and town isn't too far away."

I smiled. "Ok, then — whatever you prefer."

He started to turn away.

"Oh, and Chuy," I added.

He turned back around to face me.

"Just Riley, ok?" I grinned.

He smiled widely in return. "No problem — 'Just Riley.'"

We laughed.

Deciding it was getting late — nearly eight-thirty - I showered, fed the dogs, and hopped in my car. I had big plans for today: stop off at the café for a tasty beverage, head to Naples to snag some decorations and furniture from my to-do list, pick up some groceries, and maybe do a little browsing through the shops in town. Plus, the living-room furniture was set to arrive today, and I needed to be there to sign for it.

Stump and his crew pulled into the opposite end of the driveway as I was heading out. We conferred for a moment about his plans for the day, and I ran my request by him for a window bench in the master bedroom. He assured me he could have someone start on it today.

"Awesome," I agreed, impressed with the workers Dixie had recruited for my projects. "I'm really going to have to do something nice for her," I said to myself, deciding I would throw her a dinner party. She could invite whomever she wanted, and, of course, I would invite the guys and their crews. I loved entertaining, Dixie seemed to like to socialize, and the guys, I could tell, were going to do an amazing job, so it seemed like a win-win-win.

Cruising through town, I perused the busy streets. People here sure got an early start, I thought, noting that the restaurants looked pretty crowded. As yesterday, several people were exercising — I even recognized the two moms jogging behind their strollers. Pulling into an open spot in front of the vibrant pink café, I told Raegan I would bring him something nice. Probably a scone — he really seemed to enjoy them. Scooting up the steps, I greeted the friendly passersby and hopped in line.

Just as I was about to order, I felt someone lean over my shoulder and whisper in my ear. I'd been so absorbed in the chalkboard menu that I hadn't even heard the man sidle up behind me.

I whirled around. "Cal!" I cried, catching my breath. "I didn't hear you come in."

His face registered surprise at my reaction, then quickly changed to one of joy. He laughed heartily. "Well, I'm sorry there, darlin' — I didn't mean to scare you!" He grinned at me, his mischievous blue eyes sparkling. "I just wanted to say hey."

I nodded, telling the young barista my order. "Well, hey to you," I returned, stepping to the left so he could order. "I thought you had a tee time right about . . ." I paused, glancing at my watch. "Now," I finished, looking questioningly at him.

He stared at his expensive watch. "Oh, well, for goodness' sake!" he cried. "I didn't realize it was so late!"

For someone who owned such a pricey timepiece, I wondered how often he actually looked at it. "Uh, yep," I said, handing the kid at the cash register my card. "We wouldn't want you to be late." I grinned, tapping a finger to the side of my head. "Seeing as a good game of golf starts in the mind, and all," I teased.

Recalling yesterday's conversation, Cal broke into a smile. He was about to fire off a retort when Abby's cheerful voice called suddenly from the kitchen, "Well, if it isn't our newest town resident, Riley Larkin!"

Abby and I hugged hello, formally introducing ourselves. Cal seemed content to stare at my boobs while we ladies got acquainted.

Scurrying back around the old-fashioned glass counter, Abby continued our conversation. "You were just fantastic last night, Riley!" she gushed, piling delectable gluten-filled pastries into a large white box. "I mean, you and Bébé had me in tears." She shook her head in wonder as she piled even more dough into the box. I felt my hips widening with every one she stacked atop the next. "That's how you know someone has a beautiful voice," she said, looking over the counter at Cal and me. "When they can make you cry." She shook her head in appreciation as she deftly wound a string around the box and knotted it before I could figure out what had just happened.

I waved like it was no big deal. "Aw, thanks," I said sincerely, "but *you* were amazing. Where did you study?" I asked, knowing she must have had formal training.

Abby blushed. "Oh - well, I've been singin' since I was a little bitty girl in my daddy's church," she said bashfully, handing me the box.

I accepted it with a look of appreciation and horror; what would I *do* with all this pastry? The thing about baked goods is they looked far better on display than on my thighs.

Before I could protest, she continued, "Plus, I was a music major in college." Thinking about it, a look of amusement crossed her face. "But that was a *long* time ago!" she exclaimed. Then, growing serious, she said, "Riley," looking intently into my eyes. "Would you be interested in bein' in our holiday musical? Our director, who has some important speaking and singing parts, has laryngitis, and I haven't been able to find a replacement for her." She looked pleadingly at me. "We could really use your voice!"

By then, Cal had lost interest in my chest, and had moseyed over to a group of college girls whose tight T-shirts boasted the name of the local university. They giggled and tee-heed as the famous golfer posed for selfies with them.

Abby's question caught me off-guard. She took my look of surprise for one of repugnance, and hurriedly said, "You know what? That's ok; no biggie. If you want to, great, but . . ."

I cut in, not wanting to give her the wrong idea. "No, it's ok — I was just taken aback is all. I'd *love* to be in the musical!" I assured her. What a great way to meet people! I thought. And how nice to be asked.

Abby's round face lit up, her cheeks flushing with excitement. "Really?" She looked so pleased. "Oh, that's great, Riley! Here, let me give you my card." She trotted over to the cash register and handed me a pink-and-white card with an adorable pink-frosted cupcake on the front. "My home and cell are on there. Call my cell so I have your info, and I'll text you the time and place. We'll be rehearsing every day this week — well, for the next five days, since we perform on Christmas Eve."

I nodded, already sending her a text. "There, I just texted you." I smiled at her as I turned to leave. "Thanks, Abby — I'm really looking forward to it!"

"Oh, me, too — you'll be a wonderful addition to the show, I just know it!" she raved. "Thanks for coming in!"

We waved goodbye as I sipped my delicious caramel cappuccino. As I passed by Cal and his groupies, I offered him the box of goodies.

He put up a hand. "Oh, no thanks, darlin'; I'm watchin' my figure!" he proclaimed, putting a well-tanned and bejeweled hand on his flat stomach. He laughed, looking around at the giggling girls as they indulged his humor.

"Right," I agreed. "Well, ladies?" I asked, swirling the box in what I considered to be an appetizing circle.

They declined, looking as horrified as I had felt when Abby handed it to me.

"That's ok," I told them, not that they cared. "I've got two crews of hard-working men at my house; I'm sure they'll appreciate the carbs and calories."

As I waved goodbye, Cal graciously excused himself from his new fans and walked with me to my car.

"Say there, Riley," he began, his eyes all a-twinkle. "You change your mind about that golf game yet?"

Opening my car door, I smirked. Shaking my head, I said, "Now, Cal, you know the answer to that question - don't you?"

Unconcerned about the traffic that had slowed to swerve around him as he stood near my door in the north-bound lane on Main Street, Cal grinned as he shut my door. "Alright, alright, I'm just checkin'." He promised with a mischievous look in his eye, "As I said — you'll change your mind eventually, Riley Larkin. You'll see."

Chuckling to myself as I merged onto the street, I couldn't help but think that he was probably right. Despite the fact that Cal had a penchant for staring at my boobs, he really wasn't so bad. I mean, really - what harm could playing a little old round of golf cause, anyway, I asked myself, not seeing the curious look on Brooks McKay's face as he walked down the street toward the café, on his way to get his morning coffee.

— ◠ ◡ —

Pulling into my drive just after noon that day, I was surprised to see a small child working alongside Chuy and his crew. Figuring one of the guys had brought his kid to work with him, I turned off the engine, only to be startled by Raegan's energetic barking. He suddenly leaped from the passenger seat and onto my lap, clamoring against the window.

"Oh, gosh, Rae!" I muttered, not expecting the eighty pounds of enthusiasm to fling himself on me. "Just a second, buddy, and I'll let you out," I said, wondering what was so urgent about getting out of the car that very second.

As he continued woofing, staring intently through my window, I followed his gaze. There, standing beside my door, was the smiling face of my stepdaughter, Capri. She grinned at me, waving to Raegan. I could see that one of her front teeth was missing; I recalled that that tooth had been loose the last time I'd seen her, about three weeks ago.

"Omigod, Capri!" I exclaimed, scrambling to reach around Raegan, who was licking the glass between anxious barks.

Capri giggled, stepping back from the door as Raegan and I tumbled out. She positively glowed with excitement, her dirty-blonde hair shining in the sun. Her cheeks were rosy and the tops of her shoulders were red, which told me she'd been out here for a while without any sunblock. "Hi, Riley!" she said shyly, hugging me.

"Capri, I'm so happy to see you!" I squealed, hugging her tight. Then, pulling back, I asked with alarm, "But what *are* you doing here, honey? Is everything ok?" I kneeled down to be at her eye level. "Raegan, back," I commanded, pointing where I wanted him to sit. He wouldn't stop licking poor Capri's face.

Instead of answering, my tiny stepdaughter looked down at her feet, which were bare. Lord only knew what kind of ants or wasps lay beneath the grass, just waiting to bite her little toes.

"Capri?" I coaxed, urging her to look at me. "You're not in trouble, sweetie," I assured her. "I just need you to tell me what's going on." I held out my hand. "Come on, let's go inside and call your dad."

"No!" she protested, dropping my hand. She stopped on the sidewalk, staring up at me with a beseeching look on her face. "I don't want to talk to him!"

A couple of the yard guys looked over to see what the commotion was all about.

Squatting down, I took her hands. Ever an easy-going child, Capri wasn't one to throw fits, or even argue. That's how I knew something was wrong. "Sweetie, what's going on? If you don't tell me, I can't help you."

Finally, Capri blurted out, "Me and Alex ran away. We ran away to be with you!" Her big brown eyes welled with tears. "I'm sorry, Riley. We didn't mean to be bad; we just wanted to see you, to spend Christmas with you!" She threw herself into my arms, sobbing.

Holding her close, I cradled her head against my neck. "It's ok, sweetie. It's ok," I murmured into her hair, the way I had since she was a baby, whenever she was sick or upset.

The front door closed just then, and at the same moment, Raegan began to bark. Looking up, I was surprised to see Alex's tall figure hurrying down the walk. Her long, honey-colored hair bounced around her middle, and I couldn't help but notice that her face was worried. "Riley!" she cried, flinging herself against me and Capri.

By now, Chuy's crew had ceased their work, staring at the spectacle on the front lawn. As I stepped back from our embrace, wiping Capri's tears and stroking Alex's hair, I caught sight of them gaping at us. I smiled politely and waved. "We're ok — sorry about that," I told them. "Oh!" I said, remembering. "I have pastries!"

The men exchanged dubious looks as I ran around to the trunk. Extracting Abby's package from a cooler with which I always travel, I handed the box to Capri. "I need you to take these to Chuy for me, please," I told her.

Pleased to be given a chore, she nodded, smiling, and took off around the left side of the house.

Alex watched me warily from the sidewalk.

"Well?" I asked her, pointing to the back of my car, which was loaded down with goods. "You gonna help me, or just stand there?" I smiled to let her know she was not in trouble.

What's done was done. My fifteen-year-old stepdaughter had somehow managed to fly herself and her eight-year-old sister several hundred miles without telling a soul or asking her parents' permission. That deed was not for *me* to punish. Secretly, I was elated to see them, even more so to find out that they missed me and wanted to spend the holidays together. But I was also very worried about the circumstances that must have prompted two popular, well-rounded girls to voluntarily uproot their lives over Christmas break to go to a place they'd never been. Resolved to figure out what was going on, I decided to have the girls call their parents as soon as we got in the house.

Joining me at the back of the car, Alex asked defensively, "Are you gonna rat us out?" as she grabbed a couple of dingy-looking milk crates from the trunk. With a little paint, they would be fabulous plant stands for the back porch.

Choosing to ignore her question for the moment, I gave a noncommittal shake of my head as we trudged up the front walk. Although her misdeeds were not for me to penalize, I could not condone them, either. Alex needed to know that what she had done was not to be taken lightly. I knew that by being aloof, I could help her see her mistake by withholding my affection so she would seek my approval. "Set those down on the porch, there," I said pointing. "I'll clean them off out here before bringing them into the house."

Rolling her eyes, my teenager did as she was told. She followed me back out to the car for another load. "Well?" she asked impatiently.

I knew perfectly well what she was talking about, but didn't want her to think she'd get off that easily. "Well, what?" I asked innocently, handing Capri an ornate sconce as she came around from the other side of the car.

She was out of breath as she said in a rush, "Riley, there's a mother dog with puppies living outside your house!" She pointed, nearly dropping the patinaed piece.

"Ooh, Capri, careful!" I said, righting the object in her hands. "Please use both hands, and put it on the porch with the other things," I told her. "And, yes, I know!" I called after her. Darn, I had meant to ask Abby if she knew of anyone missing a dog, but I figured I could do that later. "Help me with these shutters," I said to Alex, whose hazel eyes had been glued to me since she'd originally asked her question.

Sighing, Alex took the ends of the six-foot shutters I intended to use for somebody's headboard. She had a way of getting an attitude when she'd didn't get her way, but I could see that this time, her attitude was born of wariness — and guilt.

As we set the shutters down against the wall, I finally looked at her and said, "You don't have to worry; I'm not mad at you. And I'm not going to make you leave."

Relief washed over her face and her posture visibly changed.

"*But*," I told her, "You and Capri have to call your dad — and mom — and explain what you did."

She started to protest, "But, Riley . . ."

"No buts," I cut in, putting up my hand. "You know that's the right thing to do." I looked at her with raised eyebrows, but she gave in, nodding resolutely. "What should you do if you know you've done something wrong?" I asked her, rehashing what Jason and I had instilled in the girls since they were little.

She looked reluctantly at me. "Apologize and make it right."

I nodded. "That's the best thing to do. They must be worried sick!"

She gave me an incredulous look. "Uh - yeah, right. My *mom* — worry about us?" she scoffed. "She's never even home anymore. And Dad," she looked away, her eyes getting all shiny. "Dad just wants us gone all the time," she murmured, trying to hold back the hurt that came out in a rush. "He just wants to be with . . ." she looked guiltily at me, not wanting to say his girlfriend's name. "You know . . ."

"Oh, honey," I said, pulling her in for another hug. Alex *never* cried. In the nine years I'd known her, I'd only ever seen her cry one time, at her grandmother's funeral. She was a tough cookie. "I'm sorry; I had no idea it was like that for you guys." I pulled back, looking her in the eye. "How long has this been going on?"

She looked down, not wanting to admit the truth. "Like," she began, knowing I wouldn't leave her alone until she told me, "since you guys separated."

I couldn't believe it. "Since last *year*?" I cried. I had no idea. Stunned, I didn't know what to say. "I'm so sorry," I repeated lamely, feeling like a terrible parent.

How could I not have known, I wondered, racking my brain. Had I been that wrapped up in my own feelings that I hadn't noticed what the girls were going through?

And then, as Alex stared silently back at me, it hit me. *That's* why, when I first moved to the mountain house, the girls had asked to go with me! They'd begged and pleaded, but I had said no, since they would have to start over in a whole new school system. At the time, I had thought — and their parents had agreed — that would be too much change on top of everything else. But that was it, I realized, feeling like I had betrayed them, like I had let them down. They had been trying to tell me what they really needed, and I had been too self-absorbed to listen. "Omigod, Alex, I'm sorry," I whispered. "I didn't mean to let you down."

She put a comforting arm around my shoulders. "It's not your fault, Riley - you didn't know. We didn't tell you." She looked at her sister as Capri ran up to us just then, her smile fading as she saw our faces. "We didn't want you to worry," Alex explained, putting an arm out toward her sister.

Standing there on my porch with my two precious daughters, I made a decision: No more self-pity, and no more secrets! I took a deep breath, looking them both in the eye. "Ok, girls," I said, as we linked arms in a circle, a habit we had done since they were little. "Here's the deal. You call your parents as soon as we get inside. Tell them everything — why you left, why you want to stay — *everything*," I repeated, seeing the looks of doubt on their faces. "I want you to stay for as long as possible, and as long as you're honest with me and with them." I dropped my arms so I could hold out my right hand in offering. "Pinky-swear: no more secrets!"

They grinned, matching smiles from two otherwise different faces. "No more secrets!" they cried in unison, locking fingers with me.

Then, as I held open the door for them, Capri looked down at the mat beneath her feet. "Hey!" she shouted excitedly. "That's the mat we gave you!"

We all laughed. Following them into the house, I had a feeling this would be a Christmas the three of us would never forget.

5

Another Piece of the Puzzle

"**R**iley!" Capri called from the front door. "The furniture's here!"

Drying my hands, I crossed through the kitchen and great room to the foyer. "Thanks, honey," I said, smiling when I saw who was at the door. "Ryan!" I exclaimed, happy to see him.

"Surprised to see me?" he teased, holding out the clipboard.

I scribbled my name, handing it back to him. As he watched me with those attentive eyes, I felt a wave of confusion wash over me. Yesterday I'd considered dating him, but less than nine hours later, I thought I'd met my Prince Charming at the bar. This was all way too perplexing, I told myself. Then, realizing he'd been staring at me, awaiting my response, I answered quickly, "Uh, no!" Smiling self-consciously, I continued in a normal tone, "Just busy. Ryan, this is my daughter, Capri." I pointed to the tiny girl who struggled to hold Raegan back from the door.

"Hi, Mr. Ryan," she said in her bubbly voice, attempting a wave as Raegan threatened to bolt. I was glad to see she was her old cheerful self again. The phone calls to their parents had been rough, and both girls would be grounded as soon as they set foot on North Carolina soil, but for the next few weeks, they would be here with me. Both had been ecstatic at the news; honestly, I think they had dreaded being sent home more than they did getting punished.

And now they had a new project to focus on: designing their own bedrooms. In the hour or so since they'd talked to their parents, both Alex and Capri had been pouring themselves into helping Stump and Randy prep their rooms for paint. When I told them they'd be able to come up with the concepts for their bedrooms and create their own space, they'd nearly passed out from excitement. As if communicating telepathically, Alex had grabbed the colored pencils from the crate of office supplies, Capri had dug out graph paper I didn't even know I had, and they'd scattered across the newly-cleaned great room floor to draw up plans for their custom-built beds. Stump seemed to enjoy their company already, and promised to build them the best rooms they could ever imagine. Frankly, I was as excited as they were. I wanted them to feel like this was home.

Doing what I thought was a pretty good job of keeping the surprise from his face, Ryan smiled down at Capri. "Hi, Capri! It's great to meet you."

She smiled politely, then grunted as Raegan pulled away. She scrambled after him as he flung himself at Ryan.

Familiar with the routine by now, the delivery man laughed, rubbing the zealous dog's ears. That seemed to pacify my pooch - somewhat. "Hey, buddy," Ryan began in a normal tone of voice. Then, without warning, he switched to that of a true (and by 'true' I mean 'crazy') dog person. "Who's a good boy?" he cooed like he was talking to a baby. "Who's a good boy? *You* are! *You're* a good boy!"

Capri and I exchanged a look. Hadn't seen that coming.

Taking Raegan's leash from beneath the old bench I'd scored at an antique store outside Naples this morning, I clipped it on his collar. Handing it to Capri, I said, "How about you take him to the back veranda? Make sure he has a water bowl out there, and then round up your sister to help us in the great room."

Capri eagerly obeyed, hurrying the boisterous dog to the back of the house.

Alex came down the hall just then, her jean shorts spotted with primer. "Help you with what?" she asked, looking questioningly at Ryan.

Although he hid it well, Ryan's face registered just the slightest hint of surprise, this time at the word 'sister.' "Hi," he greeted her, clearly wondering how many kids I had, and, probably, where they had come from.

"Ryan, this is my daughter, Alex," I told him, making the introductions.

"Hey," she returned with the noncommittal air of a too-cool teen. Pulling her hair back from her face, she directed a question at me: "Riley, Stump and I are almost finished with the walls; are we still going to be able to pick out our paint colors today?"

I looked at my watch and nodded. Quarter to two. "Sure. Let's get the living room furniture inside, then we can go into town for paint and a late lunch."

"Awesome," she said with a smile. Then, realizing she'd revealed more emotion than a teenager was supposed to around adults, she quickly slipped back into her jaded façade. She rolled her eyes at the amused expressions on our faces. "I mean — whatever."

"Right," I said with a laugh. "Well, why don't you *whatever* yourself into the great room and make sure the floor is clear so we don't trip over anything?" I asked with a smile. Glancing past Ryan, I saw two guys coming around the back of his truck, carrying what appeared to be my new couch.

Ryan was looking at me again. "So," he said casually, stepping aside as the guys crossed the threshold.

I pointed them to the great room.

"You have daughters?" he asked.

I nodded, wondering what the big deal was. "Yeah, aren't they great? Unfortunately, they don't live here full-time, though," I answered. "They're staying with me for the holidays." Then, realizing what he was *really* asking, I explained, "I'm divorced. They're my stepdaughters, bio-logically speaking, but I couldn't love them any more if they were my flesh and blood."

He nodded, looking relieved. "Phew — for a minute there, I thought there might be a *Mr.* Larkin in the picture."

I smiled politely, feeling a little awkward. He was cute, and really nice, but I wasn't about to lead him on. "Look, Ryan," I started, wishing I didn't have to give the dreaded 'I'm not exactly into you right now' speech. "I'm not really . . ."

But he cut in, putting a hand up to stop me. "Looking for anything right now?"

I gave him an apologetic look and shrugged. "Yeah, basically." I paused, feeling like an idiot. I totally hadn't meant to give him the wrong idea yesterday, and racked my brain for anything I might have said or done to make him think otherwise. "I'm sorry if I gave you the wrong impression. You seem like a really great guy."

He looked down at his feet, an embarrassed smile on his face. Clearing his throat, he met my eyes. There was that thoughtful way of looking at me again, which made me feel like an even bigger jerk. "Well," he said simply, "you seem like a really great girl." He stood up taller, tucking his clipboard under his arm. "You know what? Don't even worry about it," he told me. "I understand. But, hey," he called, as I turned to go into the house. "If you ever decide you need someone to explore the town with . . ." His voice trailed off for a second. Smiling, he shrugged. "Give me a call."

I nodded, giggling. "Thanks, Ryan."

Capri accosted me before I had turned back around. She grabbed my hand, pulling me toward the great room. "Riley, come on!" she said excitedly. "You have to see how Alex and I arranged the furniture!"

Oh, Lord help us, I thought reflexively. Then, as I stepped into the great room, I was stunned. I stopped, speechless.

Alex and Capri stared at me, anxiously awaiting my reaction.

Capri tugged on my hand. "We put the rugs down ourselves," she said, pride shining in her eyes.

"And," Alex added. "We told the guys where to put the couch and chairs," she said proudly, holding her arms out to the sides, showcasing their work.

I stood there for a second. Tears unexpectedly sprang to my eyes. This was the stuff I would miss when they were gone, these little, yet indescribably big moments. I knew then and there that this one precious moment would become a memory I would never forget.

Capri's voice broke into my thoughts. "Riley?" She squeezed my hand. "What do you think?" she asked, glancing over at her sister uncertainly.

"Girls," I whispered when I had found my voice. "It looks *fantastic!*" I squeezed Capri's hand in return and beamed at them both. "It's just perfect," I said, wiping my eyes, feeling like an emotional idiot - but a very fortunate one.

Without speaking, Capri threw her arms around me. Alex hurried over to hug us both. Holding them tight, I just stood there a moment, drinking it all in.

"Ah-hem," Ryan said tentatively from the threshold behind us, not wanting to intrude. "Sorry, Riley, but, uh - where would you like this?" He looked apologetically at me as he and his crew held a buffet of charcoal gray vintage metal lockers.

"Oh," I said, with a self-conscious laugh. Wiping my eyes, I pointed just a few steps back from where they stood in the doorway. "Right behind you, actually."

They placed the buffet on the wall that linked the foyer to the kitchen and great room. "Ok," Ryan announced. "That's everything! Enjoy your new furniture, ladies," he said warmly before turning to leave.

As Raegan and I walked the guys to the truck, the girls scurried around the room, arguing over where to place the fixtures I had picked up earlier. By the time we left for town, the great room and entry hall looked like we'd lived there for ten years. It was amazing; I had to admit that the girls had a natural talent for decorating.

Pulling into a parking space near the old inn, I thought that even after they had gone back home, every time I hung out in the great room or walked through the hallway, I would always feel my girls right there beside me.

— ⁓

By three-thirty that afternoon, my already-interesting day had gotten even more intriguing.

The hardware store was our first stop. Alex and Capri picked out their bedroom paint, which, surprisingly, turned out to be a pretty pain-free experience. Normally, a simple trip to the mall resembles some form of mental torture; one child wants to go to one store, the other doesn't want to be seen with her stepmom and "stupid sister," one needs more money, and the other can't make up her mind between two shirts that look exactly the same - and that's just the first half hour. But today, the girls were not only as good as gold - and suspiciously courteous of one another - but they also knew exactly what they wanted. According to Capri, the plans she and Alex had drawn up for Stump actually provided for every little detail, right down to the wall decor and furnishings. It's funny, but until today, I had no idea they had such a penchant for interior design!

Then, as we were leaving the hardware store, we literally bumped into Bébé and her kids, five-year-old twins Henri (pronounced the French way, 'Ahn-rii') and Lise (said: Leeze). The extremely hyper Henri seemed to take a liking to Alex. And Lise, who was mature for her age, hit it off with Capri. Bébé was her usual take-charge self, so it wasn't too difficult for her to persuade us to join them for lunch at The Hop, the fifties-style diner located in the heart of downtown.

Inside the white-and-black tiled restaurant, which featured more sparkly red vinyl than I had ever seen, we stuffed ourselves with milk-shakes and other American delicacies, while listening to Golden Oldies playing on what looked to be an original fifties jukebox. Alex entertained the exuberant Henri, while Capri and Lise exchanged facts about butterflies — a shared subject of interest - as they completed the puzzles on the back of their placemats. As the kids amused one another, Bébé and I got to know each other. We talked and laughed and shared stories like old friends.

I don't know if it was the magic of the holiday season, or the fact that the girls were staying here with me, but *something* infused us with a celebratory air. It seemed that opportunity abounded, that good energy glowed within and around us that golden afternoon. I found myself believing what the town's motto claimed: that life really *was* a little brighter in Two Moon Bay. Whatever it was, we feasted like kings on the tasty and incredibly fattening food. Even I indulged, and ordered fries (gasp!) with my grilled chicken. We were, at present, preparing to roll our gluttonous bodies out of the red-vinyl booth and back to our cars.

Alex slunk down against the backrest and moaned. "Oooh, too full."

Capri, still working on the last riddle with Lise, told her sister, "You shouldn't have eaten so much. You know you always get a stomachache when you eat red meat."

Rolling her eyes, Alex groaned again. "Don't remind me!"

After viewing *Food, Inc.* last year, Capri had sworn off all meat entirely. Alex, on the other hand, struggled with the ethical dilemma of being a carnivore, but was mostly successful in her efforts. It was times like this, though, when she fell off the wagon, that she inevitably regretted her decision and paid for it by feeling queasy.

Bébé reached into her purse. She handed Alex a little tiny candy in a white wrapper. "Bite off a little piece at a time and let it dissolve on your tongue," she commanded. "You'll feel better in no time."

"Thanks," Alex said politely, surveying the candy with a skeptical look on her face. "What is it?"

"Ginger," Bébé answered. "It's great for stomachaches."

Henri, who had been completely absorbed with banging spoons against Alex's shoulder, suddenly dropped his tools and announced, "I have to pee!" He looked alarmed. "Mama, I have to pee!"

"Let's go," she told him, ushering him out of the booth since he was on the outside. "We only have so much time before an accident occurs," she told me. "Go, go, go!" She pointed down the hall, where he disappeared into the women's rest room. "Come on, Lise — why don't you try, too?"

As the elegantly-dressed little girl hopped out of the booth, she took her mom's hand and walked daintily toward the bathroom. Two people who came from the same egg could not be more different, I thought, smiling. Lise was as refined and mature as her brother was rough and rowdy.

"Alright, guys." I looked at my crew. "You ready to head back to the house?"

They nodded. Then, Capri's eyes lit up as she asked, "Wait, can we stop by the library first?" She looked hopefully at me. "It's on the way to the car."

"Sure," I said, at the same time Alex protested, "No! What do you need to go to the library for, anyway?"

Capri ignored her, but explained to me, "I have a report that's due the week I get back. It's for my history class."

I nodded, counting out some bills for lunch. "Yeah, sure, Capri. No problem."

Alex guffawed. Her life was clearly ending. "Why can't you just use the Internet?" She rolled her eyes. "Like a normal person."

Handing her drawing to me, Capri answered her, unfazed, "Because I'm not a 'normal' person," she explained confidently. "I'm an individual."

Smiling proudly at her, I stroked her hair. "Yes, baby, you are. And never be ashamed of that." I looked at the riddle she had solved. "Hey, that's neat!" I told her. "You just solved the 'Legend of Two Moon Bay' question. Huh — the answer is 'Temperance Biscayne'? I've never heard of her."

As Henri ran back from the rest room, Capri explained. "Yep — she's the lady who fell in love with Blackheart Bellacroix." She climbed out of the booth, attempting to pull her sister to her feet. "She was aboard his ship when it sank, back in 1745. Her father was the stable hand and trusted servant of a wealthy merchant here in town."

I furrowed my brow. Huh?

Grabbing her purse from the booth, Bébé interjected, overhearing, "Baby doll, you talkin' 'bout Temperance Biscayne?"

Capri nodded. "Yes, ma'am."

"That's who your stepmama's playin' in the musical — the saddest story in all of Two Moon Bay."

"I *am*?" I asked with interest. That sounded like pertinent information, but I had no earthly idea who Temperance Biscayne was. Or what she was doing on a pirate ship. "Wait," I said, confused. "She died *aboard* Blackheart Bellacroix's ship?" Out of all the reading I had done on the Web about the legend, I'd never heard any of this. For some reason, that struck me as odd.

Bébé nodded. "Yes, chère," she said, as though everyone knew that. "She was the reason the crew revolted." At my blank look, she explained, "It was believed to be bad luck to have a woman onboard a ship. Had it not been for her, they would never have been attacked, and the *Doncella* never would have sunk."

"And," Lise added in her clear voice, "The famous *treasure* would not have sunk to the bottom of the sea, either."

"*Treasure*?" I repeated, feeling like a puzzled parrot. How was this news to me? *And*, I wondered, trying not to feel left out, how did my daughter know more than I did after answering a few measly questions on a kids' placemat? I'd looked up the legend on several different websites, but had heard *nothing* of this Temperance Biscayne person - certainly nothing of her being aboard the most ruthless pirate's ship in all of Florida's maritime history!

Bébé looked at me like I was the last one to the party. "Yes, precious. Well, you sure don't know your Two Moon Bay history now, do you?" she chided as we followed the kids out of the restaurant.

Apparently I don't, I silently agreed. I was thinking it might be time for me to reevaluate my sources.

Without warning, Henri made a sudden break from the group and took off down the street. Before the rest of us could even open our mouths, Alex darted after him, reaching him in a couple of strides.

"Crisis averted," she assured us, turning her struggling captive around to face us. He flopped and flailed at her side like a fish out of water.

Bébé didn't freak out as much as I'd expected her to, but merely issued a warning. "Henri, you mind Alex now, and stay close." She gave him 'the look,' which seemed to work. With a barely-suppressed eye roll, he grudgingly stopped pulling away from Alex. But the illusion quickly faded - I hadn't even counted to two before Bébé turned her attention back to me and he promptly resumed his antics.

Seemingly unaware of everything *except* her report, Capri ignored the Alex/Henri spectacle unfolding on the sidewalk, and said excitedly to Bébé and me, "That's what my report is on! The history of Two Moon Bay!" She looked proudly at me. "I chose it because you moved here, Riley. And I wanted to learn about the treasure."

Reaching her car, Bébé snickered. "Hmm - you and the rest of the world, chère." At our quizzical looks, she continued, "Two Moon Bay attracts amateur and professional treasure hunters from all over the *world* — upwards of twenty thousand a year, they say." She hit the key fob in her hand, popping the locks as Henri zoomed up to the door, dragging Alex along with him. Bébé got it open just in time for him to barrel inside. "But even though people have been searchin' for the *Doncella's* treasure since the 1700s, no one's ever found it." She opened her door, setting her purse in the passenger seat. "And if you ask me, chère," she said to Capri, her voice mysterious, "no one ever will."

Capri's eyes glowed. "My teacher said for me to get some 'primary sources' for my report." She looked inquisitively up at me. "Do you know what that is, Riley?"

I smiled. After teaching college English for thirteen years, I had a pretty good idea. Wanting her to feel important, though, I played my clueless card. "Hmmm," I said, furrowing my brow. "I'm not sure — why don't you tell me?"

As Capri opened her mouth to explain, Bébé cut in, "Honey, if it's 'primary sources' you need, Brooks McKay is your man."

Capri repeated the name blankly. "Brooks McKay?"

Bébé shot me a knowing look, not even attempting to hide her smile. "Ask your stepmama," she said slyly to Capri. "*She* knows him." Her devilish grin reminded me an *awful* lot of one Britlee Matlin, I realized suddenly, with a little surge of panic.

Lord help me, I thought, experiencing a Dr. Frankenstein sort of moment - what had I gotten myself into, befriending this crazy woman? I glared at Bébé for her insinuation.

I swatted her, as the girls looked at me in shock.

Alex grinned, sensing a scandal. "Riley, you have a *boyfriend*?"

Capri wrinkled her brow. "Wait — I thought you just got here yesterday . . ."

Snapping her kids into their car seats, Bébé closed the door and turned to us. Her gorgeous face was animated as she bent down to Capri's level. "Chère, she *did* just get here yesterday." As she stood, she looked squarely at Alex. "And, she *does* have a boyfriend."

Then, smirking at me, she hopped in her SUV and started the engine, waving smugly as she drove off.

6

From Temperance to Backpacks

Sunday morning's sunrise service proved to be an uplifting experience.

I wasn't sure what to expect, but Bébé had insisted we join her and the kids. Apparently, it was a sacred Two Moon Bay tradition, held on the Sunday before Christmas. Surprisingly, the girls had been excited to attend — even Alex, who usually had the most church-related drama. Typically, on weekends that they stayed with me in the mountains, our Sunday mornings were fraught with battle and strife, and always involved the following three things before we *actually* got to the church: 1) Alex complaining that she didn't want to go, 2) me making her change into something more appropriate, and 3) her pouting all the way through the service. On good days, she *might* snap out of it by the time we were halfway through brunch.

But today was completely different. I was actually beginning to think these were different kids — just Alex and Capri look-alikes or something. Not only were they up before I was, but they had made my French-press coffee and taken Raegan out to pee before I was even conscious. Alex had ditched her jeans for a pretty green sundress, *and* — if seeing was be-lieving - she was even *smiling!* No fights this morning, that was for sure. Not even when I announced that we would be taking the local mode of transportation and *walking* to church. I bristled, ready for the backlash.

She stared at me. "Wait, let me get this straight. We're *walking* to church?"

I nodded. Uh, yeah — pretty sure I just said that.

"Along the *beach?*" she continued incredulously.

Capri locked eyes with me. I knew exactly what she was thinking: Alex was about to blow. The idyllic morning, full of smiles and happy thoughts, was soon to spiral into a hissy fit like none we had ever seen before. Hoping Alex would miss my subtle gesture, I held Capri's gaze and casually slid the deck door open. Maybe we could make a break for it before Alex completely lost it.

"Omigod!" she cried suddenly, sending me and Capri flying out the door. And then, to our astonishment, she said something that stopped us in our tracks. "That is *so cool!*"

Capri and I exchanged a look. This was new.

Hurrying to slip off her sandals, Alex chattered happily, remind-ing me of the bubbly child she had been as a pre-teen - when she was Capri's age, really. How rare it was to get a flash from the past like that, I thought, smiling to myself as I grabbed my clutch. "Bye, Rae-Rae!" I called, closing the door behind us.

"Bye, Rae-Rae!" the girls echoed. It was part of our routine.

"Riley," Capri asked as we sank our feet into the sand. "Does this mean that if Alex and I lived here, we would walk to *school* on the beach?"

I thought about it. Interesting question. "No, sweetie," I explained. "The school is on Palisade Way, remember? We passed it on the way to town. It's not on the ocean."

She thought about it. "But we *would* walk to school if we moved here?"

I nodded, sensing a pattern. "Yes, I suppose you would; it's certainly close enough. The town is small enough that you can walk pretty much wherever you need to go within thirty minutes. Sure beats sitting in the carpool lane, huh?"

We fell into our own silences for the next few minutes. Mulling over Capri's questions, I came to the conclusion that the girls were definitely interested in moving here. That really shouldn't be much of a surprise, though, I told myself. I mean, after all, they had planned this trip all on their own, procured their dad's credit card, booked their flights, arranged for transportation to the airport, and flown their enterprising little selves several hundred miles here to see me. *And*, they'd given up Christmas vacation with their friends, which was, like, *huge*, as Alex would say. So, yeah, I guess it stood to reason that they *might* be interested in moving here with me.

Not wanting to get my hopes up, I told myself that such a drastic move might not be the best thing for them right now. I mean, it would be incredibly hard to be away from their parents, and friends, and everything familiar to them. Then, realizing I was getting *way* ahead of myself, I resolved to address that situation if and when it arose. Having that settled, I decided to enjoy the moment and distract myself with the natural beauty around us.

Taking a deep breath, I inhaled the humid air, reveling in the dewy morning. I was just itching to get in a run — especially after yesterday's greasy fries. My eyes combed the horizon, marveling that at this time of morning, it was impossible to tell where the water ended and the sky began. Both were a deep, murky black — even the stars were muted, I noted, as a thick cover of clouds hovered oppressively above us.

Despite the brooding weather, an air of excitement buzzed around us; I think the girls felt it, too. It positively radiated in their eyes, in the newness of every moment.

Before long, our sandy feet found the pier that led to the restaurants along the bay. Stopping at the water station, we rinsed our feet, letting them air dry before slipping on our sandals.

The sound of voices — lovely, harmonized voices — arose from somewhere just beyond the tree line. We followed the people who seemed to know where they were going, the choir's pensive tune growing louder as we approached. Just before we came to Blackheart's Blues Café, we hooked a right. Traveling south along the wooden slats, not too far from the restaurants and bars on the bay, was a nature preserve that ran for miles through the town.

Following the boardwalk, my mind wandered back to Friday night and my walk with Brooks. I smiled, thinking of him, and wondered what he was doing this morning.

Capri tugged on my arm, startling me out of my daydreams. She gave me a funny look. "Come on, Riley," she urged. "The service starts in five minutes."

"I'm coming, I'm coming," I answered, allowing her to drag me along.

The bridge was crowded as people filtered silently along the walkway, forcing us to fall into single file. Alex, who was leading, turned her head every few seconds to check out her surroundings. An avid hiker, I figured she was loving this gorgeous scenery; the marshy mangrove was such a change from the mountain vistas back home. As we got to a part of the deck that widened into an expansive seating area, I slowed to appreciate the beauty around me; with views of the marsh below and beach beyond, and the gentle humming of the choir, I felt a sense of peace wash over me. Capri, who'd noticed my slower pace, caught my eye and smiled. I had a sense that she was enjoying it, too. As the sky lightened gradually around us, the gentle flicker of hundreds of tiny white candles placed artfully around the deck gave the scene an ambient glow. The choir stood with their backs to the ocean, their red and green robes a striking reminder of the season.

As we took our seats on the left-most aisle, facing the ocean, Henri suddenly ran up behind us, his tawny face dominated by a mischievous grin. He grabbed Alex's hand, pulling her toward the kids' seating area up front, to the right of the choir. She looked at me for approval.

"Go ahead!" I told her, laughing.

In the next moment, little Lise strode calmly up to us, clad in a beautiful scarlet dress with cream-colored lace. Her customary ringlets were garnished with a matching lace headband, and her patent leather shoes positively shone. It occurred to me that the grown-up little child had probably styled herself. Capri and I greeted her as her mom and grandma approached us from the middle aisle. As the preacher took his place before the choir, Lise and Capri walked quietly toward the children's area, while Bébé and her mother took the open seats beside me.

Listening to the message, my eyes wandered, combing the sea of faces, some of whom I knew. There, toward the front, were Abby and Mayor Darrell; a little further back were Dixie and Calista. On the left I spotted Stump, and as my eyes caught a shine of light, I figured Cal must be somewhere nearby.

Then, as the sky paled and more faces came into view, I caught sight of a familiar set of eyes on me, the bluest ones that had that way of holding you there with their intensity, that made you feel touched and loved with just one look. Smiling, I gave a little wave. Feeling tingly all over, I wondered why I felt so giddy all of a sudden.

Before I knew it, the ceremony wound to a close. People began streaming out of their seats, talking in the animated tones that seem to follow an inspiring service. While Bébé and I chatted about our upcoming rehearsal, her mother excused herself and walked over to some friends.

"So, chère," Bébé told me. "Make sure to wear some comfortable clothes tonight, preferably ones that won't make you sweat. It's normally hot under the lights, but ours are kind of ancient, and seem to be wired to the equator or somethin'."

I laughed. "Thanks for the tip."

Henri bounded up to us just then, lugging Alex behind him. Two teenage girls who looked to be about her age followed.

Alex introduced us. "Riley, these are my new friends - Evangeline and Ami." We waved hello as she continued, "Evangeline asked me to come over tonight for dinner. Is that ok?"

"Oh," I said, surprised; I hadn't considered that the girls would be making friends. Probably because I was still absorbing the fact that they were actually here! I thought quickly. "Evangeline, are your parents here?"

She nodded. "Yes, ma'am — my dad's here."

"I'd love to meet him, and make sure it's ok," I said, as Bébé whipped a stain stick out of her purse. She furiously set to work on a spot that had somehow cropped up on Henri's khakis.

Suddenly, a male voice called out from behind me, "Well, sure — I guess that'd be ok."

The girls smiled over my shoulder as I spun around. Seeing the teasing expression on his face, I laughed.

"In fact," Brooks continued, his eyes aglow. "It would be ok if you and Capri wanted to come over for dinner tonight, too." He raised his eyebrows. "I see you've met my daughter, Evangeline." He paused, watching as Capri, Lise, and another girl I hadn't met, who looked slightly older than Capri approached. "And, my daughter, Lily."

Wow, I thought, speechless for a second. What are the chances that our kids would not only be the same ages, but would find each other and hit it off? I smiled, awed by it all. Life sure has a way of throwing amazingly-unexpected, but somehow perfect, surprises at you sometimes.

Greeting both of his girls, I noted the vivid blue eyes that Lily had obviously inherited from her father. Both were polite, and very sweet. After we exchanged pleasantries, however, I noticed a slight lull in the conversation, as my girls eyed Brooks a bit shyly. "Oh," I said quickly, realizing that despite Bébé's slick innuendos yesterday, my kids had never *actually* met my newfound friend — and potential love interest. "Girls," I told them, "This is Brooks McKay. Brooks, meet my daughters, Alex and Capri."

Capri piped up, "Lily introduced us a few minutes ago."

"I see," I answered lamely, as Brooks shook hands with Alex.

"That's ok," he assured me. "I haven't met Alex yet."

Right, I thought, putting it all together. Apparently, Evangeline had invited Alex over without introducing her *or* asking her dad's permission. Kids! I thought with amusement.

"Nice to meet you, Mr. McKay," Alex said cordially, before she focused on me. To the un-trained Alex-eye, it was subtle, but I caught the flash of recognition in her gaze as she repeated his name. Darn that Bébé! I thought with frustration. She was really turning out to be something — planting ideas about me in my kids' heads. Never mind that yesterday's 'big reveal' about Brooks was actually/possibly/*maybe* somewhat true.

Realizing Brooks was looking expectantly at me, I snapped back to attention.

"Well?" he asked hopefully. "What do you say — dinner tonight at our place?"

Thinking fast, I replied, "That would be lovely — thank you." Then, remembering my new commitment, I told him apologetically, "Oh, but I have play practice tonight - we won't be done 'til later."

Bébé, who'd finished attacking Henri's stain and was now adjusting Lise's headband, interjected, "Honey, practice will be done by eight." She looked up, giving me a ruthless grin. "I'd say you'll have time for some supper at Brooks' house. *And* a nightcap."

Brooks beamed in amusement. Then, seeing the death glare I shot at Bébé, he quickly cleared his throat and looked down at his feet. The children watched with interest, especially Alex, who didn't miss a thing.

Narrowing my eyes at Bébé, I said, "Thank you, Bébé, for that helpful information."

Capri looked eagerly at me. "Please, Riley?"

Brooks and I exchanged a look and laughed. It seemed the kids had already hit it off and were making plans of their own. Maybe the adults should follow suit, I reasoned.

"Well?" he prompted. "Both of your girls will already be at the house," he told me. "You can join us when you finish practice," he offered. Then, with a twinkle in his eye, he added as he glanced at Bébé, "Around eight."

I nodded, feeling outnumbered. "Sure," I relented. "That would be nice, thanks."

"Great!" he exclaimed, looking pleased. "Girls, what do you say to steaks and portobellos on the grill?"

"Dad," Lily informed him. "Capri and Alex are vegetarians."

"It's ok," Capri said quickly. "Whatever you're serving will be fine, Mr. McKay. The portobellos sound wonderful."

Brooks looked first at my daughter, then at me, obviously impressed with her manners.

I smiled proudly. That had taken some doing.

"Well," he told Capri. "I guess we'll just have to make *extra* portobellos for you and your sister, then, won't we?"

Bored with the conversation, Henri made a break for it and ran off after a group of boys who sped by. The grins on their faces made it clear they were up to no good. Bébé gave us a knowing look, taking Lise's hand. "Alright, honey," she said to me with a sigh. "That's my cue to leave. Let me round up Mama and that devil chile o' mine, and I'll see you tonight at practice."

We said goodbye, air-kissing as she scurried off after her son.

"Riley," Capri began. "Where are we going for breakfast?" she looked hopefully at me. "Maybe Blackheart's Blues Café?"

"Actually," I told her, "I was thinking that today we would make our own breakfast. I'd like to break in the kitchen. Maybe some buckwheat pancakes and eggs benedict? Minus the Canadian bacon, of course."

Alex chimed in, "That sounds good — I'm hungry. Plus, I want to start on my room after breakfast." Then, she announced with the utmost authority — mostly for her new friends' eager ears, I presumed - "Stump and Randy are coming over after church; they have the lumber for my bed." As she explained her detailed plans for a custom-made bunk bed with a tree on one end and a climbing wall on the other, Capri and Lily started down the boardwalk, toward the beach.

"Uh, excuse me," I called. When they turned back around, I asked, "Where might you be going?"

Capri looked at me like I was crazy. "Home — they're walking, too," she said as if I still might not get it.

Secretly delighted that she'd called my house 'home,' a giddy little grin lit my face. Although they'd only just arrived, the girls already felt at home here in Two Moon Bay — the thought was gratifying to say the least. "Alright," I said, realizing Capri was waiting for me to say something. "See ya there."

Sneaking a glance at Brooks, I was surprised to find his eyes on me. We held each other's gaze, smiling shyly as we fell into step behind our daughters.

"So," he said casually, after a pause. "What've you been up to lately?"

I gave him a quizzical look to gauge his expression. Did my ears deceive me, or had there been just the *slightest* hint of smugness in his question? It had come off sounding a little too *knowing* to be a simple inquiry. Wondering what he was thinking, I said truthfully, "Nothing much, yet so much has happened." I shook my head wondrously. "I mean, yesterday morning, all I had in mind was to get some coffee, pick up a few things for the house, and do a little decorating. But by the time I got home, the girls were here, and everything changed."

He nodded. "Yeah, that must have been a real shocker, huh?"

I raised my eyebrows. "You have no idea."

About to reply, Brooks' words were swallowed by the sound of someone calling out my name. "Riley!"

I gazed around, trying to locate the speaker. Though the church crowd had mostly dispersed, many people lingered, posing for pictures along the scenic route, or stopping to chat before heading to breakfast. The boardwalk was busy. Early-morning exercisers bustled by on their bikes, the spokes making ticking noises, regular in their clocklike consistency. A group of runners clopped along, the spandex crew providing a veritable rainbow of neon colors against the more conservatively-clad churchgoers. Their steps were rhythmic over the wooden boards, momentarily replacing the soothing sounds of an acoustic guitar that danced along the morning air, all the way from Blackheart's patio. Trying to focus on the voice, I glanced at Brooks. "I can't tell where that's coming from," I said, shrugging.

"Riley!" My friendly pursuer shouted again.

The girls, who were just ahead, talking like old friends, paused to look back. I motioned for them to continue on.

"Riley Larkin!"

Realizing it was coming from behind us, Brooks and I swiveled around.

Ryan hurried over, an eager smile on his face. His arm was draped casually over the shoulders of a tall leggy blonde I'd not seen before. "Riley, hi!" he said enthusiastically. His energy reminded me suddenly of Raegan. Before I knew what was happening, Ryan swooped in with what you could call an 'enthusiastic' hug — one worthy of two friends who hadn't seen each other in quite some time. Surprised all over again, and feeling that we were level-jumping just a *tad* with the overly-zealous hug, I did all I could think to do, and patted him on the shoulder. I smiled awkwardly at his wondrously-perfect-looking date, who beamed at me, her flawless teeth pinging at me in a way that reminded me of Cal's. After finally releasing me, Ryan shook hands with Brooks, who handled the moment with enviable aplomb, I noticed. Then, the deliveryman introduced us to his arm candy.

"Guys," he said. "This is my friend, Candy."

My jaw dropped open.

He continued, "Candy, this is Riley and Brooks."

Wow, Candy, I thought, giving myself props for thinking of such an accurate euphemism. She was strikingly pretty, with tanned skin, blue eyes, and a body most girls would die for.

We talked for a few minutes, then Ryan announced that he and his trophy — er, date — were heading to breakfast.

"Blackheart's has the best buffet on Sundays," he told me. "Maybe we'll see you guys there."

We waved goodbye, then, as Ryan and Candy headed to the Bay's breakfast hot spot, Brooks and I fell into step once again. Musing about the interesting — and speedy! — turn of events with Ryan, I was glad that he'd moved on. Not that I'd expected him to get hung up on me or anything; we were never actually a *thing*, after all — I was pleased he had someone in his life who seemed to make him happy. He seemed like a really nice guy. Plus, I thought, glancing at Brooks with a smile on my face, I knew the man beside me was the *only* one I was interested in getting to know.

Surprisingly, however, Brooks' gaze was fixed straight ahead, his jaw set and looking about a thousand miles away. Was it my imagination, or was he extremely tense all of a sudden?

"Brooks," I said gently, wondering what on earth was going on. "You ok?"

Blinking as though he'd suddenly awakened, he turned slightly to look at me. "Uh, yeah — yep, I'm good," he assured me, sounding like he was trying to convince himself more than me.

Despite the fact that he was pleasant enough, Brooks' energy was still incredibly keyed up. I got the feeling there was something he was holding back, something he didn't know how to say. I looked inquisitively at him.

"What is it?" I asked.

He shook his head. "Nothing." But the wrinkle in his brow told me it really *was* something. Then, as I gave him a 'Yeah, right' look he blurted out, "It's just that — I'm not sure how to say this . . ."

"Just say it," I cut in. "I've found that, when in doubt, that's usually the best way."

He nodded. "It's just that, I know you're new here — and just getting through a divorce." He looked understandingly at me. "And I don't want to pressure you or anything."

Mingling with the breakfast crowd just down from Blackheart's entrance, we stopped almost near the exact spot where we'd stood and talked the other night. Although that was less than two days ago, somehow it seemed like so much longer.

"Ok" I said, trying to follow, but not understanding what he was getting at. "I don't feel any pressure." I shrugged.

"It's just . . ." he said, looking embarrassed. "Yesterday, I saw you with Cal, and . . ."

As if on cue, the booming voice of Calhoun Foxworth the Third cut through the din, drowning out Brooks' words. "Well, look who it is!" the rowdy golfer bellowed behind us. "Hey there, Brooks. Hey, Riley!"

I gave Brooks an apologetic look before I turned to greet our famous friend. It seemed interruptions were unavoidable this morning. "Hey, Cal," I replied, returning his hug. "Oh, Dixie!" I cried, surprised to see them together. Maybe they were becoming a thing, it suddenly occurred to me.

My fashiony realtor was dressed in a snappy black romper with a cream-colored open sweater and matching hat. She wore red booties and carried a red bag that probably cost as much as the monthly mortgage payment on my mountain home. "Well, hey yourself, sug," she cooed, air-kissing me hello as we hugged daintily. Her eyes went to Brooks, taking us in. "Tell me," she said, her attention focused on me. "What are you doin' here with this handsome man?" Hugging my companion hello, her eyes swept from me to Brooks, then back.

I laughed, explaining that we were just leaving church. As she made conversation, Cal's eyes managed to lock onto my chest as we talked. Sadly, I was beginning to expect that from him.

Ignoring her date's staring problem, Dixie asked us, "Would y'all like to join us for breakfast?" She pointed at Blackheart's.

"They've got the best buffet in town," Cal told my boobs.

Brooks answered for us. "Thanks, guys, but we're actually both heading home — the kids are just ahead of us, so . . ."

Dixie put her hands together excitedly. "Oh, that's right!" she enthused. "Riley, I thought I saw you come in with two beautiful girls. Let's see if I remember their names — Alexandra and . . . Capri?" she asked uncertainly. I'd told her about them when we first got to know each other back in November.

I nodded, impressed. "That's right! Wow, great memory."

She looked positively elated. "Well, that's just fantastic! I didn't even know they were comin'!"

I laughed. "That makes two of us." At her puzzled look, I explained, "They sort of surprised me yesterday." I glanced over at the girls. Then, getting an idea, I asked Dixie, "Say, why don't you come over tomorrow to meet them?" I looked at her, and *tried* to make eye contact with Cal, but he was so involved with my boobs it was like he was *talking* to them silently or something. I shook my head, then plundered on with the invitation: "I'd love for you to come over tomorrow night for dinner." At her surprised expression, I explained, "As a thank you. Dixie, you've done so much to help me. You've been amazing."

She waved a red set of fingernails in the air. "Aw, sug — it was nothin'. But, I'd *love* to! What should I bring?" She finally noticed Cal's affliction and swatted him with her purse. "Besides this one here?" she asked with an eye roll.

"Nothing," I assured her. "Just yourselves. Seven o'clock?"

"We'll be there," she assured me.

Finally meeting my gaze, Cal proclaimed, "Well, thanks, darlin' - that sounds real nice. See y'all tomorrow!"

The men shook hands goodbye, while Dixie and I air-kissed a second time. Lapsing into a pensive silence, Brooks and I watched them walk off. As the couple headed toward the buffet, they temporarily disappeared into the throng of well-dressed bodies, everyone wearing their Sunday best. Most of the men sported suits, while the ladies wore pantsuits and dresses — and more shades of red than I had seen in a color-swatch book. Everywhere you looked, shoes were shined and hair was coiffed and cut and styled with particular care. I loved that people here dressed up for church; back home, most people had worn jeans and dressed casually — a custom in which the girls and I had *not* partaken. Call me crazy, but I'd always thought that if there was one thing you dressed up for in life, it was church. Not doing so just didn't seem right.

"Bye!" I called, waving as Dixie emerged from the crowded doorway and smiled at us. She daintily scooted inside, giggling, you could tell, as Cal swatted her playfully on the behind. She turned and swatted at him, but you could tell she really enjoyed the attention. They slung their arms easily around each other's waists and hurried inside, laughing. They seemed so happy together, I thought, smiling to myself.

Then, falling into step once more with Brooks, the lightness I'd felt watching Cal and Dixie quickly disappeared. Alone once more, the heaviness that had descended on our pleasant moment draped itself unwelcomely over us again. Realizing it was now or never, I looked at Brooks, eager to get the uncomfortable-ness over with. "Ok, so - you were saying?"

"Well," he stammered, looking like he dreaded this even more than I did. "It's just that - I saw you with Cal yesterday — at the café," he explained. "You guys looked . . ." His voice faded and he seemed *painfully* awkward now. "Really . . . *close*."

I thought back to yesterday at the café, but honestly had no idea what he was talking about. "The café?" I racked my brain, trying to conjure the *closeness.* "Uh, yeah - I ran into Cal yesterday when I was getting coffee." I thought of Abby, and her cute business card, and all those deliciously-evil pastries, then — eureka! "You mean when he walked me to my car?"

He nodded sheepishly. "Yeah. Look, you don't need to explain anything to me, Riley. It's just — I have . . . feelings for you." He gazed at me, his eyes resolute now, sure of what he was saying. "Already."

Holy crap, holy crap! I thought wildly, feeling a little breathless. I had dreamed about this moment and hadn't even known it until now.

Brooks' eyes told the full story, the one that his words danced around. And even though my heart was beating out of my chest, the story his eyes told scared the crap out of me because I was feeling the *exact same way.* "And," he finished, "If you're interested in . . . other people, I can totally respect that. I just don't want to get my hopes up, I guess is what I'm saying."

"O-kaaaay," I said slowly. "So, you're asking if I'm interested in *Cal*?" I looked at him like he was crazy. "Cal, as in 'hi-let-me-stare-at-your-boobs' Cal?" I paused, waiting for him to tell me it was all a big joke. "Are you *serious*?"

He shifted uneasily. "Well, yeah," he said. "Cal and . . . Ryan."

"*Ryan!*" I cried, glancing over my shoulder toward Blackheart's. "You did see the pin-up girl he was just with, right?" I couldn't believe we were having this conversation. Here I had thought he was going to proclaim his feelings for me, and we would have a nice, romantic moment. But this? What the heck was happening here?

Determined to see it through, Brooks stammered out an explanation. "Yeah, it's just — I heard that he was interested in you, and . . . and, then I saw you with *Cal*, and — I just had to ask." He looked at me with those eyes, and I saw in them the truth.

I saw in them that what he *really* wanted to know wasn't about Cal or Ryan, or how I felt about either of them, but about something much bigger, much scarier than anything either of us was equipped to handle at that moment. And even though I knew *exactly* what he was saying, and *exactly* what he was *really* asking, I chose to be a jerk.

I chose to be a jerk because if I told him how I *actually* felt, that would change everything — and I wasn't sure I was ready for that. "Brooks," I said, betraying my instincts and my heart and doing the exact opposite of what they told me. "I, I have to get going — I'm sorry." I looked over at the girls, who were starting to get fidgety as they stared out at the water. "I'm really sorry." I held his eyes before I fled, and even though I knew mine spoke the true story of my heart, I also knew it wasn't right to leave him hanging the way I did. I was a coward, I know. I just didn't have the guts to say how I truly felt.

Seeing the hurt in his eyes, I turned away, hurrying down the walk. "Come on, girls, let's go."

Alex started to protest. "But — Evangeline and . . ."

"We're leaving," I said firmly. "Let's go."

Brooks called out to his girls, "Come on, guys — change of plans." I didn't have to see the look on his face to hear the slight in his voice. "We're having breakfast. At Blackheart's."

— ❦ —

From stage left, Bébé called out, "Enter Temperance!"

It was almost seven-thirty that night. We'd been rehearsing for an hour-and-a-half straight, no break. With show time mere days away, the general vibe was one of excitement and nervous energy. Dress rehearsals started tomorrow night; I couldn't wait to see everyone in costume, to really watch the drama of Two Moon Bay come to life before my eyes.

Since the original director had suddenly come down with laryngitis, Bébé had taken over her duties. That seemed right, I thought, Bébé being in charge; with the way she loved giving orders, and her no-nonsense way of doing — well, *everything* - she was a natural-born director. And, since she was also the lead, in addition to rehearsing her part, she was hopping around all over the place, blocking scenes - even feeding others their lines. She was handling both roles incredibly well, I thought from my place in the wings.

The weird thing was, after Bébé's cue, nobody moved. From somewhere across the stage, a woman cleared her throat. A couple of characters, frozen onstage, shifted uncomfortably. Where the heck was Temperance, I wondered, gazing around.

"Temperance!" our director repeated, louder this time, a note of impatience filling her voice.

A cute guy standing beside me nudged me in the ribs. "Riley, that's you — Temperance," he reminded me, his long, sandy-colored hair swaying as he nodded toward the stage.

"Oh — right," I muttered, squaring my shoulders. "Thanks."

Shaking off the ditzy case of new-girl syndrome I'd just acquired, I jumped into character. Stepping onto the stage, I lost myself in Temperance's world, the reality that was her pain. Bébé was right; Temperance's lines really *were* sad. Depressing, actually. Apparently, she was the best friend and maidservant of the beautiful Destina. According to the play, which was based on actual Two Moon Bay history, Temperance was the daughter of Destina's father's most-trusted servant, Bernardo. Destina's house had been like a fortress — and a prison. Her father, Dario Delgado, was a wealthy merchant who imported guns, silver, and gold from his native Spain; he was notorious for selling to businessmen and criminals — the only men who could afford his exorbitant prices. Dario's dangerous dealings meant that his home had to be guarded night and day to protect his riches, the most prized of all being his daughter.

Free-spirited and longing for adventure, the independent Destina and her loyal servant Temperance, who were rumored to have been inseparable, were reported to have pined away their days, dreaming of romance on the high seas. The girls had longed to find love, the story went, but because of their beauty and the danger that came with being the child and maidservant of the wealthiest man around, they were forced to stay locked inside the fortress atop the bluff. They were always together, the legend went, even from the time they were babies. Even more intriguing — rumor had it that they looked shockingly alike, often being mistaken for one another.

In addition to the girls' history, the play told the story of the town's most infamous battle, the one I had read about on the Internet.

Apparently, it had occurred on December 24, 1745— a Christmas Eve that had changed Two Moon Bay forever. Tragically, that was also the last day the girls had been seen or heard from again.

After learning of their sad story, it was easy to channel into my lines the terrible loneliness I had felt as a child. Not to mention the little thing of my tiff with Brooks — try as I might, I just couldn't get the hurt I had seen on his face out of my mind. I guess all those emotions sort of combined inside me onstage in a way that made me understanding of Temperance's pain. I felt a sort of kinship with my character, right from the get-go.

Feeling her longing, I was totally in the moment as I stepped across the stage. Then, as Bébé/Destina entered behind me, I wistfully combed the shore, staring out at the ocean I longed to explore. Much like my best friend, Destina, I dreamed of freedom and love. And, according to the play, we considered the sea that surrounded the castle our ticket to freedom. Legend had it that we often escaped the mansion at night, singing of our desires, plotting and planning for the lives we dreamed of, as we walked along the shore.

As our duet began — the one that led into the momentous battle in which Destina and I would disappear - I felt the sadness of my character flood through me. Sadness and guilt. What had I been *thinking*? I asked myself, wondering why I'd been such an insensitive jerk to Brooks earlier that day. As I followed the script, I poured out all the regret and frustration that had been building inside me ever since I'd walked away from him. The emotion inside me culminated in a heartbreaking note as the cannons and gunfire sounded. Fog seeped onto the stage, swallowing Destina and Temperance, erasing us as if we'd never even been there. Creeping through the fog to stage left, I snapped back to myself, feeling more clear-headed than before I had delved into Temperance's psyche. I wouldn't have thought it was possible, but exploring *her* sadness had somehow given me the clarity I needed in my own matter of the heart. I suddenly knew that I had to talk to Brooks.

Startling me back to reality with her needs-no-microphone voice, Bébé hollered out beside me, "End scene!"

Clapping, we all met at center stage, talking and complimenting one another. We sipped from water bottles and listened to Bébé's notes for tomorrow's rehearsal. "Ok, y'all, good job, good job," she began, giving us some insight on what to work on tomorrow. Finally, she dismissed us, much to everyone's relief. It had been a long rehearsal, but a good one. Everyone seemed satisfied as they packed up to leave.

Walking offstage with Abby, I had just stepped off the bottom step when someone called out my name. "Hey, Riley! You're needed in wardrobe."

I looked questioningly at Abby. "Wardrobe?"

She laughed. "Oh, yes — our previous Temperance was a smidge bigger than you are; you're tall, but a teeny little thing. I expect your costume will need some adjusting."

"Oh, right," I said. "Be right there!" I called out, waving goodbye to her and heading back up the steps to the stage.

Wandering backstage, I passed the make-up desks and set pieces, nodding to cast members as they prepared to leave. There, at the back of the stage, was a long wooden table, covered in colorful material and scores of tiny pins. The costume designer's back was to me as she bent over a pale lavender gown.

"Uh, hi," I said quietly, not wanting to startle her.

Despite my intentions, the poor girl leapt about a foot. Her long, dark hair swirled around her face as she stooped to pick up the measuring tape she'd been holding. "Omigod!" she cried through a mouthful of pins. I marveled that none had fallen out during her episode.

"Sorry," I muttered weakly. "I didn't mean to scare you."

Recovering with a self-conscious giggle, she smiled, sticking out her hand. "Hi, you must be Riley."

I nodded as we shook.

"I'm Janice."

"Nice to meet you." She looked young to be in charge of wardrobe, I thought. I figured her to be just a few years older than Alex, probably a college student at the local university. "Ok, so," she told me. "I need you to go slip this on for me," she said, handing me the gown and pointing to the makeshift dressing room about five feet away.

"Sure thing," I said agreeably. Anxious to get to Brooks' house, I dutifully scurried over to the curtained area. I stripped off my clothes, threw the dress over my head then stepped outside.

Hearing my footsteps, Janice turned around to face me. Suddenly, she stopped, her hand going to her mouth.

"Omigod," the dark-haired girl murmured through her pins. "You look *just* like her!" Glancing over her shoulder, she called out, "Hey, Harry, Jamie — come over here a second!"

Wondering what the heck was going on, I stood there while she measured me, listening to the footsteps hurrying over.

They stopped as two guys — one a middle-aged man wearing a sweater vest and glasses, and the other a high-school kid who looked like he'd just stepped off the set of a hip-hop video, gaped at me.

Watching their reactions, Janice laughed. "Yep — that's what I thought," she said knowingly, studying me. "You are *so her*," she told me, her green eyes large and round.

I raised my eyebrows, wondering what she was talking about.

Springing back to life, the older guy dug into his leather satchel. He pulled out an old leather-bound book, flipping through the pages. Hurrying over to me, he pointed eagerly to a photo. "See here?" he asked. "That's Temperance Biscayne."

I sucked in my breath.

"You look *just* like her." His voice sounded as awed as I felt.

"Dude," the younger kid breathed. "You totally do."

Ok, *now* I saw what the big deal was. I wouldn't have thought it was possible, but I had to admit that I *did* bear an uncanny resemblance to the lonely-looking girl who stared out from the picture with the sad brown eyes. Although her face was more round than mine, her features were very much the same. Our hair was long and dark, and the set and color of our eyes were basically identical. To top it all off, she was wearing the same dress — or, rather, *I* was wearing a copy of the one she wore. Eerie.

"Wow, that's creepy," I affirmed.

The older guy told me, "That etching was made on the last day of her life; the night she and Destina disappeared in the battle." He flipped to another page in the book. "This is the aftermath of what happened," he said gravely, pointing to the familiar-looking coastline. The beautiful shore was strewn with debris. And bodies.

I shuddered. "That's terrible," I said, not wanting to see any more. Something about the carnage in the artist's rendering was a little too real and raw for me.

Janice chattered like a bird as she flitted around me, cinching and pinning. "Oh, Riley," she said, pointing to the scholarly-looking man. "This is Harry, the town historian."

The older guy shook my hand with zeal and a smile.

"He's the author of the only book ever written about Two Moon Bay. He's kind of a local celebrity."

Harry beamed with pride.

"Wow," I said warmly. "That's terrific, Harry."

His chest puffed up with pride.

"Say — could I buy a copy of your book? I'd love to get one for my daughter." A wannabe writer, myself, I was always eager to support a local author. Plus, I thought it would be perfect for Capri's report. She'd be thrilled.

"Well, of course!" he enthused, digging through his satchel again. "It just so happens I have some with me." He pulled out a copy and uncapped his pen. "What's your daughter's name?"

I told him, and, as he signed it, Janice introduced me to the other guy.

"Riley, this is Jamie," she told me, gathering several inches at my waist and pinning them. I think Abby had been kind when she'd said the previous Temperance was a 'smidge' bigger than I was. Either that, or she was being really sarcastic, but that didn't seem to be her style. "He's the sound engineer," Janice continued. "And an expert with all things technology."

The kid made a peace sign in response to my greeting.

Janice stepped back to inspect her work. "Ok, go ahead, Riley — you can take that off now. Just be careful not to stick yourself."

I hurried back to the dressing room, where I managed to impale myself only once. Coming back out, Harry handed me his book before he and Jamie turned to leave. They were discussing sound effects for the big battle scene. Handing the gown to Janice, I told her, "This dress is really beautiful. Did you make it yourself?"

She beamed, smoothing the fabric over a mannequin. "Thanks! Yeah, I did. I made all the costumes, actually."

"You made *all* the costumes?" I repeated in astonishment, gazing around at the elaborate-looking pirate outfits, flowing gowns, and eighteenth-century Spanish gentlemen's clothing hanging from nearby racks.

She nodded, her mysterious bangs and Goth look unable to hide the bashful expression on her face. I could tell she loved the praise.

"Wow," I said sincerely. "That's truly incredible. You have real talent! Did you go to school for that?"

"Uh, no," she answered, looking flattered that I would even ask. "I'm still in high school. But I would love to go to school for design. It's kind of my dream," she added shyly, looking at me with hope shining in her eyes.

"You totally should," I told her. Then, glancing at my watch, I said, "Oh, I have to get going. It was nice meeting you, Janice. See you tomorrow."

"Bye!" she called out, smiling.

Hurrying toward the front of the stage, I reflected on what a great night it had been. Rehearsal had gone great, I'd met even more cool people, bought a book for Capri, and found out I looked eerily like the tragic Temperance Biscayne. The image of me in the dress—which Janice had recreated *perfectly*, by the way — reminded me of my character's sadness. That made me think of Janice, who was obviously so talented, and a child in need of encouragement - which made me sad all over again. I could tell by the way she responded to my compliments that praise was something she just wasn't accustomed to hearing. It always made me sad to meet young people who had never been told they were good at something, or that they could *be* something in life. Maybe because I had been one of those kids, that's why I was so sensitive to it. That's why I had volunteered at the high school back home; there were so many kids who needed a mentor, someone to care. I hoped I was wrong about Janice, but something told me I wasn't.

Grabbing my bag, I waved goodbye to Bébé, who was discussing the sets with the building crew. Although the conversation looked serious, she apparently wasn't *too* absorbed in what they were talking about to call out to me, "Bye, chère. Don't do nothin' *I* wouldn't do."

Hurrying down the aisle, I turned around to smirk at her. "Well, then, the possibilities are endless!" I retorted. Seeing the narrowed glint in her eyes, I spun back around, satisfied that I had sufficiently surprised Two Moon Bay's queen bee. She was really starting to remind me of Britlee, I thought with a grin. Then, making a mental note to call my BFF tomorrow, I sent Brooks a text that I was on the way.

On the short car ride to his house, I went over in my mind everything I wanted to say. Just be honest, I told myself. Although I was a little worried that he would reject my apology — and me — I felt optimistic that tonight's conversation would go much better than this morning's. But, just in case, I was keeping my fingers crossed.

Smiling, I turned into his drive, just a few houses down from the school. In a flash, I envisioned our kids walking to school together, dressed in their jeans and scarves, and wearing the backpacks we would buy them in a ceremonial back-to-school shopping trip. I could picture Alex and Capri stopping in front of the McKays' house as Evangeline and Lily ran out the door, all falling into step with smiles on their faces. The vision was there before I could rationalize it away, telling myself not to hope for something that would probably never be. Shaking my head, I smiled. The heart knows what the heart wants, my foster mother Rainie had always said. Coming to a stop before the garage, I couldn't help but think she was right.

I knocked only once before the door swung open.

Brooks' blue eyes smiled down at me.

I wasn't sure if I'd get the usual twinkle, but the twinkle was exactly what I got. A wave of relief washed over me, and I smiled back.

"Hey," he greeted me, stepping back so I could enter. As he closed the door, our arms brushed.

Startled by the electric feeling that soared through me, I looked up in surprise. He gazed back at me. I could tell that he had felt it, too.

"Hey," I returned casually, though I wanted nothing more than to throw myself into his arms right then and there. "I brought some wine," I told him, presenting my offering. "Hope you like Muscadine grapes."

He accepted the bottle with a nod. "Thanks. And I do," he said, heading past the stairs toward the back of the house. "Come on back, let me warm you a plate."

Trying not to stare, I gazed around the rooms. The house, like all of those on Palisade Way, was historical and traditional. This one had been remodeled and decorated just beautifully, I thought, wanting to break away and browse through each cozy room. You could tell a family lived here.

"How was practice?" he asked, already popping a plate into the microwave as I sauntered into the kitchen.

Leaning against the gigantic island, I told him all about the script, Bébé's directing, Abby's amazing voice, Harry's book, and even Janice and her fabulous designs.

Setting the steaming plate before me, he shook his head slightly, not saying anything.

"What?" I asked, intrigued. "What was that I just saw?" I couldn't *wait* to eat; it smelled sooo delicious. As I dug in, blowing on a piece of steak, footsteps and giggling voices wafted down the stairs. Capri and Lily breezed into the kitchen, all smiles.

"Hey Riley!" my girl exclaimed, throwing her arms around me.

Caught mid-gnaw, I choked out, "Hey," before swallowing, and hugged her back. "I got you something at practice."

She gave me a wary look.

"It's a book!" I exclaimed, cutting a piece of asparagus. The steak was really good, and the veggies looked so tender. "Mmm," I said to myself. Then, seeing the 'Well?' expression on her face, I pointed vaguely toward the front of the house. "It's in my purse - in the foyer. . ." I called after her, though she was already running to get it.

As Lily poured two cups of a pale green beverage with lemon and orange slices in it — chilled green tea, I figured — Capri scurried back to us, book in hand.

"Wow," she said, staring appreciatively at the artistry on the cover. "Thanks, Riley."

I nodded, polishing off the last of my portobello. Brooks was quite the cook, I thought. "And," I told her, "It's signed by the author himself."

She beamed, throwing her arms around me once more. "Thanks, Riley! This is great." Grabbing her glass, she and Lily exited the kitchen, talking excitedly as they went.

Brooks had been leaning against the cupboards opposite me, watching the scene with a smile on his face.

"What?" I asked, suddenly self-conscious. I wondered, with a flash of horror, if I had bits of food smeared around my mouth. Then, gazing down at my empty plate, I put a hand to my face, giggling. "I didn't realize I was so hungry!" I apologized. "But that was really good. Thank you so much."

"Glad you enjoyed it," he replied, looking pleased. Clearing my plate, he switched it out with a smaller one that contained a perfect slice of Key lime pie. The presentation was beautiful. "Sweets for the sweet," he said, holding my eyes.

Melting a little, I thought he was just too perfect. An awesome meal and dessert, too? After the way I had treated him earlier, I was expecting a completely different reception. Guilt swept through me. I lowered my eyes.

Stepping back, he said quickly, "But don't feel you have to eat it," he told me. "It's Lily's specialty — which Capri helped her make." He smiled, relaxing back against the cupboards. "I don't know *how* those two got along without each other before today," he marveled. "It's like they've always known each other."

I know what you mean, I thought to myself, thinking of how I felt about him and Bébé — the whole town, really. I'm telling you, there was truly something special about this place and the people in it.

"No, I totally want to try it," I assured him, picking up my fork. "It's just that — I owe you an apology." I took a bite, closing my eyes as the flavors dissolved on my tongue. "Delicious." I wiped my mouth and got up from the table. This was something that needed to be said in person. Up close. Woman *a mano*. "Brooks," I said, standing before him. I took his hands as I looked into his eyes. "I'm sorry for being such a jerk earlier. I was scared," I told him, throwing caution to the wind. No matter how he reacted, I had to be honest. With us both. "And I let my fear get in the way. I was wrong to do that to you, and I'm sorry."

Squeezing my hands, he smiled. "Apology accepted." He leaned in and placed a kiss on the tip of my nose. "But, Riley — what were you afraid of?" His eyes had that knowing look again.

This was it, I thought. I could feel the air quicken around us. The big moment where we either said it, or we didn't. Full honesty. I took a deep breath. "I was afraid because . . ." I paused, then rushed on, "I felt exactly the same way you said you did. And I didn't know what that would mean, or how it would change things." I shrugged, still clasping his hands. "That's why."

He stared into my eyes for a second more, then smiled reassuringly. I could see the relief in his gaze as he replied, "Well, then, let's not let anything change. Or get in the way of how we feel."

I nodded, feeling like a huge burden had been lifted from my shoulders. When you're in sync with the person you care about, life is so much lighter. Anticipation was building inside me. As it mingled with the relief I felt from my confession, it blended with his acceptance, making me giddy with excitement.

Our bodies leaned instinctively toward one another's, no words necessary. Our hearts were finally doing the talking, and, it seemed, they had a lot to say. When we pulled back from the gentle, yet sensual kiss, I felt like I was spinning.

I crashed back to reality as I heard Alex's giggle from behind. Whirling around, I laughed sheepishly. She stood in the doorway, her arms crossed and a mock-disapproving expression on her face. Evangeline and Ami tee-heed as she said crossly, "Just what do you think you're doing, young lady?"

Blushing, I turned back around, burying my head against Brooks' shoulder. He smelled nice. Like fresh laundry. I don't know why, but in that moment, I actually felt like a teenager who'd been caught making out with her boyfriend. Clearing my throat, I turned back around to face my accusers, willing my inner parent to return to the room. "Ha ha, very funny," I quipped, assuming my grown-up role.

Dropping her arms — and the façade — Alex pushed away from the door, already bored. The girls sidled up to the bar, pulling out the stools and settling in as Evangeline asked, "Dad, could we have some more pie?" She eyed my barely-touched piece.

"Sure," he said, as I stepped away to give him some room.

Ever the doting father, Brooks set to work cutting the pie, which I plated and served after Evangeline directed me to the proper cupboard. The girls helped by setting napkins and forks for everybody at the table, so we could all sit together. Brooks cut himself a slice before returning what was left to the refrigerator, then fixed a tray for coffee, and joined us gals. We talked easily. The kids entertained us with their carefree teenage banter; Evangeline and Ami gossiped about school and boys, and their plans for Christmas vacation. Before long, Lily and Capri came downstairs, not wanting to miss out on the fun — or dessert. I complimented their pie-making prowess as Capri whipped a mini-notebook out of nowhere, it seemed, and proceeded to interview Brooks for her report. In addition to running the inn, which held relics from the Bay's historic pirate days, he actually knew a lot of facts about Blackheart Bellacroix — just as Bébé had said.

After my little scholar was satisfied that she had a good start on her 'primary information,' the girls cleaned up the kitchen as Brooks and I uncorked the wine I'd brought. The kids loaded the dishwasher before trotting back upstairs to the media room, where, they claimed, they were all about to watch a movie together. Amazed that Alex and Capri could agree on a movie to watch that easily — that was usually a battle *someone* ended up losing — Brooks and I retired to the cozy enclosed porch on the back of his house, which overlooked a sparkling pool.

Snuggled up next to him, staring out into the beautiful night, I couldn't imagine anything greater than this. I felt satisfied — whole, complete. With my girls close by, and knowing they were happy and making friends, I felt like everything in that moment was right.

Thank you, I said silently, sending out a little prayer into the cosmos. Thank you for helping me to see that from the darkest places the most beautiful things can grow.

Leaning my head against Brooks' shoulder, I knew in that moment that even though I may not know exactly what the future held, I was certain that he would be in it.

And, I thought, smiling into the blueness of his eyes, it was sure to be amazing.

7

Christmas Cheer

Day one of dress rehearsals went by in a flash. Or, more truthfully, in a flash of *color*; Janice's costumes - from cool silks to warm, smooth velvet - painted a veritable rainbow across the stage. It was amazing to see how everyone transformed into their characters after donning their garbs; Joe, the friendly butcher, suddenly became the cold, unscrupulous Dario Delgado, while sweet, cookie-making Abby came to life as one of Blackheart Bellacroix's ruthless pirates. It was pretty awesome.

So, after rehearsal, and Bébé's notes, I fled the scene like a woman on the run; I had a dinner party to throw together, after all. I had *just* gotten to my car when I heard my name being called. Not now, I thought, feeling like I was working on borrowed time. It was almost six, and I still had to stop by the hardware store on the way home. Dixie, Cal, and Brooks would be at the house by seven, and I still needed to shower before putting the finishing touches on our dinner.

Suppressing a sigh, I told myself not to be impatient; somebody just wanted to catch up after practice, no big deal. Turning around, I saw

Janice hurrying toward me. She held a burgundy velvet dress, which she handed to me as she stopped near the hood of my car. "Hi, Riley!" she said warmly. "Sorry to bother you, but would you take this home and try it on? Have someone pin it if it gaps anywhere. I think it will be ok, though; I used your measurements from the lavender gown we fitted yesterday. I just want to make sure."

"Absolutely," I replied, smoothing the beautiful frock as I hung it inside the back seat. "It's gorgeous, Janice."

She beamed. "Thanks."

I started to turn away, but caught her looking expectantly at me, like there was something else she wanted to say. "What's on your mind?" I asked, curious.

She stepped forward, thrusting a brochure at me. "It's just," she began, looking uncertainly at the paper in her hand. "This is where I was thinking of going to school."

Raising my eyebrows, I scanned the page. Southern Gulf School of Design. "That's great!" I told her, nodding approvingly. "You should definitely apply, Janice!"

She nodded, putting the brochure back in her purse. "I know. I mean — that's what I was hoping you could help me with," she told me, her eyes shining with anticipation.

"Me?" I asked uncertainly. "How could I help?"

"Well — you're a professor at a community college, right?"

"Yeah," I replied. "Well — I *was*. I'm not anymore." Boy, I thought silently, amused. The Two Moon Bay rumor mill must include a full profile! Brooks had known Ryan was interested in me, Janice knew where I used to work, and from what Bébé had told me, everyone in town was aware that my kids had sneaked their way to the Sunshine State unchaperoned. I wondered sardonically if they knew what I had eaten for breakfast that morning.

She rushed on, "I was wondering if maybe you'd write me a letter of recommendation? You know — since it's a community college, and you used to teach at one — I thought it might help my chances of getting in."

Oh, a recommendation letter! Now it made sense. I tried not to hurt her feelings as I explained, "Janice, I would *love* to help you as you apply for college. But a recommendation letter usually comes from someone a student has actually taken a class with, or worked for." Seeing the crestfallen look on her face, I thought quickly. "*But*, I do have a job that requires some sewing and design work, and I could use a reliable seamstress." I raised my eyebrows. "Think you'd be interested in taking on a gig like that? Once the play's over, of course, so you'd have more time."

Janice's dejected expression quickly changed to one of delight. She squealed, clapping her hands together. "Oh, Riley!" she cried, grabbing my hands. "That would be awesome!"

I smiled. "Great! And thank you," I told her. "I need someone I can count on, and I think you're the perfect person for the job."

After we said goodbye, I hopped in my car and drove back into town, singing Christmas carols at the top of my lungs. Pulling into a spot in front of the hardware store, I didn't realize my windows were down until I heard deep, barrel-chested laughter.

"Well, hello there, darlin'!" Cal's voice boomed as I climbed out, turning as red as a fire hydrant. "You sure sound like you're in the Christmas spirit!"

Laughing, I shrugged my shoulders. "I guess so," I agreed sheepishly. "Although it's a little hard for me to believe it's Christmas," I said, looking around. "There's no snow!"

He chuckled. "Yep, that's true. A little different than the mountains, then, I guess!" He clapped me on the shoulder as he started to walk past the hardware store. "See ya soon, darlin'!"

"Bye," I answered, ignoring the fact that he was openly staring at my butt as I scurried inside.

"Ok, painter's tape," I muttered to myself as the bells jingled behind me. I texted Alex a quick message, wondering if we needed anything else while I was there. "Hi, Ed!" I greeted the owner, Big Ed Herndon, who stood behind the counter in what I'm told were his 'Christmas' red suspenders.

The red-haired giant smiled down at me, his ruddy face the picture of kindness. Although he was as big as an ox, Big Ed was the gentlest man

I think I'd ever met. His hazel eyes sparkled as he said warmly, "Why, hullo there, Miss Riley! What kin I do fer ya t'day?"

"I'm looking for painter's tape," I told him, hoping to be in and out in under five minutes.

"Oh, yeah," he said, pointing. "Second aisle on yer right, right next to the paint brushes."

"Ok, thanks," I replied, hurrying forward. "Excuse me," I said to two kids who were blocking the aisle. Their backs were to me, but I'm sure they had heard my footsteps coming.

Or maybe not; the guy spun around as though surprised by my approach. He was dressed in baggy jeans and a white T-shirt, with a black and red flannel shirt tied around his waist. He seemed jumpy, though he was nice enough. "Oh, excuse us, ma'am," he said quickly, stepping aside and giving his companion the eye to do the same. She turned to look at me then rolled her eyes dramatically. Sighing, she moved grudgingly out of the way.

"Thanks," I murmured, wondering what the heck her problem was. Scanning the shelves for the paint brushes, I couldn't help but overhear their conversation.

"Ok," the girl said in a whisper. "So this is all we need?" They each held a square-headed shovel, and he gripped a mag-lite. "You're sure?" she prompted.

The guy nodded. "Yeah — this is it. Now let's go," he said conspiratorially, casting a wary look my way.

Racking my brain to figure out what the shady twosome was up to, I put on what I thought to be a convincing show of browsing-while-ignoring. "Ah — there you are," I mumbled victoriously, spotting the paint brushes.

Apparently they bought it, for rather than hurrying away, the girl continued, "Where are we supposed to store these until then, anyway?" Her voice was impatient. "I mean — it's not like we can waltz them inside the inn, past the front desk!"

The inn! I thought worriedly. Then - Brooks, oh, no! My mind whirled as my writer's imagination conjured all kinds of horror the young criminals had brewing.

"Shh," the guy warned her. Although I was trying my best to appear inconspicuous as I pretended to search the shelves, I could feel their watchful eyes on me. "Keep it down," he told her loudly enough for me to hear. Then, dropping his voice, he said, "We can't bring them in when that owner-guy is there, so we'll just wait 'til it's the old man's shift. Until then, they stay in the trunk."

Holy crap! I thought, my head spinning. I reached out and grabbed the first roll of tape my eyes fell upon. What the heck were these two fishy kids planning? I couldn't wait to tell Brooks.

I hurried up the next aisle, hoping to beat them to the check-out counter. Although Stump and Randy didn't need tape to finish painting, the girls did. They had made me promise to let them finish the last wall in their rooms tonight, after our company left. I was hoping they'd be too tired, but given their excitement, I had a feeling that was not going to be the case.

Glancing over at the whispering conspirators, I was relieved to see that they were taking their time. I wasn't one to judge, but given the nature of their suspicious conversation, I was creeped out, to say the least. I just wished I knew what the heck they were planning. And whether or not it was bad news for Brooks.

Smiling distractedly at Big Ed, I set the tape on the counter. I dug into my purse for some bills, thinking that I was about to make it out of the store on-schedule. Maybe I could add an appetizer to tonight's menu, I was thinking, as Ed broke into my thoughts.

He chuckled. "Treasure hunters," he said, shaking his head. "You kin spot 'em a mile away!"

Following his eyes to the shady couple, I counted out the exact change. "Really?" I asked. "How can you tell?"

"Well," he said cordially, leaning forward to give me the scoop. "Fer one thing, they always buy shovels . . ." His voice trailed off as we looked over at them.

Shovels — check.

" . . . An' some sort o' flashlight . . ." he continued.

Check — check, I thought, looking away as the girl suddenly glanced up and sent a death-glare my way.

"Lately," Big Ed continued, unfazed, "lotsa people been buyin' them head lamps, but these ones is goin' fer the ole-fashioned handheld, I guess." Returning to his full height, he laughed to himself, licking his fingers before fumbling with the plastic bags.

"That's ok, Ed," I told him, grabbing the tape. "You can keep the bag."

"Oh, well — ok, then," he said agreeably. Leaning back on his heels and pulling on his red suspenders, Big Ed loomed even taller - as if that were humanly possible. The man was seven feet if he was an inch! "Thanks, Miss Riley — see ya later!"

"Thanks, Ed!" I called, hurrying out the door.

Ignoring my instincts, which told me *not* to make eye contact with the angry she-beast, I couldn't help but glance over at the couple as I scurried by. They juggled their treasure-hunting materials awkwardly, attempting to carry the shovels and flashlights while reaching for a display of large white pillar candles. The guy lost his load at the last second, muttering an expletive as it all went crashing to the ground. I couldn't help but feel a little sorry for them. They were just kids, after all — innocent treasure hunters who'd flocked to the beach with a dream and a shovel — or at least that's what I thought for one brief moment before the glowering girl scowled at me accusingly, as though *I* had run up to her boyfriend and knocked the items out of his hands myself. Whatevs, as Alex would say.

Averting my eyes, I waved once more to Ed, as he hurried around the counter to help them. Treasure hunters, huh? I thought as the door banged closed behind me. I trusted Big Ed's judgment, but wasn't so sure that's *all* they were up to.

My phone rang as I was getting in my car. Capri.

"Hey, Capri," I said into the phone, pushing the 'Start' button on my ignition. I jumped about a mile as "Rudolph the Red-Nosed Reindeer" blasted through the speakers. Man, I had really been rockin' out — no wonder Cal had been so amused! Fumbling to turn it down, I shouted, "What was that, honey?"

". . .oven?"

"What about the oven?" I asked, signaling as I turned onto Brooks' street. If I didn't have so much to do before I got home, I figured I could go ahead and pick him up now.

"It's beeping," she said, as the sound traveled through the phone. "What should we do?"

"Go ahead and turn it off," I told her. I'd been planning to be home by the time the baked potatoes were done. That's ok, they'd be easy to finish. "Make sure to use the potholder, and take them out of the stove with the tongs. Set them on the cooling rack that's in the cupboard. I'll be home in five minutes." I told her, slowing for a family at the crosswalk. "I'll need you to help me scoop them out for twice-baked potatoes."

"You're making twice-baked potatoes?!" she exclaimed. "I love those."

I smiled, thinking she sounded like I would if I'd just learned I'd won the lottery. "I know, baby; I made them just for you." Hearing her happy giggle, I paused, gratified that I could so easily make her day. "Anyway, *we're* making twice-baked potatoes," I corrected myself. "I'll need your help to make them just perfect."

I could hear smiling through the phone as she banged the cupboard doors shut.

"Anyway, thank you, sweetie," I said. "I'll see you in a few minutes."

Clicking off, I thought about how fortunate I was. I had two amazing kids who went out of their way to spend time with me, new friends who already felt like family, and an amazing connection with the man I was quickly coming to care for.

Thinking of Brooks and his blue, blue eyes, I went over last night's blissful events in my mind. Just thinking of him made me feel warm all over. I smiled, surprised by how much I was looking forward to seeing him tonight. It's funny, but I couldn't recall the last time I'd felt this way - so filled with anticipation and excitement. The butterflies in my stomach fluttered every time he came to mind. Come to think of it, I told myself, I couldn't *ever* recall feeling this way.

As I turned into the driveway, I smiled, knowing that surely meant something big.

— ~

Despite my mad dash home from practice, and the race against time to finish preparing before my guests arrived, Dixie's honorary dinner party was a big success. Considering that it was a small gathering - really just a warm-up for the *actual* surprise party I planned to throw for her, Stump, and Chuy when the house was finished, it was even better than expected. The guys would be thrilled, I knew, and Dixie would be downright delighted, which would make the surprise even better. Plus, I knew the girls would love to help me plan it. So even though tonight was more of a personal thank you to Dixie on a smaller scale, it was a great excuse to get together with some people who meant a lot to me. Dixie, especially; she really had been so helpful to me since day one. And I felt like she was a friend, now, too.

So, at about quarter to eight that night, as we sat at the large farmhouse table I'd picked up at an antique store, my guests sat back in their chairs, looking thoroughly stuffed.

Brooks tossed his napkin on the table. "That was delicious, Riley, thank you." He put a hand over his stomach. "As much as I'd like to, I couldn't eat another bite."

Alex piped up from her seat, "Riley, may we be excused?"

"You may," I told her. "*After* you and your sister clear the table." Catching the grimace she tried to hide, I gave her a look as she rolled her eyes.

Despite Alex's attitude, the girls got right to work, eager to ditch the adults and hang with their friends. Capri scurried around the table, gathering up the plates, as Alex huffed over to the sink. Evangeline and Lily talked quietly, making polite conversation as they waited for their friends to finish up with their chores.

Swallowing her last sip of wine, Dixie set down her glass. She proclaimed with an exasperated sigh, "Well, I just don't know about that Cal, y'all." She shook her head at me. "He said he was pickin' up somethin' special to go with our meal, but, shoot," she said, glancing down at her dainty gold watch. "That was thirty minutes ago!"

She was right. We'd held dinner for as long as we dared, but by about seven-fifteen, the girls had been getting antsy, and the twice-baked potatoes were starting to de-puff; they really are best when served hot. Knowing there would be plenty of left-overs for when Cal *did* arrive, we dug in.

I was just about to reassure Dixie that he would surely be along any minute now, when the doorbell rang.

Capri, holding a stack of dinner plates in her hands on the way to the kitchen, suddenly veered off course and went running for the door. "I'll get it!" she yelled, the plates clattering together, sending a ceramic panic through the air.

I flinched, expecting them to go tumbling to the floor. They were handmade by an artisan from Maggie Valley, and, even though they hadn't cost much, to me they were priceless. "Capri — be careful of the dishes!" I hollered, getting up to do damage control.

Raegan whizzed by, yapping excitedly as he followed the crazed girl to the door.

Ignoring my warning, Capri deposited the plates haphazardly onto the entryway bench. I sighed, rescuing my poor dishes while the door greeters slid across the foyer floor. So much for the artfully-placed runners slowing them down.

Peering out the window beside the door, Capri's energy level hit another high as she shouted, "It's Cal!" before throwing open the door.

As I handed the plates off to Alex in the kitchen, I called out, my back to the door, "Come on in, Cal — supper's on the table." Starting toward the front, I caught sight of Capri darting outside the open door, Raegan's tail disappearing after her. But no sign of Cal.

"Hello?" I said to myself, glancing at Dixie and Brooks, who were still seated at the table.

They shrugged in answer. Apparently, they hadn't seen him either. Dixie lifted her glass, nodding graciously at Brooks' offer for more wine.

"Cal?" I asked, puzzled. "Capri?" What the heck were those two up to? I wondered, trying to see the porch from where I stood by the table. "Raegan?" I tried, figuring it must be something involving food if my golden was still interested. It was dark enough outside that I couldn't see beyond the bright light in the entryway.

Cal's voice suddenly reached us, sounding slightly muffled. "We'll be right with you, darlin'," followed by some whispering and a woof.

Oh, Lord help us, I thought, then immediately scolded myself for thinking the worst. It's just that with Cal, you never knew what to expect. It could be a lifetime subscription to a golf enthusiast's magazine, *or* it could be a brand-new sports car. From what Dixie had told me about the man she obviously had feelings for, he was super-generous, super-kind, and super-unpredictable.

Capri waltzed in at that moment, a Santa hat atop her head. She wore the grin she'd inherited from her father — the one that meant she was up to something. Her little face positively glowed with anticipation.

"Capri?" I said suspiciously, still not seeing Cal. He must have been off to the side of the door, out of sight. "What are you doing, sweetie? You'll let in bugs with the door open like that."

In the next second, Cal stepped forward, decked out in red golf pants, a white long-sleeved shirt, and matching white and red shoes. His blonde head was topped with a Santa hat, and his face wore a big, wide grin — a grin not even the long, white Santa beard could hide! "Hey there, y'all!" he greeted us, waving at Dixie, Brooks, and the girls.

Alex sauntered out of the kitchen to see what all the hubbub was about, drying her hands on the golden retriever-themed apron I'd tried to sew a few years back. In my defense, I'd been going through a relentless crafty phase, and had intended it to be a kitschy tribute to Raegan. Let's just say it didn't go as planned.

Everyone except Capri and I sort of did a double-take as they took in the lopsided dog with big floppy ears and a tail that hung off one side. Brooks cleared his throat as a signal for his girls to stop staring. Somewhere nearby, I thought a heard a cricket chirping.

The first to snap out of it, Cal hurried forward to give me a quick hug. "Sorry I'm late, darlin', but it took me longer'n I expected to get y'all's Christmas present!" He winked at Capri. "Say there, would you mind helpin' me out here, little darlin'?"

Capri bounced eagerly on the balls of her feet. She giggled in answer, hurrying through the door.

Cal laughed heartily as she zipped by. Turning back to us, he said graciously, "If y'all will excuse us for a moment . . ." He thumbed his Santa hat at Dixie and me. "My helper and I will be right back — with the surprise!"

As the secretive Santas scurried around on the porch, Raegan supervised from the threshold of the open door. His tail wagged excitedly.

I glanced at Dixie and Brooks to get their take on the situation.

Rolling her eyes with a noncommittal shrug, Dixie languidly sipped her wine. She and Brooks looked truly relaxed at the table — both were reclined in their chairs, Dixie's arm resting on the back, one hand cradling the bottom of her wine glass, while Brooks' long legs were stretched out in front of him. Nothing like dinner and a show, I thought, amused. By now, Alex had returned to the kitchen to finish the dishes. Evangeline and Lily were dutifully drying — leave it to Alex to rope her guests into helping with her chores.

Suddenly, Cal called out, "A one, a two, a one, two, three, four!" In the next instant, Kelly Clarkson's "Underneath the Tree" began playing from outside on the porch.

We all laughed in surprise as Cal backed through the doorway, pulling a cart with what appeared to be a seven-foot Christmas tree. Its fragrant boughs were still wrapped in plastic. "Ho, ho, ho!" he called out. "Merry Christmas tree!"

Capri danced in after him, carrying an old-school boom box. Kelly Clarkson's voice trilled from the speakers as my daughter bopped to the beat, her Santa hat keeping time with the music.

By this time, Alex and Brooks' girls had re-emerged from the kitchen. Even Dixie and Brooks had perked up, suddenly waking from their food comas to enjoy the festivities. I laughed in delight, clapping my hands together. Cal and Capri danced around the tree in the entryway, while Raegan bounced and barked at their heels, delighted by the goings-on. Alex giggled, watching the scene through her phone as she filmed the spectacle. Evangeline and Lily looked on with obvious interest, then, as if spoken aloud, all three girls suddenly ran forward to get in on the action.

"Oh, my gosh, Cal!" I exclaimed, when Capri shut the music off at Cal's command. "This is amazing — thank you!" I ran over to give him a hug. Then, as everyone chattered excitedly around us, I said quietly, so only he could hear, "Cal, thank you so much, but really — you didn't have to do this."

Smiling that million-dollar smile of his, Cal pulled back to face me, holding my arms. His eyes were earnest, his voice softened by a sincerity that was altogether different from his usual lighthearted banter. "Well, sure I did, darlin' — it's the least I can do." He glanced at Alex and Capri, who were awkwardly trying to push the tree-laden cart toward the great room. "I've got to take care of my three favorite girls, now, don't I?"

In that very moment, I saw a different side of Cal. Despite his wandering eye and persistent, flirty ways, the famous golfer had a heart of gold. And it was evident that he truly cared about me and my girls. I guess this was that generous — and unpredictable! — nature Dixie had been talking about.

Hugging him once more, I hoped he could see the gratitude in my eyes. "Thank you," I said once more. Then, turning to face the kids, I said, "Wow, girls - isn't this *great*? Now we won't have to get a tree tomorrow — Mr. Cal saved us the trouble!"

Before the words were even out of my mouth, the girls erupted into excited murmurings and rushed to give him thank-you hugs.

Capri looked up at him. "Cal, you'll have to help us decorate it!" she declared, running into the craft room to where I'd stored the one tub of decorations I'd brought from home.

"Oh, well, darlin', I'd love to!" Cal replied. "Let's just see where your stepmama wants it, first."

As I gave directions, Brooks helped him move the tree to the great room, where it could be enjoyed when we sat at the table, or while relaxing on the couch. As they jostled it into place and removed the wrap, Alex, Evangeline, Capri, and Lily set to work on the decorations. Suddenly, Capri ran out of the room, smiling, with Raegan bounding joyously after her. Mere seconds later, she scooted back across the threshold, carrying a faux sheepskin rug we'd picked up for her room the other day. She knelt, placing it beneath the tree. "There!" she cried victoriously. "Snow!"

Before I knew it, the girls had Christmas carols playing on the TV, and were singing along as the adults congregated around them. Raegan pranced around, tongue lolling, thrilled by everyone's excitement.

Dixie called out suddenly, "Oh, look, Riley — you and Brooks are under the mistletoe!"

"Mistletoe?" I repeated blankly. "We don't have any . . ." I began, looking up. "Huh, mistletoe!" I exclaimed in surprise. Wait a second — "Cal!" I swatted him, as he burst out laughing.

"Well, now, darlin', I don't know nothin' about that!" He slung an arm around Dixie's shoulders, placing a kiss on her cheek.

Brooks and I smiled at one another as I stood on tiptoe to plant a kiss on his lips.

Just then, Raegan looked over at the door, as if he suspected someone was there. In the next moment, he launched into a raucous bark. He ran forward, just as the bell rang.

Everyone looked questioningly at me as I excused myself to answer it. Who could that be? I wondered. I hadn't been expecting anyone else.

I kind of thought Capri might rush to get it, since answering the door seemed to be her and Raegan's self-appointed job, but she and the girls were totally engrossed in their decorating festivities. Even the fireplace was roaring, I noticed as I looked back.

"Raegan, sit," I commanded. Waiting until his seat hit the floor, I opened the door. "Oh, Ryan!" I said, caught off-guard. Stepping back, I made room for the large box he carried. "Come on in. You can set that beside the bench," I told him, pointing. "Would you like something to eat?" I gestured toward the table, which still had remnants of our feast.

"Hey," he greeted me with a hug after setting the package down. "No, thanks, but it smells delicious — I've got a few more people to deliver to, then I've got dinner plans." He rubbed Raegan's ears, indulging my golden with some good ole baby talk. "Hey y'all," he waved to everyone from where he stood in the entryway.

The kids called out polite but distracted 'heys,' while chattering excitedly over the decorations. Cal and Brooks returned Ryan's greeting from where they stood near the dining table. As Dixie sashayed over to greet the delivery man, I couldn't help but notice the peculiar expression on Brooks' face. As we made eye contact, he covered it with a smile, but I could tell that it was forced. Getting an odd feeling in the pit of my stomach, I wondered what that meant.

Dixie's blue eyes sparkled prettily as she sauntered over to us in her hunter green velvet dress, beaming at Ryan. "Hey, there, sug," she drawled. "You're deliv'rin kinda late, now, aren't you?" Although she looked curiously at him, I couldn't help but notice that her eyes darted to me.

"Oh," he answered with a shrug. "I've got some packages on the truck that I wanted to get out tonight, is all. With Christmas right around the corner, we'll be pulling some late nights for the next few days."

My realtor nodded, her perceptive eyes picking up on something that I wasn't seeing. She glanced at me again. "Right, Christmas. Well, it sure is good to see you, sug." Starting back toward the dining area, she stopped and added casually, "And say hello to Candy for me." Her eyes slipped back to mine as she breezed back to the table to mingle with the guys.

"I sure will," Ryan responded. "Say," he said to me. "Did you hear about the storm that's coming?"

My virgin-hurricane ears perked up. "Storm?" I asked, instantly alert. "Like a thunder storm?" I inquired hopefully. I gulped as I continued, "Or a hurricane?"

He laughed. "Don't worry, it's *not* a hurricane — it's too late in the season for that," he assured me, reading into my biggest fear. "Just a tropical storm. But it *does* sound like it's gonna be pretty strong — seventy mile-an-hour winds if it stays on track."

Visions of disaster carnage I'd seen on TV, and of my new house being demolished impaired my senses. "Tropical storm?" I repeated numbly. "Seventy-mile-an-hour winds?" I fanned myself. Was it getting hot in here all of a sudden?

Ryan looked worriedly at me.

"When's it supposed to get here?" I asked warily.

He smiled in that relaxed way of his, patting my shoulder. I thought that was a weird thing to do. Talk of tropical storms does not exactly trigger a smile in my book. "That's the kicker," he told me. "Christmas Day."

"Christmas *Day*?" I repeated, as if the words were new to me. Holy crap. My mind was spinning. I started planning for the end. "We'll have to board up the house. Evacuate. Take the mother dog and her pups."

Unfamiliar with that part of my life, Ryan gave me a skeptical look.

"Pack up the girls, the presents — wait!" I clasped his arm, panicking. "We don't even *have* presents!"

I looked guiltily toward Alex and Capri, seeing them all happy and giggling as they threw strands of tinsel at the tree. What a terrible step-mother I was for not buying presents! Oh, now it was *on*. My guilt trip was just getting started. Completely ignoring the fact that I had given the girls their gifts before I left, I judged and sentenced myself to being a horrible parent and threw away the key. Now that our lives were about to end, all I could do was beat myself up for not having presents under the tree that we'd received about fifteen minutes ago. *And,* now that the storm was bearing down on us, it was too late to go out and buy any; the house was about to be demolished by a storm of biblical proportions, and we were all going to die!

Sensing an on-coming freak-out, Ryan stared at me. "Hey, uh," he looked nervously toward the others, clearly hoping for reinforcements. I think he signaled to Brooks, but who the heck knows? My senses were waning; I was starting to slip away. "It might not even come this way," he told me. "It's still early to tell."

"Too early to tell," I mumbled, falling into a catatonic state. I had already made two mental pre-hurricane checklists by the time Brooks arrived at my side.

"Hey," he said, with concern. Placing a reassuring hand at my back, he looked from me to Ryan. "What's wrong?" Ryan filled him in as I planned for a national disaster.

The next thing I knew, they were walking to the door.

"Riley, Ryan's leaving," Brooks told me.

Snapping out of it, I told myself to watch The Weather Channel like everyone else who lived in a coastal area. Be a good hostess now and freak out later, I resolved, saying goodbye. "Thanks for bringing the package by," I told him. And for the nervous break-down, I thought cryptically, thinking we were goners for sure. Waving, I closed the door behind him.

Brooks put an arm around my shoulders as we walked into the great room. By now, Dixie and Cal were helping the girls decorate. Capri laughed uproariously as she and Lily wound garland around Cal's waist. "You ok?" Brooks asked me.

"No," I told him truthfully. "I've never experienced a hurricane." I looked at him worriedly. "How are you so calm right now?"

Suppressing a smile, Brooks replied gently, "It's *not* a hurricane, Riley. And it may not even reach us; it could break up before it gets to us."

I narrowed my eyes. People kept *saying* it wasn't a hurricane, but I wasn't so sure. In-season or not, a storm that brews over the ocean for days, picking up water and wind as it swirls toward the helpless coast is a storm I want no part of.

Dixie breezed over, a full wine glass in hand. Covered in gold garland, Cal dawdled behind her, trying not to trip over the ends. They both looked concerned. My face probably foretold our destruction. "Did somebody say 'hurricane'?" Dixie asked, curious. "I just *love* those drinks."

I shook my head. We were all going to die, and she had cocktails on the brain! "Not the kind you *drink*," I replied, "the kind that destroys

property and quaint little towns on the southern Gulf Coast of Florida."
I told her grimly. "We're about to get one."

To my astonishment, the three Two Moon Bay natives burst into
laughter. I gaped at them like they had all lost their minds.

Dixie was the first to recover. "No, sug," she told me, placing a sympathetic hand on my shoulder. People kept *doing* that, for some reason.
"It's too late in the season to get a hurricane." She looked at the others
like I might have a few screws loose. "Bless your heart, sug. It's just a little
ole' storm. No big deal."

Cal put in jovially, "Darlin', you talkin' about the storm they were
discussin' on the radio today?" He finally figured out how to unwind
the carefully-layered garland the girls had wound around him and spun
around a few times. Capri and Lily giggled nearby, watching. "Ah, shoot,"
he told me, waving a dismissive hand in the air. "That ain't nothin'. We
may not even *get* that storm!"

Brooks rubbed my arm in what I'm sure he meant as a comforting
gesture. It seemed to have the opposite effect, I noted, feeling my heart
pounding in my chest. "That's what I tried to tell her," he told them.
"Riley," he said, placing his hands on my arms as he turned to face me.
"You're going to be fine." He spoke the words slowly and carefully, as
though I might not understand. "A lot can change in the next twenty-
four hours. And if there really *is* a threat, we'll have plenty of time to
prepare." He looked at his watch. "Oh, I'm sorry, but I have to go — my
shift starts in fifteen minutes."

"Oh, that's right!" I exclaimed, thinking of the inn.

He gave me a funny look.

I shook my head. "Tell you in a sec," I told him.

As he said goodbye to his kids, who were sleeping over at our house
that night, I told Dixie and Cal about the suspicious couple I'd encoun-
tered in the hardware store.

Coming back over to us, Brooks said, "Oh, those kids?" He shrugged
his shoulders. "Yeah, they're a little shady, but they're harmless. We
get hundreds like them every year — everybody's just looking for treasure. They bring their maps and tools, and after a few days of traipsing

through the swamps, they go back to where they came from with a story to tell." He kissed me on the cheek. "But I really do have to get going. Thank you for a lovely meal."

I walked him to the door, still feeling a little uncertain. Between the shifty couple at the inn and the storm looming off the coast, I was a ball of nerves. "Well — just be careful," I said lamely. I was worried, but had nothing specific to worry about. Just suspicion. "Oh," I paused, wondering if I should ask this. "Last night, when I told you about Janice," I began, watching as he made another face. "There it is! That's exactly what you did last night when I brought up her name. What did she ever do?" I asked, befuddled.

He stopped, his hand on the door. "It's not *Janice*, per se," Brooks started. He looked at me frankly. "It's just that she and her boyfriend got into some trouble last summer. Stole some things from a town nearby, tried to sell them on the Internet." He shook his head. "I think it was more him than her, to be honest with you, but they both took the fall. The charges were dropped because they were minors, and the merchandise was returned, but the only reason they're able to work on the play at all is because it counted as community service." He pulled open the door. "A lot of people in town were pretty upset about it - said they never should have been given a second chance." He blew me a kiss. "Gotta go, babe."

Hearing him call me 'babe' for the first time brought a smile to my lips. "Night," I called after him, wondering how I could feel all gooey inside and so worried at the same time. What he had told me about Janice and Jamie just didn't sound right. They honestly seemed like good kids.

Capri's voice jolted me out of my thoughts. "Riley!" she called, running out of the great room. "Riley?"

Dixie and Cal had moved into the dining room, where they lounged at the table, talking quietly over a glass of wine. They looked up as Capri hurried over to me, curious.

"What's up, Capri?" I asked, following her into the great room.

Her face was alight as she thrust a library book at me. "Look at this! It's an artist's rendering of Destina Delgado. You look just like her!" she cried, watching for my reaction.

Cal and Dixie hopped up. They peered over my shoulder for a look. Dixie's syrupy voice cried in agreement, "Oh, you do, sug!"

I studied the picture, shaking my head. "No, that's not Destina; that's Temperance Biscayne." I told them. "I saw a picture of her yesterday."

Capri flipped through the book. "No, Riley," she told me emphatically. "*That's* Temperance Biscayne," she said, pointing to a picture of a sad-looking girl, the same face and eyes I had seen yesterday at the theater. She shifted her finger to the happy, smiling girl next to her. "And *that's* Destina Delgado."

I was quiet for a second. "Huh," I finally said, puzzled. "They look so much alike." I looked at my daughter. "Flip back to that other one for a second?"

She did, awaiting my response.

"They look the same," I concluded. "I don't see how anyone could tell them apart. The only difference I see is that one looks happy and the other is always sad. Other than that, they could be the same person."

Cal piped up, "You know, my daddy is a big Delgado family expert," he told us. "You have any questions for your report, darlin'," he said to Capri, "you should ask him. His great-great-grandmama was a Delgado — descended from the Spaniards. He knows all about the treasure and the legend. I'm sure he'd be happy to talk to you about it."

"Cool!" Capri looked expectantly at me. "Could we talk to Cal's dad tomorrow, Riley?"

I put my hand on her shoulder. "We'll see, hon." I looked at Cal. "*Mr.* Cal's daddy might have something to do tomorrow," I started, hoping she'd get the hint and remember to use the Southern name prefix she'd been raised to say. At the same time, Cal cut in, "Oh, no, ma'am! All he's got goin' on tomorrow is thirty-six holes of golf!"

I paused, considering. Between hurricane-prepping efforts, I could fit in a lunch with Cal's dad.

"Shoot," he continued to Capri, "I can pick you and your stepmama up for lunch at the club so you can interview him all you want!" He smiled cheerfully at me, happy that he could be of service.

Capri grasped my hand, practically yanking my arm out of the socket in her excitement. "Oh, that'd be so great! *Please*, Riley?"

I smiled, relenting. I *suppose* I could board up the windows in the morning and watch The Weather Channel in the bar at the club over lunch. "Of course," I agreed. "What do you say to Mr. Cal?"

She threw her arms around his waist, still wearing her Santa hat. "Thanks, Mr. Cal!"

We watched as Capri hurried back to the other girls, who were putting the finishing touches on the tree.

Alex dug into the tub of decorations. She pulled out the star Rainie had given me the Christmas before I turned eighteen. It was white and shiny like pearls, and had a simple white light kit inside. I always loved how it glowed, so clean and bright. "Riley," she said, unwrapping it carefully. "It's your turn to put the star on the tree."

Cal and Dixie followed me into the great room, watching quietly as the girls and I completed the ritual that had been ours for nearly nine years. Evangeline and Lily stepped back from the tree as I took the star from Alex's hands, and gently placed it atop the tree. Before I hopped off the ottoman they'd been using as a stepladder, I hit the switch. The star lit up with a gentle glow, as white and peaceful as I remembered. Alex and Capri stood next to me, admiring their work. Without speaking, we slung our arms around each other.

"It's perfect," Capri said quietly.

I nodded my head. "It sure is, baby." I wiped a tear of happiness from my eye. "It sure is."

8

The Legend Continues

ritlee's voice was loud and obtrusive in the quiet of the morning. It was Tuesday, just three days 'til Christmas, and a blustery one at that. Tropical Storm Ida was expected to make landfall sooner than expected. Now it was set to strike the southern Gulf Coast in the wee hours of the night on Christmas Eve. Although its winds were well below the hurricane category, the storm had sped up, eager to make landfall a day earlier than expected. As Brit's video call broke into my 'Running' playlist, I slowed my pace to answer.

"Riley *E*-lizabeth Larkin," she launched right in before I could say hello. "Why on *earth* have you not called me back?!" Her brown eyes shot daggers through the phone. "I called you twice yesterday *and* the day before!"

I gave her a smarty-pants smile, catching my breath. "Well, hey, Brit, I'm fine, thanks — how are you?"

She rolled her eyes then snapped indignantly, "Well, I *could* have been dead on the side of the road, but *you'd* never know since you never called me back!"

This was a familiar routine with us — if you didn't answer or call her back *immediately*, Brit made it her job to make you feel like complete crap. Guilt was her specialty. But, I conceded silently, not calling her back for two days *was* pretty bad. I'd meant to call her, just . . . got busy. Feeling like a bad friend, I said truthfully, "I'm sorry, Brit — I meant to call you. It's just been so busy the past few days." I paused. "How are you? I miss you."

Her expression softened a bit, but her voice still had an edge. "Well," she huffed. "I'm fine. But I do have a story to tell you." Her eyes sparkled mischievously, then she added, "That's what I wanted to tell you the other day." She stopped, suddenly worried. "It's about Jason."

I furrowed my brow, watching as the eastern sky began to lighten. I looked over the dunes toward town, where pale pink fingers softened the inky sky. The breeze was gusty and the air was oppressively humid, signaling that the storm swirling just off the coast would soon make landfall. "Jason?" I asked, as though unfamiliar with the name.

She sighed, exasperated. "Yes, honey, Jason — the selfish jerk who cheated on you with a twenty-five-year-old who dumped *him* for a twenty-*four*-year-old kid." She paused, looking meaningfully at me. "*That* Jason."

I blinked. I'm sure I should have felt *something*, but all I felt in that moment was eager to continue my run. Britlee stared at me through the phone, anxious to capture my reaction. I don't know if she expected me to fall out or wail with gratitude, but I honestly couldn't have cared less if Jason had gotten dumped or married. It just didn't matter anymore. "Huh," I finally said. Screw it, I thought, picking up the pace. I can talk and jog.

Britlee gaped at me. "Riley?" She brought her face closer to the phone, as though she would be able to stick her head through to my end. "Are you *runnin'*?"

"Yes," I answered, my breath regulated by my pace. "Why?"

"*Why*?" She gave me an incredulous look. "Because that's not *normal*, that's why! When your best friend tells you your ex-husband was dumped by the bimbo he cheated on you with, the normal reaction is not to start runnin'," she said, exasperated. "I thought you might have *some* sort of reaction to my news." Her voice was petulant. "I, for one, was positively giddy when I heard it." She looked hurt. "I couldn't *wait* to tell you."

I sighed, slowing down to a walk. "Brit," I told her, not meaning to hurt her feelings. "It's just that I don't *care* what's going on with Jason anymore." I shrugged. "I just honestly . . . really don't."

She watched me for a moment, then said, "Well, I guess that's a good thing." She was quiet before she finished, "It seems like a lot has changed." Her observation was straight-forward enough, but her tone was loaded.

"Brit," I started to protest, but I knew she heard the half-hearted quality in my voice. Truth was, I knew *exactly* what she meant. "Nothing's changed, it's just that . . ." I continued lamely, but she cut me off.

"It's fine, Riley, don't worry about it." Her tone was disturbingly flat, void of emotion. "I'm glad you're not upset about Jason." She glanced over her shoulder, suddenly, as though she heard something. "Well, my children are callin' me," she said hurriedly.

I didn't see or hear anyone in the background. And at six o'clock in the morning during Christmas break, I was *pretty* sure the kids were still asleep. "Brit," I murmured, but honestly, I didn't even know what to say.

"I'm sorry to have bothered you," she said in a rush. "Bah." And then she was gone.

Sighing, I switched back to my music. Foregoing my 'Running' playlist, I went with the 'New Rock' one; with the tension I was feeling at that very moment, I would need some acoustic assistance to channel my stress into something more productive — like sprints. As Foo Fighters' "Come Alive" started out slowly, I turned my thoughts of Britlee over to Dave Grohl's voice. I knew her picking a fight with me wasn't about me — or *her*, per se - it was about the fact that she felt she was losing me, losing the friendship we'd nurtured for the past decade. And given all that had happened in the past few days, I could understand why she was worried.

As Grohl's voice crescendoed and exploded into the emotionally-driven guitar solo, I sprinted along the ocean. I ran and ran, until long after his voice had faded in my head. I ran until all thoughts of Britlee and the hurt I had seen on her face were wiped clean from my memory. I ran until the sun came up.

I didn't stop until my weary legs and my burning lungs drowned out the pain in my throbbing heart.

— ⁓

Capri's head swiveled one way, then the other, craning to study the diners around our table. "Which one do you think he is?" she asked me, pointing to a group of golfers who were making their way out of the restaurant, to the outdoor dining area where we sat.

I shook my head. "None of those guys," I told her. They were in their thirties — plus, Cal wasn't with them. "Oh, wait," I said, looking over her shoulder to the driving range that abutted the back of the al fresco seating area. The blustery morning had turned into a calm afternoon, though the wind blew the trees and grasses beyond the covered eating area. As we watched, Cal and a distinguished gentleman who looked remarkably like him strode toward us, talking animatedly with their hands. Their voices boomed in the same hearty tone.

Catching sight of her new best friend, Capri jumped up. Unbeknownst to her, the buttercup-colored dress she wore caught on the back of her chair. With catlike reflexes, I reached across the table and managed to unhook it just as she took off toward him. Phew - that could have been *disastrous*, I was thinking, as she threw herself at the famous golfer. "Cal, Cal!" she cried.

The flashy golfer laughed, catching her in a hug. He introduced her to his dad.

"Well, hey there, darlin'!" Calhoun Foxworth the Second exclaimed, bending to look her in the eye. "It is truly my pleasure to meet you, Miss Capri." He paused, shaking her hand. "Now - I hear you've got some research to do?"

Capri nodded. "Yes, sir — I'm writing a report on the legend of Two Moon Bay. And the treasure!"

Cal Sr. chuckled appreciatively. "Well, darlin', that's just fantastic!" He rose to his feet, still beaming down at my daughter. "You know," he dropped his voice to a conspiratorial tone. "I happen to be a Delgado-family expert," he told her. Then, glancing at Cal, he declared, "Whaddaya say we set down an' see if we can help," he bellowed, clapping his son on the back. "Come on!"

Beaming, Capri ran back to the table, eager to introduce me to her new friend. "Riley, this is Cal's dad — *Mr.* Cal!"

I laughed, thinking that we still had some work to do with adding the respectful title consistently to *both* Cals' names. Standing to shake 'Mr. Cal's' hand, I greeted him. "Hello, Mr. Foxworth." I smiled, a little star-struck. "It's a pleasure to meet you, sir." I had grown up watching Cal's dad on the pro golf circuit — the man had been unstoppable in the seventies and eighties — even into the nineties. Considering he must be near eighty now, he was remarkably spry. He was tall and fit — Cal had inherited his build — and his blonde hair was only mildly sprinkled with gray. He was tanned and flashy, but not nearly as vibrant as his son.

Our waitress popped up almost immediately, seeking our drink orders. As we made small talk, Cal Senior brought up the storm — my new least-favorite subject.

"Well," he began, glancing at the outdoor TV's weather report. "It looks like you ladies are about to experience your first-ever tropical storm." He looked from Capri's eager face to my panicked one. "Y'all are in for a real treat!" He laughed, glancing at his son for agreement.

Cal smiled a thank-you at the waitress's butt as she deposited our drinks and hurried away. "Yes, sir, that's right!" he agreed. "But, unfortunately," he told me, "we'll have to tough this one out without a party."

I took a sip of my water, wondering if I'd heard correctly. "I'm sorry," I asked, furrowing my brow. "But did you just say 'party'?"

Cal and Cal Senior exchanged a knowing look. "It's a tradition," Cal explained. "When there's a storm comin' in — one we don't have to evacuate for, of course — we party! Everybody stocks up on food and water — and beer — and we get together and have a good ole time." He raised his glass. "But, with this one gettin' weaker and weaker, and comin' in right at Christmas time, I'm thinkin' people will just stay home, for the most part. Maybe just party at the inn tomorrow, then go home to ride out the storm overnight."

Capri, following our conversation, looked at me as if I'd deliberately withheld vital social information from her. "Mr. Brooks is having a party?" she asked before shooting me a look of betrayal.

Cal Senior nodded his head. "Well, yes, darlin'. It's a long-standing Two Moon Bay tradition — ties in to the legend," he told her knowingly.

She leaned in with interest. "Really?"

"Yes, ma'am," he assured her. "Ya see, the inn's been around as long as the fort — which is what this club used to be - Destina's home, as you probably already know." She nodded vigorously as he added, "And later, it was a stronghold that served as protection for the town."

Capri's eyes were riveted. She discreetly extracted her pink pen and matching notebook from the little handbag I'd given her for fancy occasions, waiting for him to go on.

"Well, because the inn is so old, it's become sort of a museum of the town's history. Plus, Ole Man McKay — he's been collectin' relics from the Bay's pirate days ever since he was a boy — well, recently, he's bought pieces off the Internet that've been traced back to the 1700's — the days of Blackheart Bellacroix and his crew." He nodded at his son for agreement. "An' every year on the day before Christmas Eve, Ole Man McKay hosts a party for the entire town at the inn. All the guests stayin' there are invited, too." He paused to take a swig of his bourbon.

Capri asked him, "How come the party is held on December 23rd, Mr. Cal?" Her brow was furrowed as she absently chewed on the fluffy decorative end of her pen. "The day before Christmas Eve is kind of an odd day for a party," she reasoned.

Cal Senior replied, "That's a mighty fine observation, there, young lady," he told her. "December 23rd is symbolic because it's the day before Two Moon Bay was changed forever — the day before Destina and Temperance disappeared in what we now know as the worst pirate battle our town has ever seen. The yearly party is a mighty important affair for us; why, it's the biggest event o' the year for us Bayers!" He gave Capri a special nod. "They even have a real live treasure hunt for the kids!" He smiled at her, his blue eyes twinkling, as he took a healthy swallow of his drink. "Oh, yeah," he finished. "Y'all are gonna love it."

"Wow, a treasure hunt," Capri whispered to herself as she flipped to the questions she'd prepared. I could see her mind whirling, and wasn't surprised when she transitioned to the *real* treasure. "Speaking of treasure, Mr. Cal, what can you tell me about the *Doncella's* treasure? Was it really as valuable as people say?"

Cal Senior chuckled. "Oh, well, darlin', no one knows for sure, since it's never been found." He paused. "But, based on logs that were kept by other sea-faring merchants at the time — people that Bellacroix did business with — yes, that treasure was rumored to be worth about three hundred million dollars." He looked at us for emphasis.

My jaw dropped open. *Three hundred million dollars!* I couldn't even wrap my mind around how many zeroes that was. One thing I *did* know, three hundred million was an unfathomable amount of money, especially back in Temperance and Destina's day!

Ever the professional interviewer, Capri scribbled furiously in her book, seemingly unfazed by the staggering sum. "And how would someone know if an artifact was actually part of a buried or sunken treasure?" As Cal Senior considered the question, she went on, "According to treasure hunters on the Internet, they come across relics from various wrecks all the time. But how are the items validated if they're not found aboard the *actual* ship?"

Wow, she sounded like a pro, even to my ears. Cal and I exchanged an amused look as Cal Senior answered, "Well, darlin', an item would have to be listed on the ship's log in order to be connected with the actual treasure." He shrugged. "Since the boats get torn apart as they sink, and' get blown around by hurricanes and storms, their items get scattered for miles and miles around." He shrugged. "Without a record o' the goods that were aboard a ship at the time that it sank, anybody could claim that somethin' they found was a part o' the treasure, even if they got it somewhere's else."

She nodded, checking off the next question as she asked, "And do you know of any items that were reported to be on Blackheart Bellacroix's ship when it sank?"

Cal Senior thought about it, pausing as the waitress brought us our food. After she left, he responded, "Well, darlin', I don't know of any per-ticular items — but I do know a *person* who was rumored to be on that ship the night it sank."

"Person?" she asked, intrigued.

Cal and I stopped eating to listen.

With a dramatic pause, Cal Senior said in a hushed voice, "Yes, ma'am. That person was none other than the beautiful Temperance Biscayne." He took a bite of his steak, chewing thoughtfully before continuing. "You see, she was rumored to have been in love with Blackheart Bellacroix. She dreamed of romance and riches and the glamorous life she imagined would be hers if she escaped her lot in life and ran off with the most ruthless pirate of her time." He shrugged again. "She was in love."

"No way!" Capri cried, scribbling away.

Catching her excitement, Cal jumped in, adding, "And you know what else, darlin'? Temperance was actually plannin' to *elope* with Blackheart Bellacroix on the night the town was attacked. That's why the ship coasted into the Bay that night in the first place — the lovers had planned it!" His blue eyes twinkled as they watched Capri's reaction.

"Wow," she breathed, putting down her pen to stretch her wrist. Her eyes were wide with wonder. "This is *so* much better than anything I've read on the Internet!"

Swallowing the bite of my salad, I asked the Cals, "This is exciting information, guys, but I'm just curious — how do you know all this?" I'd only been able to find out basic stuff about the legend — like what Brit had read to me that night on the Web. Come to think of it, everything I'd read was about Destina, and made *no* mention of Temperance whatsoever. Even the books Capri had gotten out of the library didn't say anything like this.

Finished with his meal, Cal Senior leaned back in his seat. He sighed contentedly, placing his hands behind his head. "Boy, that was a good steak, there, young lady," he told the waitress as she cleared our plates. Then, focusing his attention on me, he replied, "Well, darlin', most o' that's what my daddy used to tell me — the stories were handed down the line from my great-great-grandmama, who was a Delgado. My daddy's granddaddy — now, *he* was a real live treasure hunter; he was said to've been hot on the trail of the *Doncella* when he passed, but whatever he knew of its whereabouts, the secret died with him."

Cal nooded. "That's right, he was a well-known treasure hunter around here. And," he told Capri, "Daddy and me did some cleanin' the other day, and found a box of old Delgado family relics just gatherin' dust in the attic," he said, looking to his father for confirmation. "We thought someone should go through it — you know — really take their time, sort through everything to determine if it might be worth somethin'. Maybe even find some relics from an old treasure — you never know just what might be in that box!" He glanced at his dad, whose eyes sparkled with the same excitement as his son's. Looking back to the enthralled Capri, he raised his eyebrows questioningly. "Do you know anyone who might be interested in an undertakin' like that?"

Capri leaned forward in her chair, practically leaping out of it to answer, "Me, Cal! I'd love to sort through it!" She looked anxiously from Cal the Third to the Second, then to me. "Pleeeease?"

We laughed.

Cal stood up from the table, chuckling. "Aw, well, shoot. I guess it would be a blessin' if you were to take that box off our hands. What do you say we go to my car to get it?" He smiled as she grabbed his hand, dragging him behind her as we passed the driving range.

Winding past the front of the club, I marveled at the gazebo and concert area that overlooked the craggy bay. This was where Destina and Temperance had lived, it suddenly occurred to me. Despite the fact that we'd been having play practice here for the past few days, I'd been so busy learning my lines that little tidbit really hadn't sunk in until now.

Feeling an immediate connection with the lonely, willful girls, I wondered if they had *truly* walked along the cliffs at night, longing for a better life — or for love, as Cal had said. It was one thing to read a fantasy-like legend on the Internet, or in the pages of a book, but somehow being there — at the home that, with its isolation and guarded doors - must really have *been* a prison to the free-spirited girls — their story suddenly went from being just a romantic notion to a tragic real-life drama. The thought struck me, and I suddenly felt closer to Temperance and Destina, no longer seeing them as mere characters in a play, but as real people who longed to be free.

"Riley?" Capri's voice broke into my thoughts. "Could you pop the trunk?" she asked, nodding toward our car. We had stopped behind Cal's flashy convertible, which was just a few down from my Jeep.

"Oh, right," I said, digging through my purse. Hitting the switch, we waited for the hatch to open as Cal lifted an enormous box out of his trunk. Holy load of Delgado family items! I thought, amazed by how much old stuff was crammed into the box.

A brass urn lay atop what appeared to be old candles, and a copper helmet that looked like it belonged on a medieval knight started to topple over the side as Capri caught it. Her eyes positively bugged out of her head as she stared at the ancient relics. I knew she would be busy for the next several days with this.

"Whoa," she murmured, mesmerized. She set the helmet carefully on the floor of my car as Cal deposited the box inside. "Thank you so much, Mr. Cal — and Mr. Cal Senior!" she cried, hugging them both. "I'll take good care of all of your family's items, I promise."

Cal Senior nodded, grinning. "Well, I know you will, darlin' — you're just the young lady for the job, and I thank you for helpin' us out. It'll be real good to know what-all my great-great granddaddy found all those years ago."

As Capri scurried into the back seat, I paused to hug both gentlemen goodbye. "Hey," I asked Cal as his dad headed back to the club. "Are you sure you want to do this? There might be some actual treasure in there." I nodded toward the inside of the car.

Cal chuckled, waving a hand in the air. "Aw, darlin' — there's nothin' in there from the *Doncella*, that's for sure, since ain't nobody ever found it. Though there's likely some actual booty from some of the other wrecks he found." He looked through the back window, seeing Capri leaning over the seat so she could dig through the items that lay on top. "And if she *does* find somethin' valuable — good for her. She'll go back to school with a great story and the best report on treasure her teacher's ever read." He laughed. "She's a good kid, that one."

I nodded. "She really is. And you know what?" I asked, feeling a sudden wave of gratitude come over me. "You're pretty great, yourself," I said impulsively, hugging him again. Seeing how much he and his dad were willing to help out my daughter gave me an even deeper appreciation for them both. "You're the best, Cal."

"Aw, darlin'," he said, glancing at my chest as I hopped in my car. "It's my pleasure. Y'all be good now!"

I waved and honked the horn as I followed the winding road along the top of the hill. The blue-green waves crashed into the rocky shore of the bay below, while the wind blew in fitful gusts, not letting us forget that a storm hung in the balance, just off the coast, waiting to make landfall. Just like in the staging of the play, the squall threatened in unpredictable fury. The surreal setting made me appreciate even more how much the formidable Mother Nature must have complicated the infamous battle that night - and, according to the Cals, the planned escape of Temperance and Blackheart Bellacroix. Navigating the Jeep down the road, I wondered if Capri really *would* find any items that could be linked to actual shipwrecks and treasure - or the infamous pirate.

But, no matter what she found, I knew the whole experience was already cast in gold for her. Capri could find joy in any situation, it seemed, and this adventure echoed with all the romance and possibility that poor Temperance and Destina had always dreamed of.

As we drove home that blustery afternoon, I smiled to myself, knowing that no matter what my daughter uncovered, just being given the box to dig through was her golden nugget, her treasure chest of riches.

9

The Storm Comes Marching In

As the excited murmur of pre-Christmas, pre-treasure hunt, pre-tropical storm party conversation rose to a roar, Brooks took his place before the crowd. Ever the gracious host, he smiled warmly at the anxious horde, his eyes lingering as they made their way to mine. I blushed, feeling like a teenager experiencing her first crush all over again. I thought he looked mighty cute in his smart red blazer, with a matching shirt and tie.

"Good evening, and welcome," his voice, smooth and sexy, filled the room.

The chattering fell away, as everyone focused on the host. Expectation hung heavy in the air.

With the floor-to-ceiling windows of the ancient inn's dining room for a backdrop, the formal space was the perfect setting for a mystery, I thought appreciatively. It seemed appropriate that relics of the town's greatest mystery were housed here, in the inn that had stood even before Temperance and Destina's day. I gazed around, waiting for Brooks to begin, taking in the dimly-lit room. Everywhere you looked, hundreds of snow-white candles glowed in golden splendor from black wrought-iron candelabras, and sconces on the walls. The setting was ripe for mystery and mayhem, I thought excitedly, my writer's mind inspired.

Brooks continued, "I'm so happy you could join us for our yearly Two Moon Bay tradition." He paused, heightening the suspense. If the room were a balloon, it would be just about to pop. "The much-awaited Two Moon Bay Inn's treasure hunt is about to begin!"

A cheer went up from the eager children and adults.

He laughed, then channeled his appreciation into a serious announcer voice. "Alright, kids — are you ready?"

The sea of children, grouped together at his feet, nodded up at him and shouted a collective "Yes!"

"Ok, then, now - you each hold in your hand, the first clue."

Some kids shifted, glancing down at the white slips of paper in their hands. I could tell they were just *itching* to read the first clue.

"When I count to three," Brooks explained, "you will open your papers and read the first clue. Remember to work in pairs, save all your clues, and when you have found the treasure . . ." he paused as some of the children giggled nervously. "Use the whistle you were given - blow three equal blasts." He demonstrated using the scarlet whistle that encircled his neck. "Then stay by the treasure until I reach you." He gazed around at the enthusiastic faces looking back at him. "Are you ready?"

The kids whooped in answer. Some tooted excitedly on their whistles.

Brooks laughed, raising his hands to quiet them. "Ok, ok. Treasure hunters, on your marks, get set . . . read your clue in one, two, and *three!*"

A tense hush fell over the competitors as they scanned the clue on their little slips of paper. Then, in about three seconds, they began to disperse, whispering conspiratorially with their partners as they dashed out of the room.

The adults watched with interest, sipping from their drinks and chatting animatedly as the kids took off.

As Brooks stepped away from his platform, a sudden gust of wind rattled the massive windows. Conversation faltered for a moment, as if the night's gaiety had temporarily slipped the revelers' minds. But in a matter of seconds, the reminder faded to a mere memory, as the celebrating resumed. Brooks made his way around the room, speaking to the townsfolk and few hotel guests who had apparently decided to brave the weather and stay. Despite the raging storm that threatened to make landfall in less than six hours, the air inside the ornate hotel was as festive as Santa's workshop.

My conversation partners were the usual suspects: Bébé and Dixie, with Cal not too far away. Bébé stood to my left, facing me. The merlot in her glass matched the deep scarlet dress she wore. Her springy curls were arranged in an elegant French twist, accentuating her striking features. "So," she said to me, appraising me with those unabashed eyes of hers. "You ready for your first major storm, chère?"

Choking on the swig of wine I had taken, I sputtered, "M-major?" I coughed, covering my mouth. "I thought it was only a *tropical* storm." My eyes were as round as saucers as I stared at my friend. Ever since Ryan had dropped the bomb about the impending weather, I had sensed our doom. But darn those misleading news reports that tried to tell me we were safe; I *knew* it was going to be a hurricane - I just knew it! Although Ryan and the Cals - and Brooks - had tried to dissuade me, I *knew*. And now, here was Bébé practically telling me we were all going to die!

Interrupting my panic attack, Bébé's laugh was both caustic and amused. "Oh, it is, honey. But a tropical storm has winds of up to seventy-three miles an hour." She cocked an eyebrow at me. "You ok with that?"

Dixie waved a hand at Bébé, shaking her head no. "Unh-unh, honey, don't you go scarin' our newest resident now." She gazed at me with sympathetic eyes. "It's alright, sug," she assured me. "We're goin' to be just fine, but if y'all would feel more comfortable, you're welcome to stay with me."

Bébé rolled her eyes. "Scarin'? Hardly. This chile needs to know what she's in for, is all. This isn't a mountain shower, chère; this is a real-live, honest-to-goodness just-below-a-Category-One tropical storm." She looked at Dixie. "I'm just tryin' to help her out, is all."

Torn between Bébé's alarmingly accurate description, and Dixie's unfazed attitude, I wasn't sure who to believe. Before I could think more of it, I felt an arm on my back. I guess I was feeling keyed-up with all this talk of the *supposedly* non-life-threatening storm, for I jumped about a mile. I whirled around. "Omigosh, Janice!" I cried, putting my hand to my heart in relief.

"Oh," she murmured, stepping back in surprise. "I didn't mean to frighten you." She smiled and waved to Bébé and Dixie, who greeted her politely, but a little coolly, I thought. "I just wanted to tell you that I have the information you need for my letter — it's in the car." She pointed vaguely over her shoulder toward the street.

"Ok," I said, thinking. "Why don't you just get it to me before we leave? Or — if you leave before I do, just set it inside my car — it's unlocked."

Janice nodded. "I will. Thank you so much, Riley - I really appreciate this." Her green eyes glowed with excitement.

Suddenly, a low, halting voice called from behind, "Yo, Janice — Janice, over here."

We all looked toward the entrance of the formal room to see Jamie standing in the doorway with that shady couple from Big Ed's hardware store. They looked impatiently back at us. As I met the mean girl's smoky eyes, she glared at me.

Janice gave us an embarrassed look, her face coloring. "I'm sorry," she told us. Her dark bangs fell in her eyes, shading the expression she tried to hide. "Excuse me a moment."

I nodded, smiling understandingly as she hurried away. As she scurried over to hush the loud threesome who looked sorely out of place amidst the sea of people dressed up for the occasion, I turned back to Bébé and Dixie. They descended, however, before I had even spun all the way around to face them.

"What," Bébé asked incredulously, "was that all about?"

She and Dixie pressed in on me, their wine glasses raised loftily as they glanced past my shoulder to Janice and the others.

"What do you mean?" I asked, taking a sip of my drink. They were making me extremely uncomfortable. "I'm just helping out a friend."

"*Friend?*" they repeated, guffawing. They exchanged a look.

Just then, Brooks and Cal sauntered over, laughing about something.

"What friend?" Brooks asked curiously, as Cal boomed, "Well, I'm your friend, darlin'. Come give your ole friend a hug!" He chuckled as I smiled and gave him a quick hug hello. Honestly, I was glad for the reprieve from Dixie and Bébé's grilling.

Bébé filled them in, casting her eyes toward the three in the doorway. "Oh, that would be Riley makin' friends with *Janice*."

Brooks nodded, following her gaze. "Oh, right," he said. "Still giving her the benefit of the doubt, huh?"

Wow, this was going to be a long night, I thought, downing the rest of my drink. "Look, I, uh, think she's a nice person. With a lot of talent." I shrugged. "I'm writing her a letter of recommendation for college, ok?" I held up my glass, anxious to get out of there. "I'm going to get a refill."

Hurrying past them, I waved hello to the people I knew on the way to the bar. Abby and Mayor Darrell, Apple and her partner, Charice, Cherry and some people from the play I knew. By the time I made it to the rear of the large room, to where the baroque silver beverage cart was set up before the windows that overlooked the marsh, I felt markedly relieved. Everybody's hating on Janice was really starting to get to me. The poor girl, I thought, feeling empathetic toward her. How would she ever get ahead in this town if everyone continued to hold her past against her? "Shiraz, please," I told the bartender.

Nodding, he gave me a fresh glass, smiling in thanks as I placed a tip in his jar. As the next customer stepped up behind me, I inhaled the wine's bouquet and strode toward the stately windows. The wind howled outside, screaming as though it yearned to come in. Staring out into the blackness, I could just make out the lengthy balcony that extended far out over the marsh. It struck me then, as the moon peeked out from swiftly-moving clouds, that the ancient balcony surrounded the inn like a moat.

Lost in my thoughts, I was startled when a throng of children rushed by the doorway to my left. Following their laughter, I poked my head through the threshold. It looked to be an old drawing room of some sort.

As another wave of kids ran by, I wandered inside, curious at all of the artifacts that lined the walls. Surrounding the luxurious red velvet couch and matching chairs were various relics that looked Spanish in style. There was a suit of armor against one wall, dingy-looking enough to be the real thing. I wondered how old it was — it looked medieval, so I was guessing pretty old. Along the wall to my left, which bordered the front entrance and reception area, were beautiful mahogany built-in shelves surrounding the door's frame. Scattered amongst the shelves were various items that were, if what the Cals had said was true, relics from old pirate shipwrecks: silver and gold candlesticks, rusted lanterns, shiny doubloons, ornately-patterned mirrors of all shapes and sizes, bronze busts, china figurines, and then, finally, on the wall before me, a beat-up piece of metal that looked to be an old battle shield. Beneath what appeared to be dents dinged across the top third of it was an etching of some sort. A family crest it looked like, but the letters and pictures were so faint and the dings so many that I couldn't make out what it said.

"Riley," I heard a voice say suddenly behind me.

Jumping into the air, I recovered quickly, but not fast enough to prevent some of my wine from spilling onto the dark wood floor. "Oh, Capri, you scared me half to death," I told her, bending to wipe up the liquid with my napkin.

"Sorry," she said quickly. "Can Lily sleep over tonight?"

"Honey," I said, pausing as yet another stream of boisterous children traipsed past us. "Aren't you looking for treasure?"

She nodded impatiently. "Yeah — Lily and I already solved it. She's on the way to claim the treasure now, but I wanted to ask you if she could come over. You should hear her," she paused as a whistle tooted three distinct times, "blow the whistle any second now," she finished excitedly. "Can she? Please?"

"Capri, Lily can stay another night, but tonight the storm's coming in. I think she should be at home, with her family."

My daughter gave me her seldom-used but oh-so-effective "That is so unfair" look before storming away. That was an Alex move if I ever did see one.

"Good luck with the treasure!" I called out lamely. Shrugging, I crossed back into the dining room to see a swarm of adults scurrying after Brooks, who was running toward the front of the inn. I guess everyone was anxious to see who had won the loot.

Surveying what was left of the crowd, I saw that Bébé, Dixie, and Cal were standing exactly where I had left them. As I made my way over, I noticed that Janice, Jamie, and the odd couple were nowhere to be found. Maybe they had gone to see about the treasure, too.

"Well, hey there, sug," Dixie greeted me. "We were wonderin' where you'd gone off to."

I pointed toward the drawing room. "I decided to check out the room with all the relics," I explained. "That place is like a museum. Some of that stuff must be really old."

Dixie nodded. "Oh, it is," she agreed. "Mr. McKay has been collectin' antiques since before ole Brooks came along. And," she broke off, noticing that Cal was pensively studying my breasts. "Some of those items are reportedly very valuable. Many are from the *Bella Lucia*," she explained, swatting her date.

"What's the *Bella Lucia*?"

Bébé replied, "It's one of the more famous sunken ships off Two Moon Bay's coast." She looked to Dixie for agreement. "The wreck was discovered back in the eighties by some professional treasure hunters from over in Sarasota." Her eyes widened as she said, "Although an actual 'treasure chest' wasn't found, the items onboard were valued at over fifty million dollars. And ole Mr. McKay has some of it hangin' on his wall." She shook her head in awe.

Before that fact had time to sink in, shouts erupted from the drawing room. Thinking it was the kids, we were surprised when a group of adults came stumbling in from the other entrance to the relic room. Their faces were awash with worry, some with anger.

"It's gone!" someone shouted. "It's really *gone!*"

Abby's face was ashen as she hurried down the steps into the dining room. She scrambled over to us. "Oh, y'all, it's just terrible," she told us. "I just can't believe it!"

Mayor Darrell and Apple stood at the foot of the stairs, talking in hushed tones. Others milled about, conjecturing and muttering under their breaths. Some whipped out their phones and appeared to be texting furiously. What could possibly be wrong?

Bébé's brow furrowed. "What is it?" she asked Abby. "What's gone?"

Abby put a hand to her chest, breathing as though she'd just run a race. "It's the . . ." She paused to catch her breath. ". . . shield," she finished, glancing over her shoulder as her husband approached us.

My jaw dropped open. "The shield is *missing*?" I asked incredulously. "But I just saw it!" I pointed futilely toward the doorway, envisioning the worn metal surface, looking as though it had seen better days.

Mayor Darrell took over. "How long ago was that, Riley?" he asked gravely.

"About ten minutes ago," I answered, at a loss for words.

He and Abby exchanged a look. Both glanced toward the doorway behind me, then back at each other knowingly.

"What?" I asked, wondering what the heck was going on.

"It was that *girl*," Abby said distastefully. "And her horrible boyfriend. They took it."

Stunned, I gazed from one uncomfortable-looking face to the other. Bébé nodded her head, sipping her drink as if inserting the period on Janice's guilty sentence. Dixie suddenly wouldn't meet my eyes, but I could tell by the fixed expression on her face that she agreed. Cal stared at his shoes, reluctantly raising his eyes to mine. At least he seemed to feel badly about it, rather than smug like the others.

"Are you *kidding*?" I asked all of them, shocked by their rush to judgment. I felt hurt for Janice, and angry that they would turn their backs so swiftly on her.

Mayor Darrell shook his head, then said gently to me, "Riley, we know you don't know their history and all, but . . ."

I broke in, feeling completely offended. "I'm sorry, Mayor, but I *am* aware of their history. I know all about what happened." At his surprised look, I continued, "I know what Janice and Jamie did last year." I searched his eyes, then the others', hoping for a glimpse of understanding. "But I don't see how what they did in the past has anything to do with *this*." I pointed toward the relic room. "I mean — they weren't even anywhere *near* the drawing room, so I don't see how you think it could be them."

Before Mayor Darrell had a chance to respond, Brooks hurried over. His expression was grim. "I just heard," he said. "Do we know who did it?"

Bébé nodded. "I'll give you two guesses," she said cryptically. "And both start with a 'j.'"

My jaw dropped open. Did she hear *nothing* I just said? I felt hurt and betrayed all over again.

Brooks stared at Bébé. "You're kidding."

Dixie piped up, "Well, sug, who else could it be? They're the only ones around here we know who steal, and conveniently — they're gone." She pointed to the doorway where the accused kids had stood just moments before.

Just then thunder clapped loudly beyond the window, rattling the panes. Everyone was silent for a moment, listening tensely as the angry weather raged outside.

Bébé suddenly leaped into action. "That storm sounds like it's gettin' closer, y'all," she said, swallowing the rest of her wine. "I'm goin' to round up my children and get on outta here." She gave us all a quick hug goodbye. I smiled stiffly as she took my hands and said, "You get scared durin' the storm, honey, you come to my house. I mean it."

"Thanks," I murmured, feeling grateful for the offer, but resentful that she was so quick to condemn Janice as being guilty. "You know what?" I said to the others. "I'm going to find the girls and be heading home, too. Before the storm gets any worse."

Honestly, I couldn't wait to get out of there. I was so surprised and disappointed that the people whom I considered friends, and who had treated me with nothing but warmth and kindness since I had arrived, could be so critical of someone else. I said my goodbyes.

Cal took an extra few seconds to break eye contact with my boobs, but, once he did, he hugged me warmly. "Let us know if you need anythin', darlin', or if you want to ride out the storm with some seasoned locals," he told me, glancing at Dixie for agreement. "I'm just a few houses away."

Dixie added, "That's right, sug. The party will be ragin' 'til the sun comes up or the wind stops blowin' — whichever comes first." She laughed, raising her glass to toast her own words.

"Thanks, guys," I answered. "I appreciate that." To Brooks I said, "I'm sorry about what happened. And I hope you find the shield." *And*, I added silently, I hope that when you do, it's as far from Janice as we are to the nearest galaxy. "Thanks for having us over. Good night," I said stiffly. Although it was a polite goodbye, and a sincere one, I couldn't *wait* to leave. I turned and fled, anxious to get to the car.

Brooks broke off from the others, hurrying after me. He obviously knew I was upset. "Riley, wait." He grabbed my arm, pulling me around to face him.

Standing in the doorway, I looked back at him, not bothering to hide my frustration.

"Why are you so upset?" he asked. "Is it because of Janice?"

I gaped at him as a flock of kids ran into the room, their chatter just as clamorous as before the treasure hunt. Some of the grown-ups corralled their children, ushering them toward the door. I think everybody was getting the urge to get home before the storm descended. As the mob dispersed, I repeated, *"Janice?"* I shook my head in disbelief. "No, I'm not upset because of *Janice*; I'm upset with the way everyone is *judging* her. There's absolutely no reason to think she had anything to do with the shield being stolen."

Brooks stared silently back at me, listening. Although I could see by his fixed expression that his mind was already made up, I also saw the concern that shone through his eyes. This man cared about me, that much was evident. I instinctively understood that he didn't want me to go away mad — *and* that there was no hope for us to see eye to eye on this one. "Riley," he started. "You don't know her like we do. People don't change. . ." he tried to explain.

But I cut him off. "That's where you're wrong, Brooks. Some people do. And even if I don't *know* her, or the history she supposedly has, I don't think it's fair to condemn someone without knowing all the facts." I shook my head, starting to turn away. I could see he was about to protest, and I just didn't want to hear any more, didn't want to see that judgmental look in the eyes of the man I was falling for. "Look — I really need to get going. Thanks for a . . ." I tried to muster a heartfelt sentiment, but it ended up sounding forced. "Lovely evening."

At that moment, Capri and Lily bounded into the room, excited looks on their faces. They each held a gilded picture frame in their hands. Must be the prizes from the treasure hunt.

"Capri, get your sister," I said to her. "It's time to go." At her crestfallen look, I headed toward the front door. "I'll be in the car."

"But, Riley!" she began.

"No buts," I responded without looking back. "We're going home before the storm gets any worse. Say goodnight, and tell Mr. Brooks thank you."

As I closed the heavy wooden door behind me, I hurried into the night, into the driving rain. By the time I reached the car, my hair and outfit were soaked, much like my mood. Nervous about the impending storm, my mind was crowded with images of tree limbs through windows and the roof blowing away. Not to mention visions of poor Janice being hunted by the angry villagers, chasing after her with condemning words and burning torches. Wondering what would become of the girl who had so much potential, I couldn't help but think that with everyone assuming the worst of her, it would be all too easy to erode what was left of her self-confidence. Thinking how unfair it was that some people had it so hard in life, I was startled from my stormy thoughts as the passenger doors suddenly opened, and the driving rain poured in.

As Alex and Capri scrambled inside, I started the engine, anxious to get home. Thanks to Stump and his crew, we were all boarded up and ready to ride out the worst of it. I turned up the radio to hear the latest report:

"Well, Two Moon Bay residents, you'll be happy to hear that Tropical Storm Ida has broken up and is no more; all you can expect are a few more hours of rain, with winds reaching top speeds of less than thirty five miles an hour."

I breathed a sigh of relief. Although that sounded *much* better than the national emergency I had prepared for, I was still worried. Gripping the steering wheel, I told myself I would feel better when we were home, tucked away behind the close-fastened shutters. Just a few more hours, and the effects of the storm would be well away from us.

"Hey!" Alex cried suddenly, shifting on the front seat. She pulled out what looked to be a folder. "What's this?"

My heart sank as I realized what it was. "That's Janice's," I answered. "Put it on the back seat, please."

As she handed it to Capri, who set it on the seat beside her, I told myself once again that there was *no way* the hate-filled horde was right. Janice *couldn't* be involved with stealing the shield; she had likely put the folder in my car around the very time that the relic was pilfered inside. Yep, I told myself, satisfied that I had all the proof that was needed to free her from blame. It *definitely* wasn't Janice.

As the girls recapped the night's events, I couldn't help but ponder what Dixie had said earlier; the timing *was* just a tad coincidental. After all, the foursome had been seen in the next room right before the shield went missing, and just seconds later, they were gone. Shooing away the nagging thought, I told myself that coincidental timing doesn't necessarily equal guilt.

Sighing, I signaled as I turned into our driveway. Putting the car in 'Park,' I just hoped that, however things turned out, Janice's leaving the party had nothing to do with the stealing of the very valuable shield.

And, I reasoned, peering through the sheets of rain that drove against our windshield, if Janice did, in fact, have something to do with it, I prayed that she'd be smart enough to stay as far from Two Moon Bay and the fuming, vengeful mob as possible.

10

Cleaning Up

Christmas Eve morning was as beautiful and sunny as the day before was stormy and gray.

I woke before the sun that Thursday morning, having slept very little in the night. The storm's remnants continued to roll through the Bay in the wee hours of the morning, though the wind and rain were the last things on my mind. Wondering where Janice was, and how she was faring the night, I had prayed she was somewhere safe. With the rain thrashing against the rooftop and the wind rattling every door and window like uninvited guests, I had listened for every sound, hoping it was Janice outside, begging for me to let her in. Although I seemed to be the only person on her side at this point, I felt the burden of the town's disapproval as though it were my own.

After we'd gotten home from the party, Alex had retired to her room to shower and video chat with her friends from North Carolina, while Capri camped out in the living room with Raegan and the lab, whom, I learned, the girls had lovingly named Ruby. Thankfully, we'd managed to gain the mama dog's trust, and had gotten her and the pups inside the house; the last thing we wanted was for them to weather the storm out on the veranda, since it was surrounded by glass. Even though the worst of the squall was supposedly over, we weren't about to take any chances. Tucked inside the great room, safe behind the plantation shutters, Capri made a fortress of blankets before the raging fireplace for herself and Raegan, while Ruby and her babies lounged nearby in a large bed we'd gotten from Sarasota that resembled a big fluffy inner-tube. While my little researcher pored through the box the Cals had given her, I attempted to watch reruns of my favorite show on Netflix, while touching up my pedicure. Every time the wind whistled hauntingly through the eaves, however, I jumped, spilling Dusky Sunset on the towel I had fortunately thought to lay out. As the winds finally tapered off around four that morning, I drifted off to sleep, waking with a start less than two hours later. Anxious to check out the damage, I threw on my running clothes, grabbed my phone, and crept through the silent house.

Capri lay fast asleep in her blankets on the floor, surrounded by library books and items from her box of treasure. Her breath came in quick, rhythmic puffs as she dreamed, her mind probably filled with silver and gold and pirate ships sailing into the bay in the dark of night. I smiled, taking in the scene. One arm rested on Ruby's side, while the other was slung across Raegan's back. Unlike their human counterpart, both dogs were wide awake. Judging by their eager eyes, I figured they were ready to go outside and do their business.

"Hey girl," I whispered to the mama dog.

Ruby's amber eyes sought mine as I sneaked by. She wagged her tail in quiet greeting before slipping out from under her babies' tiny sleeping forms.

"What's up, Rae-Rae?" I asked my boy.

As if he'd been waiting to hear my voice, my enthusiastic golden escaped Capri's embrace and trotted toward me. He paused to stretch by the door, and gave a sleepy yawn.

"I know how ya feel, buddy," I told him, rubbing his ears. "I didn't get much sleep, myself." As we sneaked out into the darkness, I closed the veranda door without a sound.

Surveying the backyard, I was surprised by the lack of carnage I saw. Nothing was damaged, thank goodness. Lots of downed limbs littered the yard, along with some items from the neighbors' property. As I circled the house, I let out a cry of relief; we'd gotten off pretty easily, thank the Good Lord. Everyone had survived, no windows had been broken, and the roof was still intact. All we'd have to do was some yard clean-up, it looked like. Thank you, Tropical Storm/Not Tropical Storm Ida! I cheered silently. As I queued my 'Running I' playlist, I hoped everyone else had been as fortunate. I was just about to dial Bébé when I realized it was still too early to call; she and her brood were probably still sleeping, as most *normal* people were at that hour. I'd call her and Dixie as soon as I finished my workout, I decided.

After twenty minutes of self-imposed torture, I turned around, heading back toward the house. As the sun crept over the horizon, people began to crawl outside their homes, scurrying around like busy ants, picking up debris and removing the shutters and boards from their houses. I kept a strong pace, feeling upbeat and filled with hope. It was a new day.

Christmas Eve, in fact, I remembered as I neared our house. I had managed to order some last-minute presents for the girls, wanting them to have something to open on Christmas Day. I'm sure Ryan would be bringing my 'guaranteed before Christmas' packages by sometime soon. Good, I thought - that would give me plenty of time to get them wrapped and under the tree before Capri woke us tomorrow morning before the sun came up - a ritual she had practiced every Christmas since she could walk. Even though she knew the real story of Christmas, she was always the first one awake that morning, anxious to delve into the goodies that Santa had brought her.

Heading through the back door, I was surprised to see the patio furniture back in place. And the hose was on, filling the water Stump had drained from the pool yesterday. "Huh," I said aloud, watching as Raegan bounded around the side of the house. "How could the girls have lifted this all by themselves?"

A male voice answered from the great room, "Oh, they had a little help, I'd say."

I started, missing the counter as I attempted to set my phone on the docking station. "Oh, my gosh, Brooks!" I cried, clutching my heart. "I didn't know you were here."

He smiled, putting up a hand in apology. "Sorry, didn't mean to scare you. The girls and I wanted to come over early to see how y'all fared the night. I hope that's ok," he said quickly, searching my face. His eyes were big and blue, earnest as always. I knew what he was really asking. "You *are* alright, aren't you, Riley?"

I nodded, stepping toward him. Wanting to put last night behind us, I reached out to embrace him. His body was warm and strong against mine, and he smelled fresh, like spring. "We're fine. Look, Brooks — about last night, I . . ." I started, but he put a hand up to stop me.

"Riley, listen. You don't have to say anything. I acted like a jerk last night, and I'm grateful that you helped me realize it."

"But, I . . ." I muttered, needing to clear my conscience.

Brooks rushed on, his eyes imploring. "You helped me realize that I was wrong for judging Janice; just because she stole something last year, doesn't mean she did last night, too. You're right that some people *can* change. And I'm willing to give her the benefit of the doubt that she's one of them." He squeezed my arms, pulling me toward him once again. "Besides," he added. "We have a tape — security cameras in the drawing room. The monitoring company's in Naples, which was hit a little harder than we were, so as soon as their communications have been restored, we'll know *exactly* who's responsible."

I was speechless for a second. "That's great!" I finally managed, pleased that we would soon have an answer to the mystery. My phone rang, just as I was about to add something else. "Oh, hang on," I told him. "It's Bébé." Hitting 'Answer,' I put the phone to my ear.

She launched right in before I had time to say hello. "Well, hey there, chère." Her voice became muffled as she hollered to Henri in the background. "No, chile — put that down. Henri!"

I smirked, happy to hear that things were faring as they always did in the Beauchamps household.

Uncovering the phone, she asked me, "So how did y'all do last night in your first tropical/not tropical storm? Your house still intact?"

I laughed, reflecting on my doomsday prepping. I *had* gone just a tad overboard, maybe. "Yes, the house is fine. We're all good, except for my fingernails; they're pretty much bitten down to the quick." I nodded at Brooks as he went out the back door, presumably to check on the pool. "How are you guys?"

"Oh, we're fine, honey. We're fine. Henri is runnin' around like a chicken with his head cut off; I swear I don't know where that boy gets his energy. Mama's fine, and my Samuel just got back from Tampa; the roads were closed last night, but thank-you-Jesus he is safe and helpin' the neighbors with their yards."

"That's great, Bébé. I'm glad to hear that you're all together, safe and sound."

Before I could go on, like a herd of buffalo, Capri and Lily came running into the house from out back, their feet covered in mud.

I called out to them, halting them in their sodden tracks, "Unh-unh - leave your shoes by the door, please." Coming back on the line, I said to my friend, "Thanks for checking on us, Bébé. Let me know if you guys need any help cleaning up."

"Alright, chère. Y'all do the same. Bah!"

"Bye!" I answered happily, clicking off.

As the girls dutifully kicked off their shoes - slinging mud on the wall, of course - I got a paper towel and sanitizer out of the cupboard. Completely oblivious to the mess they had left in their enthusiastic wake, they took off toward Capri's bedroom, giggling all the way.

Just then, a knock sounded at the front door, as a booming voice called out, "Well, hello there, darlin'!"

I looked up to see Cal's blonde head and gleaming teeth through the glass beside the door. "Cal!" I exclaimed, throwing away the paper towel as I called, "Come on in — it's unlocked."

Today, the flashy golfer was as dressed-down as I had ever seen him, wearing khaki cargo shorts, a white Izod T-shirt, and a pair of tan-colored flip-flops. His grin, as always, was wide and white. "Well, hello there, Riley!" he greeted me. As he reached out to hug me, Capri came tearing out from her bedroom, roping him around the waist. He laughed good-naturedly, hugging her back.

"Cal, Cal!" she hollered. "You have to see what I found in the box!"

"Capri, let Mr. Cal come in the house, please," I told her, smiling despite myself.

At her crestfallen look, Cal put a reassuring hand on her shoulder. "Aw, now, little darlin', I'd love to. Soon's I finish talkin' to your step-mama here, I'm all yours." As she smiled in satisfaction, he said to me, "I just wanted to check on y'all, see how y'all made it through the storm." He looked out front. "Looks pretty good — no damage!"

I nodded. "Yeah, we were pretty lucky," I said gratefully. "How about you?"

"Yep — we're all good, too; Daddy and me cleaned up the yard a bit this mornin' — all we had were some downed limbs from the wind. Coulda been a lot worse, that's for sure."

I nodded, happy to hear that they had fared well. "And Dixie?" I asked, hoping she had been as fortunate as the rest of us. "She's ok, too?"

At the mention of his sweetheart's name, Cal's sparkly smile blinged like diamonds. "Yes, ma'am, Dixie and her house are ok, too." I swear he blushed. "She stayed with me last night — we were entertainin', havin' a little tropical storm/not tropical storm party." He shrugged, grinning. "What can I say? It's one of our most favorite traditions."

I giggled. "Well, next time, I just might join you," I told him, feeling courageous enough to weather a future storm with some seasoned pros.

"We'd love that, darlin'," he said, and I could tell he meant it. "Well," he said, clapping his hands together as if he were about to leave. "I just thought I'd come around and make sure my northern gals fared well in our southern storm last night." His eyes twinkled. Glancing at the back yard, he observed, as he turned to leave, "Looks like y'all have some help early this mornin'." He nodded to where Brooks — and Stump, I was surprised to see - had made a pile of debris.

"Huh!" I exclaimed, pleased. "I didn't know Stump was here."

Cal smiled at me. "Well, it seems that you have some people here who really care about you, Riley." It was a serious comment, one that took me a little by surprise, coming from my ever-teasing new friend. I was just about to agree when the sound of Capri and Lily's laughter erupted from the bedroom, breaking the moment. Cal's eyes relit with their usual sparkle, as he said, "Well, I better go see what the young'n has to show me."

"Right," I agreed, smiling, watching him go. Deciding I would head outside to resume my clean-up duties, I couldn't help but ponder what Cal had said. Even though I'd only been in Two Moon Bay a short time, it somehow felt like home. The people here felt like friends, as though we'd known each other our whole lives. I felt overcome with gratitude in that moment, as I stepped out through the veranda, onto the pool deck.

I greeted Stump, thanking him for coming over to help, and had just set to work when Alex came around from the right side of the house. She must have been working out front, I figured. Dressed in gym clothes and gardening gloves, my eldest announced, "Riley, Ryan's at the door."

Brooks glanced up, a funny look on his face. As I met his eyes, however, he quickly busied himself with moving a rather large piece of driftwood.

"Be right there," I told her, nodding as I removed my dusty work gloves.

"Ok," she answered, hurrying back out front. Evangeline's head suddenly appeared from around the corner, as she waited for Alex to rejoin her. Like Alex, she was dressed in work attire, rain boots and a garbage bag full of limbs to complete the look.

Teenagers — willingly working, I thought with a sense of awe. What was it about this place that motivated my usually not-so-helpful daughter to take chores upon herself? Whatever it was, I thought, thanking my lucky stars, I was *not* about to wish it away. A girl could get used to this, I thought, smiling to myself. Then, catching Brooks' eye, I said, "Hey, save that, will you? I have an idea."

Nodding in agreement, he set the piece of wood on the outdoor dining table. I'd always wanted an authentic driftwood decoration, and this would be just perfect.

Hurrying around to the front of the house, I wondered what was up with Brooks' barely-noticeable-but-still-evident evasiveness. I thought we were past that funny business about Ryan. Resolving not to worry about it right then, I made a mental note to ask him about it later. It may be nothing, I told myself.

Rounding the corner, I took in the bounty of packages already littering the driveway. Holy load of goodies, I thought, worried that maybe I had over-shopped just a *tad*; it looked like Santa's sleigh had toppled over right there in my yard. "Hey, Ryan!" I greeted the delivery man, dismissing my over-indulgent spending as a well-deserved first Christmas here for the girls.

His muscular arms were raised above his head as he hoisted another box from his truck. "Hey there, pretty lady!" he called out warmly, hugging me with one arm as he lowered the parcel with the other.

"Here, let me help you with those," I told him, grabbing a long rectangular box that would become one of Alex's favorite presents - once I put it together, of course. "Follow me to my top-secret hiding spot."

Intrigued, Ryan raised his eyebrows. He followed, a package in each arm. "Top secret, huh?" he asked skeptically as I led him into the empty three-car garage. "How can you be so sure?"

"Well, my friend," I replied conspiratorially, "When the girls were little, we made the garage into a TV/game room/hang out spot, thinking they'd *love* it, treat it as a sort of refuge, a place to hang out their friends. . . " I paused, setting my box down. Ryan deposited his next to it, then stood up, hooking an eyebrow at me to go on. ". . . Well, they *never* set foot in there, not once!" I threw up my hands as if to prove my point. "We even got a pool table."

Ryan snickered. "So *this* garage," he said, glancing around at the bland, cavernous space. "Will *definitely* keep them away."

"There you go," I told him, pleased that he'd seen my point.

We made several trips, traipsing the Christmas loot into the garage one package at a time. Remarking about the storm/non-storm, we made small talk as we worked. Raegan followed close by, trotting around with a newfound stick in his mouth, grinning like he'd just won the doggie lottery.

"Hey," Ryan whispered on our last load. He nodded imperceptibly toward the front porch, where Alex was pretending to *not* watch what we were doing. "I think someone might be onto you."

"Well, yes she is," I murmured back, so only he would hear. "Watch this." With my free hand, I waved boldly at Alex, calling her bluff. "Hey, honey!" I called merrily. "You girls are doing a great job!"

Before the words were even out of my mouth, Alex had ducked her head, scrambling to look busy. Clutching the broom she'd been using to idly sweep the already-swept porch, she swiped it across the window shutters — as if any cobwebs could possibly have survived the wind and rain we'd gotten yesterday. I smirked, amused. Yep, she'd been caught, alright. "Busted," I muttered, nudging my friend.

Ryan laughed. "Totally. Say, you want me to help you hide these somewhere else?" he asked, stopping at the back of the truck.

I shook my head. "Nah, that's ok — while they're eating breakfast, I'll stash them in the storage closet inside the garage — it has a lock," I said craftily, wiggling my eyebrows.

He grinned. "Ah — that'll keep 'em out," he agreed.

"Yep," I told him, tapping the side of my head. "I'm always thinkin'." I laughed, then asked him, "Busy day today?"

He nodded. "Oh, yeah — slammed, actually. We knock off at five tonight, and I'm paying two drivers holiday pay. Lots of packages to deliver before the dinner bell rings tonight."

"Well, that's great," I told him. "Good for business, plus, you're making lots of little boys and girls happy by helping Santa to deliver their packages early," I clapped him on the shoulder. Realizing how relaxed I felt around Ryan — someone I had briefly considered dating not so long ago — I was relieved that there was no awkwardness between us — just a comfortable friendship.

Thinking how nice the moment was, the conversation quickly took an unexpected turn to my new least-favorite subject, as Ryan asked, "Say, you hear about the inn last night?"

I nodded. "Yeah - I was there."

His eyebrows rose. "Oh, so you were actually *in* the room with the thieves, then." My heart sank, but I listened, hoping he wasn't going to utter the dreaded words as he continued, "I can't *believe* those kids were stupid enough to steal from Old Man McKay — while virtually the whole town was there to witness it! Pretty stupid if you ask me."

I froze. Not this again. "What — what kids?" I asked warily. Please don't say Janice; I pleaded silently. Please don't say her name. I didn't want Ryan to be against her, too.

"Oh," he said, nodding understandingly. I could tell he was thinking that I wasn't up on my Two Moon Bay history. "Maybe you don't know, but these two kids got arrested for stealing a bunch of stuff a few months back. Some girl and her boyfriend. A bunch of criminals, from what I hear."

There it was. Another guilty verdict. It was time to end the conversation. "You know, I have a ton of work to do before the play tonight," I explained, not wanting to be rude. I pointed toward the house, as if it were calling my name. "I should really get back to it. Thanks for bringing the girls' presents by," I said quickly.

"Yeah, sure," Ryan said, surprised. "No problem." Then, heading toward the front of his truck, he turned around to call out, "Hey, good luck tonight — or, 'break a leg,' I guess I should say."

I smiled. "Thanks. And Merry Christmas."

Thumbing his hat bill at me, Ryan hopped in the cab. A few seconds later, the engine rumbled to life.

As I started toward Alex and Evangeline, who had resumed their yard work, I absently studied the large pile of limbs they'd gathered on the side of the lawn. Without meaning to, I felt a ripple of worry run through me. Yet another townsperson against the condemned couple — for some reason, I was surprised that Ryan wasn't willing to give them the benefit of the doubt. Somebody *else* who assumed the worst, that Janice and Jamie were involved with the inn's theft. Did *everyone* in Two Moon Bay think they were guilty? I wondered fretfully.

My thoughts were heavy, brewing up a storm of their own, when I heard the swiftly-moving vehicle approach the house. As I bent to pick up some trash that had blown into the yard, the car slowed just enough to pull swiftly into the drive. Looking up, I was shocked to see Janice come to a quick stop beside Cal's convertible. "Janice?" I said aloud in wonder, feeling like she wasn't real.

Though her face betrayed little emotion, there was a tenseness about her shoulders as she hastily put the car in park. The gears whined a little, creaking in stubborn protest.

I glanced over my shoulder, making sure no one was around who would possibly scare her away. Seeing only Alex and Evangeline, who were loading the piled limbs into Stump's wheelbarrow, I moved slowly toward the drive. Feeling like a precious bird had ventured near to me, hesitating about whether or not to trust me, I resolved to do nothing to scare her away.

"Janice," I said again, this time so she could her me. "What are you doing here?"

From inside the car, her keen eyes met mine for just a moment. Just enough to take me in, pinpoint my intentions. Then, just as quickly, they searched the yard from beneath her dark bangs. She was probably trying to size up who *else* might be here. I hated that she was being treated like a fugitive of the law. I guess she felt it was safe, for she quickly unfastened her seatbelt, opened the groaning door, and hurried toward me.

"Riley," she breathed, her voice urgent with worry. "I'm sorry to bother you at home, it's just . . ." Her voice trailed off as she looked nervously toward the house. Cal's voice roared with laughter inside. "I didn't know how else to get ahold of you."

I furrowed my brow. "What do you mean?" I asked, confused. "We'll see each other tonight, at the play."

She shook her head. "No," she said hurriedly. "We won't. Look, Riley, that's what I came to tell you. I won't *be* at the play tonight. I'm leaving. Now."

"Leaving?" I repeated. "Why would you leave? The play's *tonight!*" I insisted dumbly, as though she didn't get it.

"I know, I know," she replied, telling me slowly, like *I* didn't get it. "But everyone's costumes are made, so it's not like they need me. And," she broke off, her eyes looking wary as Brooks appeared suddenly from the side of the house. Seeing her, he quickly set to work helping the girls with the limbs. Janice continued, more quickly this time, "It's just that everyone thinks I did something wrong — something I *didn't* do," she declared. I could see the truth in her eyes. I so wanted to believe her. "I just don't want to stick around for another trial, you know? This time the charges probably won't go away like last time."

"But," I protested. "Why would you leave if you didn't do it?" I asked earnestly. "Leaving makes you *look* guilty." I put my hand on her arm. "Janice, please don't go."

She shook her head. "Riley, it's not that simple." She studied me, her cat-like eyes both wise and sad. I could see the wheels turning inside her head - probably weighing how much to explain. Then, dejection crept into her gaze. It clouded over the keenness, waving a little white flag of defeat. Like everyone else, she probably figured I wouldn't understand. "If you're guilty of something once," she told me in a monotone voice, like she'd rehearsed it many times before, "you must be guilty again — that's the way it is." She shrugged. "And I have no one here to support me, anyway, no reason to stay. My mom's who knows where, my dad's in jail. . . ." She broke off, her green eyes suddenly glassy. But before the tears could start to form, she blinked them away. "It's just me." She shrugged, the emotion seeming to disappear with the movement. She looked me straight in the eye. "Anyway, I just wanted to say thank you. For believing in me." She started to turn away, then added, "Oh, and you won't need to write me that recommendation letter, after all." The cat-like eyes blinked again, and before I could even process what was happening, she fled, hurrying to her car.

"Janice, wait!" I called, running after her. I couldn't let her leave. My mind whirled, grasping at straws. "What about Jamie? You have him."

Reaching her car, she stopped beside the rusted door. Shaking her head at me, she said, "No, Riley, I don't. I don't have anybody." The hinges moaned once again as she opened the door. Settling into the seat through which the inner springs were poking, Janice sighed in resignation, putting her key in the ignition.

It was then that I saw all the stuff that was crammed in the backseat of her old Toyota Celica. That must be all of her belongings, I thought sadly. Her whole life is in that car, I realized with a pang. She has no one to care for her, nowhere to go.

"Janice," I pleaded, placing my hand on the window. She rolled it down by hand. "Where will you go?" I asked, silently willing her to reconsider. "What will you do? Do you have any money?"

She looked plainly back at me, as if answering what the weather would be like that day. "I'll be fine. I've been on my own before." The green eyes blinked at me once again, looking far too defeated for someone her age. It wasn't right. "I'll get through this, too. I mean — what choice do I have?" With a flick of the wrist, she turned the key, urging the old car to life.

Her words echoed in my head, pinged hollowly inside my chest. Someone so young shouldn't have to say those words, shouldn't know what it's like to be truly alone. It wasn't fair. "Janice, you're wrong," I said, raising my voice to be heard over the engine. Her car made a squealing sound for a second, then evened out. "You *do* have someone who cares about you."

She looked evenly back at me, though her eyes were sad.

"You have me," I told her, needing her to believe me. "You can stay here — with me and the girls. No one has to know, if you want to lay low 'til all this blows over. Please, Janice — stay."

Her lips quivered, her gaze softened, and her lips parted as she started to say, "Mayb . . ." but just then Alex called out from behind me, "Riley!"

Without looking away from Janice, I held up a hand for my daughter to wait. Darn it!, I thought frantically. I had finally gained the trust of my little precious bird, and now she was about to fly away.

Sure enough, Janice's eyes darted toward the sound of Alex's voice. The next thing I knew, the guarded expression was back, covering over the vulnerable one that I'd thought meant she was going to stay. My heart fell. The little bird sensed danger, and was about to fly away.

Glancing anxiously in the rearview mirror, Janice put her car in gear. The angry villagers were not far from her mind; Alex had unknowingly reminded her of that. "Thanks, Riley, I appreciate that. But I don't want you to get involved in this mess. You've done enough to help me already." As she backed away, she looked at me one last time. "Goodbye, Riley. Thanks for showing me what it feels like to have a friend. I haven't had that in a really long time."

And with that, she continued out of the driveway and onto the street, never looking back.

I watched until her car disappeared from sight, feeling numb from the inside out. It wasn't until I felt Brooks' hand on my shoulder that I turned away from the road. What would become of Janice, I wondered to myself. Why didn't I do more to stop her, to make her stay?

And what, I thought warily, will happen once Brooks has the tape and can clear her name? How will she ever find out that she'd been freed from blame?

The worst thing of all, I thought, taking a deep breath and staring into the sky as a flock of birds flew overhead, their cries both plaintive and sad, what if something happens to her, and no one is there to help? What will become of Janice? And why does no one care?

"Riley!" Alex's voice broke into my darkened thoughts once more. Quickly, I sent a little prayer out into the cosmos. A prayer for her to be safe from harm. Maybe, just maybe, I thought hopefully, one day, the little bird would fly home, safe and happy and free.

— ~

11

Christmas Eve Secrets

$\mathcal{I}$ didn't have to wonder for long.

Janice had pulled out of my driveway around eight that morning, and before the play had even started at dusk that night, the whole town was abuzz with the news that *no* Two Moon Bay resident was responsible for the crime. Due to the ongoing investigation, however, no names or identities could be revealed as yet — at least that's what the investigators had told Brooks. The rumor mill was running on overdrive, of course, churning out conjecture and unfounded supposition - and more pointed fingers about who could have done such a thing if it wasn't 'those two kids,' after all.

While I was elated that Janice had been exonerated, I still didn't have the heart to face the crew before the play — didn't want to hear their words of shame. As far as I was concerned, it was *their* fault that Janice had quit the play. It was *their* fault she'd given up on her dreams and left town feeling alone and condemned. She might as well be walking around with big fat scarlet letters on her forehead. 'W.A.', they would say, for 'Wrongfully Accused.' But instead of being *her* punishment, *her* penance, the letters would be the town's cross to bear. Every time they looked at her, those who had said she was guilty would be forced to face *their* ugly truth, to avert their eyes in shame.

Their judgment and subsequent remorse that night was a tragedy I just didn't want any part of, so I rolled into the theater about fifteen minutes before curtain. I already felt guilty enough for not insisting that Janice stay, for not telling her about the tape; if I had, she would undoubtedly have agreed to lay low at my house until the security people in Naples could email Brooks the file. How tragic that less than six hours later, her name was not only completely exonerated, but people were shamefully regretting their rush to judgment. Too little too late.

One *good* thing about Christmas Eve, however, was that the play went off without a hitch. Everyone remembered their lines, the lights and sound worked perfectly, thanks to Jamie and Harry. And no one had a wardrobe malfunction — thankfully, since Janice wasn't around to sew up the mistake. Aside from the fact that one of our key crew members was gone, everything was just perfect.

And, at one point, in one magical moment when Bébé and I were onstage just before the culmination of the battle scene, singing our sad, lonely song, actual tears had coursed down my cheeks. Suddenly more enmeshed in Temperance's character than any I had ever played, I channeled all of the hurt I felt for Janice, all of the pain she must be feeling, into my performance. It was like something came over me in that instant, something real and pure and true. I don't know what you'd call it, but it was almost like I, and everyone else in that darkened auditorium that night, were in some sort of trance. It came over me in a flash, as though somewhere far above the stage, my fairy godmother had waved her magic wand, casting me in her spell of truth. It gripped me, raised the little hairs on the back of my neck until the cannons boomed and the crackling gunfire rang out. It was an awesome moment, almost spiritual in its power.

And now, hours later, as Christmas Eve waned and Christmas Day approached, the entire town gathered for the after-party at Blackheart's Blues Café. People of all ages celebrated another successful performance of the town's commemorative drama, while the Christmas spirit charged the air. After hitting the buffet, adults crowded the dance floor and bar, while the kids gathered in the gaming room. To the right of the main dining area, which, like The Real Macaw, opened onto an outdoor deck, were rows of pool tables, dart boards lining the walls, and old-school arcade games. Since the night was warm and muggy, still in the low eighties, despite the fact that it was almost nine o'clock, the outdoor bar was open for business. The blues palace lived up to its reputation of serving the best food on the Bay, including a delectable Southern supper complete with fried chicken, collard greens, potato salad, barbequed ribs, and good ole banana puddin'. The house band played all the hits, sounding remarkably like the original blues masters themselves. A celebratory vibe infused the air, buzzing like invisible electric currents.

Although I was worried about Janice, I maintained a convincing attitude of gaiety as I danced with Bébé and Dixie, met a whole slew of new faces, and kept feeding five dollar bills to Capri, who invariably turned them into quarters for the games. According to the rumor mill, Alex was a wicked pool player, cleaning up by beating all the boys who dared to take her on. I wondered why Capri kept coming to *me* for money, when her sister was striking it rich in the other room.

On her sixth request for more dough, I decided to ask Capri about it. From the raised dance floor, I looked down at her, a skeptical look on my face. "Hey, if Alex is so good at pool, why aren't you draining *her* of cash? I'm beginning to feel like an ATM."

With the practiced air of a true diva, Capri rolled her eyes at Lily and Lise, who stared at me as if I'd just sprouted two heads. I could see the invisible 'duh' on their faces, felt their disdain for the old clueless cash-cow/parent. "Riley," Capri told me in her snottiest voice. I *knew* she had learned that from Alex. "She won't *give* me any money. She's stuffing it in her bra, where she claims it's 'safe'." She shrugged helplessly as though everyone in the world knew this but me.

Meanwhile, in my paranoid, worst-case-scenario, over-protective mind, alarm bells were going off. Somebody had hit the 'panic' button, and I couldn't seem to shut it off. My eyebrows shot to the ceiling.

"Her *bra*? What does her *bra* have to do with anything? Is her bra *exposed*? Or her stomach?" The questions kept coming, each one more panicked than the last. Call me crazy, but I was picturing the modest black-and-red plaid, button-down shirt-dress she'd been wearing over leggings tied fashionably above her belly button. I blame the nineties' twisted sense of fashion that seemed to be making a comeback.

Capri narrowed her eyes questioningly. "No, why? Every time she wins, she turns away from the table so no one can see, and stuffs the money into her bra." She shrugged at her friends as though befuddled by the line of questions.

I breathed a sigh of relief. The screaming alarm suddenly fell silent. For a second there, I was worried that the stomach-baring fashion of my twenties had somehow cycled back around to haunt my daughter. Not a good feeling. With my mind clear, I was able to focus on Capri's sudden attitude. "Um, ok, little miss *duh*, thank you for explaining that to me." I repressed the urge to roll my eyes at Bébé. "Anyway, this is the last of my cash," I told her, holding up a twenty. "Unh unh," I corrected, her, pulling it back as she attempted to snatch it from my fingers. "I would like for you to ask the bartender for change, and to bring it *all* over to me. I'll give you your cut then."

She sighed. I was truly inconveniencing her life. "Why can't you just do it?"

I raised my eyebrows in mock surprise. "Oh, really? Ok. No problem. I *will* do it myself - when I go pay my tab in a couple of hours. Ok, then, bye-bye. You girls have a good time!" I said jovially, tossing the bill back into my clutch.

"No, wait!" she cried, looking worried. "I'll change it for you."

It was my turn to be dramatic. "Oh, well - are you sure?" I asked with mock concern. "I don't want you to go to any trouble for me."

My sarcasm was not lost on Capri. Despite that, I could see she was just *aching* to roll her eyes at her friends. To her credit, though, she maintained a polite — yet strained — expression. The conflicting emotions on her face were hilarious. She was caught between a rock and a hard place of trying to appear indifferent to her friends, yet respectful to me. The strain of it all caused her to shift uncomfortably. "Um, no, it's no problem, Riley. I'll be right back," she said with forced politeness, accepting the bill I held out to her.

When they were out of earshot, Bébé and I giggled like schoolgirls.

"Kids," Bébé said, shrugging.

We boogie-oogie-oogied to James Brown's "Get on Up" and half of The Doors' "Light My Fire," when the change-monger came back, her too-cool pre-teen posse in tow. Capri held out the change to me, looking humbled.

I made a big show of counting out the change. "Let's just make sure this is right," I said, not ready to let her off the hook quite yet. "Bébé, would you hold out your hand for me?"

My Creole friend suddenly snapped to attention beside me. "Oh, well, of *course*, Riley. Anything for a friend." She grinned at Capri and her friends, dutifully holding her palm out to me.

"Thank you so much. Ok," I said, counting slowly. "Here's ten, and five — that makes fifteen. And here's one, two, three . . ." I broke off suddenly, furrowing my brow. "Wait, was that two I said, or three?"

"That was three," Bébé said helpfully, her grin widening.

The girls fidgeted anxiously. Capri cleared her throat, but held her tongue.

"Right, three — thank you, Bébé. So that's three, four, and five ones. That makes twenty." Taking the stack from Bébé, I smiled victoriously at Capri. "Ok, honey, here you go." I handed her the ones. "Five more dollars for games. Spend them well."

Capri snatched the money and took off, dying to get away. "Thanks," she muttered over her shoulder.

Watching them peel away toward the game room, Bébé and I burst out laughing.

"Oh, that was mean," she said, wiping a tear from her eye. "You could have at *least* given her the ten after putting her through all that."

I tucked the rest of the money back into my clutch. "I *could* have," I agreed. "But then she wouldn't have learned that little girls need not act like adults with their *I'm-so-grown* attitudes. A little humbling goes a long way sometimes."

She nodded, sipping from her drink. "Amen, honey. My Henri needs a slice or two of humble pie every day." Draining her cocktail, she grabbed my hand. "I think it's about time for a refill, don't you?" she asked, pulling me along before I had time to object. "Let's go to the outside bar — the line's shorter."

"Good idea," I agreed, realizing how loud and crowded it had gotten inside. As we stepped onto the outer deck and up to the bar, I looked out past the tables that lined the marsh. Seeing the cool moonlight reflecting off the crashing waves, I had a sudden urge to be out there, near the water, listening to the soothing surf. "You know what?" I asked Bébé, pointing toward the marsh. "I'm just going to get some air. Catch up with you in a few."

She nodded, waving as I broke off to the left, dodging the mob surrounding the bar. I could hear her strident voice cascade in musical laughter behind me; somebody already had the popular Bébé Beauchamps' ear as she leaned over the counter to order another drink.

Weaving between the throngs of people, I waved to the familiar faces. Calista and Cathy, Ryan and Candy, Abby and Mayor Darrell, and a handful of people from the play. Seeing Harry with Jamie, I just wished Janice were here to celebrate with us. Dixie, the Cals, and Brooks were in the middle of what sounded like a serious discussion on real estate, so I scooted by, pointing to where I was going as Brooks raised a questioning eyebrow. Cal the Third just watched me quietly, nodding his head as I passed.

My footsteps echoed hollowly on the wooden boards. Drinking in the dewy evening air, my mind wandered as I followed the deck that curved along the bay. This was one of the town's most famous spots, I reflected, most likely due to its natural beauty. Here, the water crept inward toward the town, creating a safe harbor - a place where boats could hide from pirates during Blackheart Bellacroix's day. Funny how my thoughts found their way to the character I had played, and now felt so connected to. Gazing out over the stillness of the bay, it occurred to me that this very spot could have been where the willful Temperance and Destina had lost their lives the night they disappeared. Although it was miles from their home, miles from *the* bay, the one for which the town was named, it was possible they really *had* descended the craggy coastline to the beach below. The path that led from the castle — now the club — down to the water's edge was rocky and covered with dunes, from what the locals said. They must have been incredibly bold to have braved the rough terrain in the dark of night so many years ago.

Unless, I thought, gazing up at the silvery crescent in the sky, they had waited for the moon to guide them. I could just picture them: eager eyes lit by the flames of their glowing candles, long dark hair and pale flowing gowns, guided by the moon's ghostly double. Many a ship had crashed into the craggy coastline, following what they thought was the moon in the sky, but was actually the reflection along the water. The articles I'd read on the Internet explained the phenomenon as some sort of specular reflection; the light bouncing off the still surface of the bay supposedly creates a mirror-like illusion. I didn't really understand it, but apparently it was a real thing.

The sound of footsteps approaching me from behind suddenly broke into my thoughts. I'd been so absorbed in studying the play of light on the water that I hadn't noticed someone had crept up behind me. I sucked in my breath, whirling around.

The booming voice and gleaming teeth, however, put me immediately at ease. "Whoa there, darlin'! I didn't mean to scare you," Cal apologized. He put a reassuring hand on my shoulder before leaning over the railing. Gazing out over the water, he took a deep breath, seeming to need the quiet as much as I, and said softly, "Just thought I'd get a little fresh air, is all."

I nodded, staring back at the sea. It seemed that you could see forever — so far that the water and darkness almost appeared as one. "Yeah, me too. It's so peaceful," I remarked, enjoying the sounds that filled the calm. Night creatures chorusing, rhythmic and soothing, like a lullaby.

A comfortable silence passed, neither of us rushing to fill it.

"You know, Cal," I said pensively, after a while. "There's something really special about this place. I'm so glad I moved here."

"We-ell," he returned, drawing out the word. I could almost hear the smile in his voice. "I'm real happy to hear that, darlin'." He continued, in a serious tone, "You know, some of us are real happy to have you here." He paused, and I could feel his eyes watching me. With a lighter tone, he continued, "I can think of at least *one* person in particular, who's especially pleased." He chuckled. "Yep, you've made quite an impression on one fella, that's for sure."

I smiled, thinking of Brooks. Teasing Cal, though, I nudged his shoulder with my own and gushed, "Aw, thanks, Cal, that's so sweet!"

He snickered appreciatively. "Well, darlin' you know I'm talkin' about Brooks!" He slung an arm around my shoulders in a friendly embrace. "He sure has fallen for you."

I shook my head, marveling over all that had transpired in the course of six days. Looking out over the water, it was easier to confess my feelings without someone staring back at me. "Well, don't tell anybody," I said conspiratorially. "But I've kind of fallen for him, too." Wow, I thought, how liberating it was to say that out loud! And such a turning-point for me; rather than hiding behind my emotions all the time, which was kind of a hobby of mine, it felt so empowering to just face the truth and say it aloud. Inspired by my newfound self-honesty, I acknowledged that I really *should* get around to telling Brooks how I felt about him sometime soon - whenever the time was right, that is.

Turning to look at Cal, I continued, more boldly, "You know – I just can't believe I've only been here a week – not even!" I shook my head again. "It feels more like six months. It's crazy – like I'm in some sort of time warp, or something. I don't know what it is, but there's something truly . . ." My words broke off as something splashed in the water nearby.

We both turned, following the sound.

The moon glowed feebly from behind a cloud, its light dimmed so that all we saw was the heavy darkness.

Probably a dolphin, or a night bird, hunting in the darkness. I was grateful for the delay, though, for it gave me time to gather my words. ". . . I know it sounds insane, Cal, but it's true; there's something almost . . . *magical* about this place."

Cal's eyes lit up. "That's right – this place *is* magical, darlin'. Like our slogan says, 'Life's a little brighter in Two Moon Bay.'" He smiled mischievously. "There's a reason the moon tricks people with its light," he whispered theatrically. "And there's a reason it bounces off the water, luring ships onto the shore."

"Specular reflection," I answered confidently, proud of my knowledge.

Unimpressed, Cal guffawed in amusement. "Aw, darlin', you can't believe everythin' you read on the Internet!"

I scowled, recalling all the times I had warned my students of the same thing.

"No, that ain't no specular reflection," Cal assured me, shaking his head. "That's somethin' far simpler, and as old as time itself." He paused as I turned to look questioningly at him. "You said so yourself about this place, darlin' — it's *magic*."

Watching his face, I waited for him to laugh, but he didn't. I could see by the earnest expression on his face that he wasn't joking. "You can't be serious," I said dismissively. "I mean — that's just a manner of speaking, right?"

Cal shook his head. "Not at all, darlin', not here in Two Moon Bay. It's somethin' that all of us locals know; we just kinda keep it to ourselves. Things are a little different here, you'll see," he promised.

I nodded quietly, staring back at the ocean. Whether I wanted to admit it or not, I had to acknowledge that ever since Raegan and I had crossed into the town's limits, *everything* had changed. And in only six days! I went from being the new girl in town to one of the family — even meeting someone to fall in love with, because that's obviously what was going on between Brooks and me. Stuff like that didn't exactly happen every day — or *ever*, for me, until coming here. Maybe Cal was onto something.

"You know," he continued offhandedly, "I found some more stuff for Capri — some more information about the legend."

I looked over at him, curious. Though he acted casual, I got the feeling his news was more important than he was letting on. "Oh?"

He nodded, still staring out into the distance. "Yep. A couple of journals. One was written by Temperance Biscayne." He paused, turning to look at me, his tone suddenly excited. "And the other — by Blackheart

Bellacroix himself. It was dated in the same year he died — the same year the girls disappeared." He watched my face as the information sank in. "Riley, the shield that was stolen yesterday. . ."

I raised my eyebrows, shocked by what he had just revealed.

". . . It was aboard the *Doncella* when it sank; I found it on the manifest Blackheart had copied in his journal."

I looked blankly at him, unable to believe what he was saying.

Cal continued, "Yep, apparently ole Blackheart was known for makin' a copy of all of his ships' logs; the one I found was mixed in with a bunch of stuff ole Granddaddy had found years ago. The shield wasn't armor at all — or an antique. That's why it was stolen."

I furrowed my brow, not getting it. "Why?" I questioned.

Sighing, Cal explained, "The shield *looked* like a breastplate of armor, but it was actually made of a malleable material. Somethin' soft enough that dings could be hammered in to be used as a map; a map to the treasure Blackheart's crew was accused of stealin' off a Spanish galleon they raided not long before they came ashore that night." He took a breath, then continued, "Darlin', before his ship was attacked that night, he buried the treasure."

I shook my head, fumbling to connect all the dots. "Ok, so what does the shield have to do with the buried treasure?" I was confused; the shield wasn't part of the booty Blackheart had stolen from the Spanish ship, so what was the big deal?

Cal put his hands on my shoulders, turning me to face him. "Darlin'," he spelled it out for me. "The shield *was* the map; ole Blackheart drew a copy of the map next to the shield on the manifest." He looked frankly at me for emphasis. "That's why it was stolen yesterday; the thieves somehow figured it out, and took the shield in order to find the treasure."

I gaped at him, speechless. When I finally found my voice, I mumbled, "That means," I started, unable to grasp all those dollar signs. "You mean . . ."

Cal nodded, reading my thoughts. "That's right," he answered. "Blackheart Bellacroix's treasure is buried here in Two Moon Bay. And I know where to find it."

12

Buried Treasure

As the cold sand squished between my toes, I went over Cal's words again in my mind.

"I know where to find it," he had said, his blue eyes intense in the darkness. "Blackheart Bellacroix's treasure is buried here in Two Moon Bay."

Shaking my head, I trudged along, unable to believe that I had not only sneaked out of my house in the middle of the night — on Christmas Day — to find three-hundred-year-old buried treasure, but I had left my two sleeping daughters in the house alone.

"What the heck is *wrong* with you?" I asked myself in exasperation, stopping suddenly. I debated about whether or not to turn around. "You should go back," my conscience prompted me to say. But then, my other mind rationalized, the girls *were* asleep. Plus, it was after midnight; I would be back by one, no doubt — it wouldn't take Cal long to realize that the "map" he was convinced he'd found was no more than a random drawing. I mean, really - who ever heard of a ruthless pirate making copies of his ship's manifests, anyway? I'm no pirate scholar, but copying the map seemed to go against everything I'd ever known about hiding treasure. I would tell Cal as soon as I saw him, and then be on my way.

"Let's see," I said aloud, trying to distract myself out of my anstyness. "How much further?" I wondered, feeling like Capri on a road trip.

Couldn't be much longer. Looking around, I got my bearings. I'd only been to this part of the beach a few times, on some of my longer runs. It was several miles from my house to the club, and, judging by the fact that the homes had now disappeared as the marsh popped up along the sand's edge, I figured the club was not far away.

Sure enough - the next thing I knew, the calm, still waters of the Bay were in sight. This was where the coastline jutted out into the sea, forming the protective barrier for which the town was named. Here, the cove looked deceptively larger than it was, with the sheer rock cliffs reflecting the moon's cool light, somehow replicating the panorama of the sky along the craggy walls. The pristine waters of the bay loomed much larger than they actually were; I chalked it up to that whole specular reflection phenomenon.

A sudden vibrating startled me out of my skin. You would have thought the boogeyman himself had snuck up behind me and tapped me on the shoulder — I could not have jumped any further if he had. Then, realizing it was *not* my worst nightmare coming true but just a simple text, I laughed off how lost in thought I'd been, breathed a sigh of relief, and pulled my phone from my pocket.

Brooks: Hey beautiful. U and the girls still at the par-tay? Y'all need a ride home?

Giggling like a girl who'd just received her first Valentine, I texted him back a quick thank you, explaining that I was sorry to have missed them. The bar had been so packed by the time I'd rounded up the girls to leave that we hadn't gotten to say goodbye. But how sweet of him to try to see us safely home.

Brooks: No worries. Y'all be good tonight — Santa's on his way! Santa emoji, gift emoji, smiley face.

How cute was he? Grinning, I typed back: 'On an adventure,' smiley face/wink. 'Tell you all about it tomorrow.' Christmas tree emoji, blushing smiley face.

Then, with a twinge of guilt, I tried to ignore the fact that I had *conveniently* left out the part about buried treasure. Ah, well, I rationalized, when I saw him tomorrow to give him his gift, I would most happily rehash tonight's temporary insanity and my hasty trip to track down Blackheart Bellacriox's booty with Cal.

Stuffing my phone back into my pocket, the outline of the old castle suddenly came into view. Its silhouette atop the cliffs looked even more medieval from a distance, I noted creepily. The turrets rose formidably into the night-dark sky, looking lonely and intimidating at the same time.

"Holy creepy castle," I mumbled under my breath, wondering how the place I'd rehearsed and performed in for several nights running was now almost unrecognizable to me.

A sudden shiver snaked its way down my spine.

"The beach path must be along here somewhere," I said to myself, studying the shoreline, hoping to see Cal nearby.

But glancing around, I was disappointed to see that I was alone. To my left, the dunes disappeared into the marsh that wove through town. Beyond that, rocky bluffs rose up the steep hill to the club, which I couldn't stop thinking of as Destina and Temperance's prison. Trying to keep my mind off the uneasiness that hovered around me in the cool night air, I wondered what this area must have looked like back in their day.

Stopping for a moment, I closed my eyes, picturing the way it must have back then. This part of the beach — so secluded from town, and even from the closest neighbor, must have been ghostly quiet — I mean, it certainly was *now*. Feeling the breeze against my face, I breathed deeply of the night. Poor Temperance and Destina, I thought, empathizing with them. Willful, independent girls who longed for adventure and romance — and the vastness of the world . . . who could blame them for sneaking out at night, running to the beach below?

Something stirred suddenly - a rustling - startling me all over again. My heart slammed wildly in my chest as I looked around, my eyes combing the deserted beach. Hoping it was Cal, I realized with a surge of disappointment that it wasn't him. Subtlety was *not* his strong suit; he was about as quiet as a herd of wild mustangs under normal circumstances — and, tonight, since he had promised to bring treasure-digging materials like shovels and lights, I knew I'd hear and see him *long* before he became aware of me. No, whatever this sound was, it was quiet, almost unnoticeable, as though someone were walking discreetly through the dunes that lined the beach. Seeing nothing, I waited to hear it again, but didn't.

Just then, the grasses stirred gently in the breeze. Letting out the breath I'd been holding, I felt like an idiot. I laughed in relief. "Oh, wow," I murmured. "You are *really* on edge!" I vowed to take a long hot bath when I got home. That would settle me down.

Resuming my walk again, I hummed a few bars of the duet I'd shared with Bébé just a few hours earlier. I wondered vaguely who had written the beautiful music — as a late-comer to the play, I'd been so concerned about learning my lines that I hadn't even thought to ask. Must have been somebody who knew the history of the town extremely well. And somebody who'd lived a *long* time ago, since the play had been performed every year since the girls had disappeared. Such a lovely song, so plaintively beautiful, yet filled with a yearning for something more, something out of reach. The sad song of a lonely girl's heart.

A sudden whisper in my ear catapulted me into a frenzy of motion. In the same moment, unseen fingers trailed along the back of my neck. My heart thundered wildly in my chest.

Whirling around, I expected to find someone standing there, but there was nothing — no one.

Feeling unsettled, I finally understood what it meant to be 'chilled to the core'. Unable to explain what had just happened in any *rational* way, I ran my hand along my neck, as if that could make the lingering, ghostly touch disappear.

"Come on, Cal," I said aloud, my eyes combing the empty stretch of beach once more, the softly-swaying grasses.

Shivering — more from apprehension than from being cold — I drew my hood up around my head. No more creepy whispers and spectral contact for me. I had *no* idea what was going on, but I didn't like it.

"Cal, please hurry," I urged him.

Looking up, I studied the stars to divert my thoughts from whispers and touches from a person who wasn't there. Then, as I recognized the pattern in the night sky, my breath caught in my throat. "Oh, my gosh," I whispered. "That's what was on the shield!" I exclaimed. "Now it all makes sense."

So *that's* what Cal had been talking about, I realized, feeling like a dummy for not putting it all together sooner - and like a bad friend for doubting him about the map. Seeing the stars overhead, the missing piece of the puzzle suddenly fit into place. Blackheart had etched the pattern in the shield and buried the treasure at the base of the cliff where his true love had lived. In *fact*, I bet if we could find the path that led from the castle to the shore, that's where the loot would be!

Gazing back toward the rocky wall, I felt a little giddy that I'd finally figured it all out.

"This is it!" I exclaimed, feeling elated and a little overwhelmed to be standing near one of the biggest — and most famous — buried treasures of all time.

But my excitement didn't last long. Despite being warmed by my revelation, a shiver danced down my spine once again. That creepy feeling was back. Whether it was the memory of the ghostly hand, or the whispery sound of the grasses stirring in the breeze, I attempted to distract myself from the eeriness I was suddenly feeling. I texted Cal a quick "Where r u," hoping for a speedy reply. Resuming my solo, I hummed the next few bars, rubbing my hands along my arms to rid myself of the chill that lingered like an unseen spirit.

The next thing I knew, the rustling sounded again, just off to the left. Thinking it was the ocean breeze, I didn't make much of it until I realized that the swishing was coming from one particular area, rather than sweeping along, as the wind would do. I stared out over my shoulder, toward the marshy dunes. It was so dark back there, where the swamp disappeared against the cliffs. So dark that I couldn't see anything at all.

Just then, a whispery voice wafted along the air.

"Temperance," I said automatically, without even thinking. Feeling that someone was watching me, I turned around, slowly.

There, before me, singing her lonely song, was the girl from the pictures — the girl whose role I had played just hours before.

"Oh, my God," I whispered. Was this really happening?

The fact that she looked *real* — like a person, and not some wispy, ghostly image — told me that what I was seeing was *actually* happening. Even more astounding was the fact that the filmy lavender gown she wore actually *blew* in the breeze. Unbelievable as it was, she really *was* there, and not just a figment of my imagination.

Just like in the pictures Capri and Janice had shown me, Temperance's hair was long and dark, trailing in waves down to her waist. The song I recognized, as well; it was that same sad song I had heard a week ago, first when watching the sunset from the little bench in my backyard, then again when I was walking to the bar. Now, staring at her, at the girl from the legend, I felt I must have stepped back in time, to a moment that had *actually* happened to someone else, long ago. Wondering what she must want from me, why she was sharing this moment with me, I yearned to ask, but could not seem to form the words.

Speechless, I studied her, afraid to move lest I scare her away. Temperance's eyes were big and round, and as dark as night. The Cupids bow lips were parted in song, her words imploring me to listen. I felt, for some reason, that she was singing to *me* - that she needed *me* to hear her, and understand.

I stood there, spellbound, my feet rooted to the spot.

Overcome with a sudden sadness, I somehow understood that it was Temperance's emotion that abruptly consumed me. She was communicating with me; I just didn't know what it was she was trying to tell me.

And then, without knowing why, I reached out my hand.

Unexpectedly, she reached back.

Feeling as though I had stepped outside myself, I watched the next few seconds unfold as though from a distance. Without realizing it, I surrendered to her pain, her yearning, wanting desperately to understand what she was trying to show me. What was it, I wondered frantically, sensing that we were somehow running out of time.

We strained toward one another, but try as we might, our fingers just wouldn't touch. It felt like something was holding us back, keeping us apart. Something unseen, and far more powerful than we were.

"Temperance!" I called out, as a sudden wind whipped through the bay.

But what, I wondered, could have caused the calm waters to suddenly churn with the vehemence that now stirred them into waves? I couldn't make sense of it, but I knew, without a doubt, that something beyond words, beyond simple understanding, was happening here tonight.

The wind rushed in my ears, blowing my hair around my face. I had to shout to be heard over the angry torrent. "Temperance!" I hollered, straining once more for her hand.

She reached back, staring me straight in the eye. I could see she was about to speak when her eyes suddenly went wide. She froze, a look of fear crossing her face. She pointed over my shoulder, crying out, "No — *don't!*"

That feeling of foreboding gripped me once more. But before I could turn to see what had frightened her, I felt a crushing pain against the back of my skull.

And in the next instant, the world went black.

─ ⌒ ─

Bickering voices were the first thing I heard as I awoke. Careful not to make a sound, I stayed exactly where I was, squinting just enough to get my bearings. The last thing I needed was for the jerk who had knocked me out to realize I had come to. No, better to listen and gather what information I could. Besides, I thought, wincing from the throbbing in the back of my head, I had a *pounding* headache. To top that off, my hands were tied behind my back.

I gazed around, wondering where that light was coming from. Had someone made a fire? Cal certainly wouldn't do that; he was planning to bring head lamps, he had said, and a fire would be way too obvious. So what was that glow that lit the area?

Looking to the left, toward the cliffs, I saw a path of large white pillar candles stuck into the sand, their lighted wicks shining through the darkness. The trail of candles wrapped around a bend in the swampy grasses, but that was as far as I could see.

Glancing around, there was something else nearby, just a few feet from my right hand. Squinting, I struggled to bring the burnished item into focus; it looked to be an old copper pot, propped in the sand. But as I stared, my breath caught in my throat — that was no copper pot! That was the missing shield! The one I had appraised on Mr. McKay's wall just moments before it'd been stolen. That made sense, I thought — whoever had stolen it knew that it was the map, and had stuck it in the sand for safekeeping while digging.

Now that *that* part of the mystery had been solved, I was on to who had taken it. Guessing it was the same person who had knocked me out, I squinted at the culprits whose backs were facing me. Unable to tell much — besides the fact that there were two of them - I gauged that they — and Cal — were about twenty feet from me. I was lying not far from where I'd stood; apparently, whoever had conked me over the head had let me lay where I fell. Even more interesting? By my estimation, I was smack dab where Temperance had been standing when the interloper had hit me.

No longer feeling her presence — and that overwhelming sadness — I figured she was gone. Which left me with . . . whom? I still couldn't tell, until they started to raise their voices.

"Look old man," a female voice quipped, sounding angry. "You need to get out of here — *fast!*"

Oh, my God! I thought frantically, wriggling my hands, attempting to loosen the restraints. It was the glaring girl from Big Ed's store! The shady couple who'd been buying shovels and candles — treasure-hunting materials! Dang, I was getting good at putting all these little clues together. A regular Nancy Drew.

As my eyes adjusted to the darkness, I figured I had only a brief amount of time before Bonnie and Clyde realized I was awake. Or, before they did something to poor Cal. Who knew what kind of weapons these creeps had on them?

Speaking of weapons, I looked around to see what I could find. Continuing to twist my hands, I felt the restraints begin to loosen. Somebody had done a pretty shoddy job of tying them, since I was able to wiggle free so easily.

Cal's voice boomed into the night. "Now, I don't know what y'all are thinkin'. Everyone *knows* you stole the shield!" he gestured toward the map in the sand. "You were caught red-handed on tape! It's only a matter of time before the authorities catch up with you!"

As the guy fired off a nasty retort, my eyes fell on my cell phone, lying about five feet away. It must have fallen out when I'd hit the ground. Perfect! I thought, eyeing the couple, who was still busy arguing with Cal.

Inching my way toward the phone, I managed to pull free from the cloth they'd used to bind my wrists together. I grabbed my phone, typing a quick text to Brooks. Hopefully, he'd get it, and call the cops. If he was asleep — well, let's just say Cal and I were doomed.

Making sure the volume was off in case he texted back, I stuck it in my pocket.

Now — on to a search for weapons. These two were not going to outsmart me twice - that was for sure.

Spying a shovel off to my left, I ever so slowly pushed myself to my hands and knees. My head swooned, but I had to focus. Grasping the handle, I tiptoed toward the couple, careful to stay out of their periphery. Hoping Cal wouldn't give me away, I had the shovel poised, ready to swing, when he cried out, "Riley, behind you!"

I spun around.

And looked into the muzzle of a gun.

"Jamie!" I exclaimed, more surprised than scared. "What are you doing?"

He smirked sarcastically at me. "What am I doing?" he repeated in a mocking tone. Then, glancing over my shoulder, toward the couple, whom, I could tell, had inched up behind me, he continued, "What I'm *doing* . . ." His tone was icy. "Is getting ready to put a bullet in you — and the old man," he added, glancing at Cal. "And whoever else gets in my way."

Cal rushed forward. "Now you listen here, young man," he began, then thrust his hands in the air as Jamie pointed the gun at him. "Don't do nothin' rash," he cautioned. "Riley and me aren't gonna stop you from what you were doin'." He took a tentative step forward. "We can work this out. Just put the gun down."

Jamie snickered sardonically. Ignoring him, he aimed it at me once again. "You — on your knees."

Exchanging a look with Cal, I did as the gunman bid, and lowered myself to my knees. Distract him, I told myself. Get him talking. "So it was you all along, wasn't it, Jamie?" I asked him. "You and these two clowns," I added, motioning behind me. "But you let Janice take the fall." I scoffed. "Kind of a cowardly thing to do, don't you think?"

Jamie squinted at me, suddenly angry. He hurried forward, the gun raised as if to strike.

Cal darted in front of me, shielding me with his body.

Jamie shouted, "How dare you!" but stopped abruptly, as a haunting female voice started to sing.

We all glanced around, wondering where the sound was coming from. It seemed to be emanating from the dunes, which swayed with a music all their own.

Temperance? I wondered vaguely. Funny, but I didn't feel her presence, not the way I had before. And this song, though sad, was a little different.

As we listened, spellbound, the mournful tune wafted out of the marsh, out of what must have been the trail that led down from the cliffs. We watched, frozen in place, as a girl with long dark hair stepped out of the grasses and onto the beach, her shimmery dress silvered by the moonlight. Though much of her face was covered in shadow, I could see her Cupid's bow mouth moving in time to the music. Like the fair maiden I had seen just moments earlier, this was no apparition, but a real, live person. And as she stepped gingerly toward the ocean, everyone fell under the magic of her spell. All, that is, except for the criminals, who instead became incredibly spooked.

Jamie's voice trembled as he muttered, "Omigod — *omigod*! That's her! That's the ghost of Temperance Biscayne!"

"Holy crap!" the other guy shrieked as his girlfriend cried, "Let's get outta here! That's a *ghost*, omigod!"

Without another word, the threesome hightailed it down the beach. They scrambled into the dunes several hundred yards ahead, where a public beach access was built over the marsh. From there, they could reach Beach Boulevard, where they'd likely parked their car.

Watching them flee, Cal and I burst into laughter. He put his arms around me, hugging me close. "You alright there, darlin'?" he asked, looking down at me.

"I am now," I assured him, offering an arm for the apparition as she walked toward us, a smile on her face. "How about you, Alex?" I asked. "Are you ok?"

She giggled. "Well, for a ghost," she answered. "I'm feeling pretty darned good right about now."

Hugging them both with relief, it occurred to me how much my daughter actually *did* resemble the young Temperance Biscayne. She wore my dress from the play, which helped to set the scene, plus she had similar facial features, and Temperance's large almond-shaped eyes. Although Alex's hair was lighter, in the darkness on the beach it had looked much darker. Despite the fact that I had recognized her voice immediately, I gave her credit for being a pretty convincing ghost. Enough, anyway, to scare away the superstitious kids! I laughed, recalling the horrified expression on Jamie's panicked face.

As the crazy scene with the treasure-stealing kids ran through my mind, I realized I had a *ton* of unanswered questions to account for. Namely, how Alex had known where I'd be? *And*, how had she known to wear the dress and act the part of a long-dead ghost?

Turning to her, I asked, "Hey, how did you know?" At her inquisitive look, I gestured toward her outfit, as if that explained it all.

Alex looked down at the dress, swishing the flowing gown from side to side. The moon cast off its pale color with an ethereal glow. "What, you mean the dress?" She asked, aloof. I could tell she was dodging my question.

I snickered sardonically, trying to figure out the reason for her evasiveness. She was *definitely* up to something. "Uh — *yeah*, the dress, the singing, the pretending to be a ghost in the moonlight . . ." My voice trailed off as I looked at Cal, hoping he'd chime in with some useful information. Something told me our golfing friend knew more than he was letting on. Studying him, and the mischievous expression he tried to hide, I saw that little tell-tale sparkle in his eyes. Another piece of the puzzle fell right into place. "Ah, I should have known," I said, understanding, sort of. "But, Cal," I began, then paused. It was almost too much to put into words. "How did *you* know . . .?" With so many puzzling questions filling my brain, my words faltered, hanging in the humid air.

But instead of answering, he stepped forward and put an arm around my shoulders, reassuring me, "It's a long story, darlin'. And we'll be happy to fill you in." He pulled his phone from his pocket, saying, "Let me just find out where our *other* partners-in-crime are first." Cal glanced conspiratorially at Alex.

Oh, good Lord, I thought in exasperation. Who else could *possibly* be involved? Congress? The Pope? I threw a suspicious look at Alex.

She shrugged, not bothering to hide her grin. "What?" she asked innocently. "All I did was show up and do my part, I swear." She pointed at Cal, whose face glowed with a bluish tint from the light of his phone. "*He's* the man with the plan."

I nodded silently, giving up for the time being. It would all come out soon enough, I reckoned. Then, in the next second, it suddenly occurred to me: since Alex was *here*, that meant Capri was at the house all alone. Oh, God! I thought, panicking. I'd abandoned my eight-year-old child. What a horrible, horrible person I was! I fought to keep my voice calm as I asked meekly, "Um, Alex — does Capri know you're here?"

To my complete surprise, Alex laughed. "Uh, I don't think you have to worry about her," she replied almost smugly, glancing at Cal. "I'm pretty sure she's fine."

A surge of relief ran through me, but I raised a questioning eyebrow. "So my baby's not home alone? Please tell me."

"Aww, darlin'," the professional golfer — and now trickster — chimed in, coming to Alex's rescue. He looked up for a moment, about to explain, when the light from his head lamp hit me full force in the eyes.

I squinted, putting a hand up to block it.

"Oops, sorry about that," he said quickly. Pushing the lamp higher on his forehead, it faced upward, like a spotlight cutting through the inky darkness. "I can *promise* you that the little darlin's safe and sound."

At my dubious look, he nodded emphatically, returning to his phone as it dinged with a new message.

"Oh, thank God," I muttered, taking a deep breath. These two shady-cats could be as aloof as they wanted to, so long as my baby was safe. I might as well just keep quiet and save my questions for later.

Realizing I had nothing left to worry about, I thought back to my encounter with the *actual* Temperance Biscayne. How real she'd seemed, standing before me, singing. Then, reaching out, straining for my hand. God, I just wish I knew what it was she'd been trying to tell me.

Cal's cannon-like voice boomed through the air, breaking into my thoughts. "You alright there, darlin'?" he asked, his eyebrows knitted into a frown of concern. "Capri's ok, I promise, she . . ."

But before he could finish, an anxious little voice called out from the darkness of the marsh, "Riley? Riley, where are you?"

"Capri?!" I exclaimed in surprise.

Not seeing her, I ran blindly toward her voice. It sounded like she was near the beach path. Looking toward where the cliff lowered to the shore, I could just make out the deck that led to Beach Boulevard. Blue lights spun into the darkened sky, and there, where the parking lot met the beach access, was a police cruiser. The cops! They had gotten here in time to catch the criminals! I breathed a sigh of relief.

"Capri!" I shouted, spotting her running toward me, the glint of the moon shining off her hair.

"Riley!" she hollered, her shoes clattering down the deck and onto the sand. She paused to kick them away, then plundered toward me.

I laughed, thinking how amazing it was that in all her excitement — and probably worry — she could remember a little detail like removing her shoes. That was my daughter! "Hey, honey!" I shouted, catching her as she launched herself at me.

"Riley, I was so worried!" she gushed, pulling back from our embrace. And then it all came out in a rush. "I was reading one of the journals Mr. Cal gave me and figured out the legend, and when I went to your room to tell you, you were *gone*!" She glanced over her shoulder as the tall, athletic form of Mr. Calhoun Foxworth the Second approached her from behind. "I called you and Cal, but you didn't answer, so I called *Mr.* Cal," she explained, looking up at him. He placed a reassuring hand on her shoulder. "And he told me he knew just where to find you."

By then, Cal and Alex had hurried toward us.

"Oh, honey, I'm sorry to have worried you," I gushed, drawing her tightly to me once more. Then, pulling back to look into her face, I added, "I *promise* I won't leave you like that again."

She nodded, already forgiving me.

Still struggling to put the rest of it together, I looked squarely at the person I presumed to be the ringleader of this whole sordid operation. "Ok, can you clue me in now?" With Capri still close by my side, I stood up, returning to my full height. "I'm dying to know how the plan went from you and me locating the treasure, to Alex dressing up as Temperance and foiling the criminals' attempt to steal it using the map?"

Cal smiled at my confusion, his teeth pinging at me like stars in the night sky. His booming voice explained, "Well, darlin', after Capri called Daddy, he got me on the line, figurin' I'd told you about the treasure. . . ." His voice faded as Cal Senior added, "That's exactly right, there, darlin'. Word had gotten 'round that it was those crazy kids from the inn who'd stole the shield. When I heard *that*, I reckoned they'd laid low long enough and were most likely goin' to dig it up tonight — they'd wanna get on outta town as quick as possible. So I called a buddy of mine on the force to alert 'im of the trouble we were expectin' here at the beach."

Capri broke in, "And Mr. Cal told me and Alex he needed our help to invoke the legend — in order to scare them away . . ."

"That's right," Cal Senior corroborated. "I thought we might need a little help from our friend Temperance — and the legend . . ." He looked at the puzzled expression on my face, not knowing that I was thinking that's *exactly* who I'd seen — the *real* Temperance, just moments before they'd arrived, probably. But the only ones who knew it were her and me.

Speechless over it all, I shook my head.

Cal Senior shrugged, amused by his little scheme. "And lo and behold — it worked!" he chuckled to himself.

"Wow . . ." I finally muttered. Then, a bolt of realization hit me, razor-sharp, like lightning. What they were saying — without *actually* saying it — was that they had known about the treasure all along! I swatted at the other Cal accusingly. Unfortunately for him, he was the only one *to* smack — I mean, he was closest, and, besides, I wasn't about to swat an old man, even if Cal Senior *was* incredibly spry. "Cal, you *knew*? All this time?"

He chuckled in amusement. "Well, now, darlin', o' course I knew!" He fended off another blow, laughing good-naturedly. "I *am* a Delgado descendant, after all."

Alex cut in, "I just find it hard to believe that you *both*," she began, pointing at the two Cals, "knew that Blackheart's treasure — the most famous one in all of *history* — was buried here in Two Moon Bay, and you never dug it up!"

The men exchanged a knowing look then shrugged.

She continued, "And you never *told* anybody?"

Capri interjected, "Forget about *telling* anybody — why *didn't* you dig it up?" She looked from one beaming face to the other.

We all laughed.

"Capri's right," I agreed. "But so is Alex," I continued, confused. "It *is* hard to understand. I mean - weren't you the *least* bit curious to unearth what Blackheart buried so many years ago?" At their blank expressions, I finished, "You'd not only make history, but you'd be rich!" I realized, as I was saying it, that I was talking to two professional, world-class, champion golfers. *Rich* was something they had always been. But still – *three hundred million dollars?* I was about to burst a blood vessel just trying to fathom that kind of money.

Cal Senior chuckled. "Aw, darlin'," he told me. "It ain't about the money — never was! My family has known about the treasure for generations and never dug it up." He looked at his son, his voice dropping. His expression grew serious as he looked us each in the eye. "I know it's not what the rest of the world would do, but things are a little different here in Two Moon Bay — but I think y'all are startin' to realize that." He chuckled softly, then said reflectively, "Like my daddy told me, and his daddy before him - some secrets — especially when they're not your own - are better left untold. And some treasures are meant to stay buried." He paused. "Now - whatever y'all decide to do is your business. But I, for one, am goin' home and goin' to bed." He looked at his watch before nodding to the girls and me. "Night, y'all," he said to us, starting toward the deck. "Oh, and," he added as an afterthought. "Y'all will be happy to know that the criminals have been apprehended. They'll be spending Christmas Day in the county jail. Merry Christmas, y'all!" And with that, Cal Senior turned, and was gone.

We all stared after him, lost in our own thoughts.

Alex spoke first. She looked at Cal and Capri, who were the only ones who knew exactly where the treasure was located. "Well?" she asked expectantly. "Where is it?"

Cal pointed toward the shield. "Right about where that young'n attacked your step-mama," he said.

I furrowed my brow. "Wait — I thought it was buried at the base of the cliff."

Cal gave me a curious look. "Why would you think that, darlin'?"

I opened my mouth to answer when Capri broke in, "Riley, are we going to do what Mr. Cal said, and leave the treasure?"

Blowing out a breath I didn't realize I'd been holding, I gazed back at her, considering what we should do. I kind of agreed with Cal Senior that the best thing was to leave the treasure where Blackheart had buried it. Maybe the older man was right; maybe some secrets *were* better left untold. "I don't know, honey," I said truthfully. "Maybe we should." I looked at my daughters, then at Cal.

All were staring toward the shield, lying in shadow just a few feet from the path of candles. It was hard to believe that if what Cal had said was true, beneath it lay hundreds of millions of dollars. My mind swam with a mixture of dollar signs and question marks. What was *right*? What was the right thing to *do*?

Being in the immediate vicinity of something so valuable was *slightly* intimidating, to say the least. An awe-inspired, "Wow," escaped my lips as I turned back to study the pensive faces around me. Must be they felt it, too. Letting my eyes blur as I stared into the candle's flame, I couldn't help but think of the amazing lives we could have with our own cut of the fortune. I was not a greedy person, nor did I crave extravagance, but man! With that kind of money, the girls could go to any college they wanted — debt-free — *and* I could start those non-profits I'd always dreamed of. So many peoples' and animals' lives could be changed for the better because of that money. And all it would take was a little digging.

Suddenly, Capri jogged over to the shield, leaning close so that her head lamp shone against its marred surface. Studying it, she looked back up at the sky. "Huh," she said, her brow furrowed. She glanced over her shoulder again, then back at the relic.

Alex trotted over to her, suspicion in her voice. "Huh, what?"

Capri shook her head. "I don't think this is right," she said, looking at Cal and me.

We stood beside her, staring down at her puzzled face. "What do you mean?" I asked.

Without answering, she shone her flashlight toward the dunes, past the trail of glowing candles. Apparently, she was on to something, for she hurried forward, following the candles' path. Suddenly, she disappeared behind the tall grasses, and hollered, "Uh — Riley? Cal?" she paused. "I think you're gonna wanna see this."

Cal and I exchanged a look, hurrying forward.

Not wasting a second, Alex sped past us. We heard her gasp in surprise. "No way," she murmured.

Hot on her heels, Cal and I rounded the bend. We came to a sudden stop. Standing at the lip of the hole in the ground, we all stared in disbelief.

"Oh . . . my . . . *gosh* . . ." My voice was a whisper.

"You can say that again," Alex agreed.

Cal whistled. "Well, look-a there," he muttered, shaking his head.

There, partially covered with sand, was a large wooden chest. Surrounded by a ring of glowing candles, its wood was old and dark, the lock barely visible beneath the sand. Two shovels had been abandoned nearby, probably after the couple had knocked me out and Cal had happened upon them. They would have leaped away from the hole so he wouldn't see, which meant someone else was on lookout — no doubt the armed bandit, Jamie.

Capri broke the silence. "I was wrong — I assumed that the dings were a constellation, that *that* was the map," she explained.

I nodded in agreement; I had thought the same thing.

She continued, "But then I noticed that the shape on the shield and the one in the sky are a little different — the one on the shield is actually a bird - a nightingale, to be exact." She quickly disappeared around the grasses, leaving us to ponder what she'd just revealed.

"A nightingale?" I repeated blankly. What did a nightingale have to do with the treasure?

Cal interjected, "But nightingales haven't been seen in Two Moon Bay in nearly three hundred years . . ." His voice trailed off as a look of recognition came over his face. "Oh . . ." he said, nodding in understanding.

I gazed at him, not following. "Huh?"

Capri came forward, carrying the relic. "Here," she said, adjusting her head lamp so it pointed down toward the shield. "Look *beneath* the dings — you can see part of the etching. It looks like some sort of crest."

"Yeah, like an old family crest," Alex put in.

"Right," Capri agreed, excited that someone was following her. "But it's not. It's actually the *map* — I remember seeing it in one of the journals

Mr. Cal gave to me," she said, glancing up at him. "But I didn't think anything of it, or even remember it until now. See here?"

We nodded silently as she pointed to what appeared to be part of a full moon, partially obscured by the marks.

"That's the moon. The song in the play — and the legend on the Web — both say that Temperance and Destina disappeared under the light of a full moon. That was when they were supposed to meet Blackheart! To disappear together, when the moon was full." She gazed at us, her brown eyes twinkling beneath the light from her lamp. "And this?" she said, moving her finger. "This is the nightingale — it was mentioned in your song, Riley!

At my look of recognition, she explained, quoting the song, "'On the eve when the moon is full and bright/the nightingale sings in the lone dark night.'" Her eyes grew round as she added, "Temperance *was* the nightingale! She was the one singing along the shore, on Christmas Eve, waiting for her love."

She watched our awed faces, observing as we took it all in.

"I never would have gathered all that from the shield, Capri," I mumbled finally. How had she put this all together? It was truly overwhelming.

She shrugged like it was nothing, staring out wistfully toward the bay. The moon's double glowed on the glassy surface. "*That*," she said, pointing to the bay, "is the clincher."

I furrowed my brow.

"There's more?" Alex asked, reading my mind.

Capri nodded. "See here on the map?" She pointed to a craggy outline just below the bird, her voice filled with excitement. "That's the coastline. Where we're standing is that *exact* spot." She swiveled around, pointing up at the cliff. "Which is perfectly aligned with the coast," she clarified, looking toward the edge of the bluff.

Alex gazed wonderingly at the map. "Wow, so the marks weren't a map of the stars, after all?"

Capri shrugged. "Could be — *or*, we could have just read into it what we wanted; it's easy to think that the dings represented a constellation because lots of legends claim that pirates made maps by charting the stars in the sky." She looked at Cal and me. "But *my* guess is that the dings were really put there to distort the *actual* map. If anyone found the shield in Temperance and Destina's day, they'd overlook it, thinking it was just a piece of art. Since nightingales lived here then, it would look like any old nature etching, but *not* a treasure map."

"Hiding the map in plain sight," Alex mused. "That's brilliant."

I was just thinking that both my girls were rather brilliant - Capri especially. Leave it to her to figure out a centuries-old mystery that had eluded discovery by *thousands* of treasure-hunting adults over the years!

"Wow," Cal said, letting out a whistle. "Those're some pretty astute observations you've made there, little darlin'." He patted her shoulder approvingly.

She turned slightly to gaze up at him, beaming with pride.

Alex asked, "Ok, so that explains how Blackheart hid the treasure all those years, but . . . now what do we do?" Her eyes searched mine, then Cal's. "I mean, do we walk away, like Mr. Cal said? Or do we dig it up and claim it?"

I sighed. "Well, that's the question, isn't it?" I replied with a shake of the head. The three-hundred-*million*-dollar question. I honestly had no freakin' idea what to do. What we *should* do was call the authorities immediately and let them handle it. But staring down at the trunk that was chock full of gold, reason went right out the window. All our needs could be taken care of with just a *fraction* of what was in that chest. Heck, we could even skim off a little more to help out others, too. It would be so easy - all we had to do was finish what those kids had started, and our lives would change forever . . .

Shaking his head, Cal exhaled, breaking into my thoughts. From beneath his head lamp, I could see his eyes moving from the ancient chest to me and the girls. "Well, darlin'," he looked at Alex, answering her question that hovered in the air around us. "I think that those kids have already gone and done all the work for us, so what would be the harm in us digging it up?"

I gaped at him in surprise. "Cal!" I exclaimed, shocked. Hearing him say aloud what I'd been considering made me realize just how wrong we both were. Oh, man, I was a horrible person for even *thinking* such greedy thoughts!

Ignoring my reproach, he continued as if I hadn't spoken, "You can be sure those kids won't be tellin' the po-lice what they found, either. That puts us in the clear to claim it. We could explain to the law the truth - that the kids found the treasure and started to dig it up. We just happened along afterward, and laid claim to it all." He shrugged. "Ain't nothin' wrong with that, right? Since it's the truth and all."

"Cal . . ." I interjected, but he cut me off.

"On the other hand," he rushed on, raising a hand to stop me. "If we *don't* dig it up, y'all — if we let Blackheart Bellacriox's secret lay where it rests, those crooks are gonna hurry over here and uncover it the first chance they get." He shook his head. "And I would *hate* for that to happen. Such dishonest people layin' claim to all that money. . . ." His voice trailed off.

I nodded in agreement. "Yeah, I would hate that, too," I agreed. "*But,* is it up to us to decide who gets to claim the treasure and who doesn't?" I shrugged. "I mean — if a professional treasure hunter dug it up, would we object then?" I looked him square in the eyes. "Would we care if we thought the money would go to someone good?" I wasn't so sure that I wanted the responsibility of choosing who got what; that wasn't for me to decide. "Like you, I don't want some greedy kids who don't mind stealing from others to get all that money either, but still . . ." My voice trailed off as I eyed him through the beams of the flashlights. "If we were to claim the treasure tonight, we would essentially be stealing from those who found it in the first place — we would be no better than thieves ourselves."

Alex suddenly grabbed one of the shovels. Apparently, she'd heard enough. Before anyone could react, she dug into the sand and tossed a shovelful onto the chest.

Without a sound, Capri picked up another shovel, her face determined. Cal and I watched, silently at first, taken aback by the resolve of their unspoken decision. Watching them in the pale moonlight, through the rays of the flashlights, I thought I had never been more proud.

After a few moments, I regained my powers of speech. I glanced at Cal, shrugged my shoulders and said simply, "Well — it looks like Blackheart's secret will be kept just a little while longer."

He chuckled, then tossed me one of the shovels he'd brought. Beneath the cool moonlight, we worked quietly, as though performing some sort of ceremony. Without words, we helped the girls bury the infamous pirate's secret, to return it to the earth, to the sand and sea, and the mysterious legend of Two Moon Bay.

Finally it was done. Looking down, Cal proclaimed, "Well, I'd say that just about does it, y'all." He looked at me and the girls. "What do y'all say we grab these tools and head on back to our beds?"

"Yes!" the girls and I chorused, sounding sleepy and tired. It'd been a long night.

We trudged along, stopping intermittently as Cal and I blew out the candles that lit the path.

"You know," I said as we headed toward the beach access. "Even though it's Christmas *Day* . . ." I continued, glancing first at Capri, then Alex. Even though they were older, they were still kids — and it was Christmas, after all. ". . . It's still technically the *night* before Christmas - since it's the middle of the night and all . . ."

Alex gave me a weary look. *Really*? I could just hear her thinking. Wow, she really *was* tired, I realized, hoping at least Capri would share my enthusiasm.

"Anywho," I continued, ruffling Capri's hair. She looked at me and smiled. "We need to get to bed as soon as we get home so that Santa can stop at our house!"

My younger daughter smiled up at me in that grown-up way of hers. "Riley," she said, clasping my hand. "He's already stopped at our house."

Not sure what she meant by that, my smile got all wobbly. What did *that* mean? Had someone broken into our house and left presents beneath the tree while I was skulking along the beach in the dark of night with Cal? Did we have an *actual* Secret Santa who'd gifted us with his generosity? Not bloody likely! "Huh?" I asked.

Alex answered with an exasperated sigh and an eye roll. "Uh — Riley? All those presents you stashed for us in the garage?"

My face fell. They *knew*!

"They're wrapped and under the tree."

What the . . .? I wondered, then shot a look at Cal. So much for my secret hiding place!

Seeing how my famous golfer friend's posture suddenly stiffened, I realized what must have happened.

But *how* he had known about the gifts — and where I hid the key — were questions I would *love* to know the answer to. I figured I'd cast a line and see what I might catch. "Say, Cal?" I asked, super cool and casual. "You don't happen to know anything about that, do you?"

At his innocent expression, I explained, "You know - how my secret stash of gifts for the girls *mysteriously* wandered out of their hiding place, and came to be wrapped and under the tree?"

He shook his head, but I could see the twinkle in his eyes. "Uh, no, ma'am," he answered, his eyes darting over to mine for just a second. Beneath the light from his lamp, I saw *everything* I needed to know. "Don't know nothin' 'bout that."

I nodded, feigning like I believed him. "Right, yeah. Course you don't. Well," I said, playing along. "You wouldn't happen to have any plans for Christmas dinner now, would you?"

He chuckled. "Well, darlin', my mama always has us a Christmas lunch, which we call 'dinner,'" he teased. "But if you mean 'supper,' why no, I got no plans for Christmas supper." By now we'd turned off our lights, but I swear I saw him wink at me through the darkness.

I laughed, appreciating his Southern semantics. "Well, I *did* mean 'supper,' actually, so that's perfect — why don't you join us around five?"

"Well, that'd be real nice, darlin'," Cal answered, pleased. "It would be my pleasure."

I nodded, smiling, feeling a sense of peace. Tired beyond belief, but peaceful. I couldn't wait to crawl into my gazillion-count sheets and comfy bed.

Lapsing into a comfortable silence, we strolled along, allowing the moon to light our way. Finally, we mounted the steps to the beach access. Capri and Alex scurried ahead, anxious to get home, their shovels clanging against the wooden slats of the walkway.

I gestured to the girls, grinning, and said to Cal, "I know a couple of elves who sure will *love* to spend Christmas with their favorite Santa. I'm really glad you'll be joining us for our first Christmas in Two Moon Bay, Cal."

Reaching the truck, the girls promptly dropped their shovels to the ground, groaning with relief. As Alex stretched her muscles, Capri ran over to Cal, wrapping her arms around him. "I'm glad you're having Christmas dinner with us, too, Cal," she told him, gazing up at him. "And I'm glad we buried the treasure — it was the right thing to do."

He chortled, hugging her back. "Well, I'm pleased as punch to be part of y'all's first Christmas here, little darlin'," he assured her, patting her back. "And I do believe you're right — we did the right thing with that treasure."

Alex sauntered over, looking sleepy, but I could see the smile on her face. She gave Cal and me a hug. "I agree — now Blackheart's secret will *stay* a secret forever — I hope," she added pensively.

Listening to the girls, I beamed with pride. They sure were some pretty amazing kids, I told myself, not for the first time. Bending to toss their shovels into the back of Cal's snazzy crew-cab truck, I silently agreed that we had made the right decision. One I could definitely live with.

Coming over to my side, Cal took off his head lamp and set it inside the bed. He clicked the locks on his key fob, saying to the girls, "Little darlins? What do you say we all hop in Santa's sleigh?" He opened the back passenger door, gesturing like a valet. "As you can see, there's plenty of room for my little elves."

"Oooh," Capri murmured, peering inside. "It's nice!"

Alex accepted his hand and hopped inside. "It sure is," she remarked.

"Well, thank you," Cal said, helping Capri inside. His truck was so tall even the sideboard was a stretch for her. "I do love my truck."

I chuckled, loading more of our gear in the back. "I wouldn't have taken you for a truck person, Cal, but I must say — this suits you." I nodded appreciatively at the smooth black Cadillac Escalade beast of a truck. It was rugged yet fancy. Just like Cal.

He smirked. "Well, darlin', I'll take that as a compliment." As we tossed the last of our load into the back, he joked, "Lord knows I had to have somethin' big enough to hold all of our treasure-buryin' materials — all these darned shovels!"

We laughed, clambering inside to join the girls. Although we were worn out from the emotional and physical stress of the last few hours, Cal cranked up the volume as "Jingle Bell Rock" came on the radio. Singing at the top of our lungs, we cruised along Beach Boulevard with the windows down, bellowing Christmas cheer into the night.

As he let us off in the driveway, the girls whispered conspiratorially to one another. Then, as he circled around toward the road, they called out to him, "Ho, ho, ho — Merry Christmas, Santa Cal!"

Seeing his look of surprise, they dissolved into giggles.

Without missing a beat, Cal leaned out the window and boomed, "Merry Christmas to y'all, and to y'all, a good night!"

13

She Smiles

Christmas morning flew by in a whirlwind of presents, joy, and tissue paper.

And more red tartan plaid than I remembered seeing in the entire movie of *Braveheart*.

Before you knew it, it was after noon. The girls and I took our first-ever — and first *annual*, according to Capri — Christmas pictures on the beach. Decked out, of course, in red plaid, as we did every year. Maybe next year we could do something more subtle — less-*overtly* Christmasy. I would have to broach that suggestion delicately, I knew, and only when armed with the girls' favorite chocolate truffles. They were kind of obsessed with plaid, especially at the holidays, so the truffles would help to smooth things over — I hoped.

Raegan, the poor dog, was cajoled by his sisters, in their usual Christmas cheer, to wear the red and green antler ears, the bane of his existence. It had started out, innocently enough, as a simple school project a few years back. Alex had sewn the ears for Home Ec, coincidentally, around Christmas-time. The ears had turned out pretty well, which convinced her that she was an *amazing* seamstress, who was obviously destined to be a famous clothing designer.

And the idea just sort of steam-rolled from there. Capri oohed and aahed over the ears, holding them atop her head, and fawning over how cute they would be on a headband. Also innocent enough. But then, *somehow*, the project had morphed into being the perfect gift for Raegan - *just* for Raegan, Capri had decreed, his special Christmas antler ears. I didn't have the heart to tell her that *no one* in their right mind would want to wear the ears, especially not a dog.

The worst of it, though, was the ears' most recent incarnation, which involved the ultimate auditory symbol of Christmas, according to Alex — bells. Of course — it made *perfect* sense, she insisted, that *no* dog's red and green and plaid antler ears would be complete without jingle bells. We'd gone through at least two full cartridges of hot glue to affix those darned bells, which meant *several* emergency trips through the snow and ice to Alex's second-favorite place in the entire world, Hobby Lobby.

So after two *more* glue sticks and way too many more jingle bells, my crafts-loving daughters had deemed the ears complete. Fast-forward to this Christmas. As much as Raegan probably *hoped* the ears had gotten lost in the move, they somehow made their way to Florida, and onto his pretty red head.

Poor Rae-Rae endured Christmas presents *and* pictures in those blasted ears, jingling all over the house and yard. I felt guilty, listening to him jangling through the kitchen, thinking that I should have made those ears go bye-bye — I could so easily have blamed their unfortunate disappearance on the move. But I'm pretty sure one of the girls had brought them along for the ride in their suitcase.

Finally, as the afternoon rolled into evening, I couldn't take it anymore. Hearing him dashing down the hall after Capri that afternoon, ringing all the way, I made up my mind to relieve the poor Golden of his Christmas ears. As my buttery homemade rolls came out of the oven and the aromas of our feast signaled that it was time to eat, I called him into the kitchen and slipped the antlers off when the girls weren't looking. I could see the relief in his eyes.

Rubbing his head in apology, I handed him a roll. "Here ya go, buddy," I told him. "It'll be our little secret."

As he trotted silently to the back veranda, I sensed his appreciation. Standing in the threshold, he looked back at me with gratitude in his amber eyes, then slipped through the door to enjoy his buttery treat in peace.

After that, it was time to eat! With the dogs napping on their beds after being served their very own portions of Christmas ham, it was time for the hungry humans to chow down. And that we did!

Cal and Dixie joined us for the meal, which was full of laughter and fun and a couple decanters of wine for the adults. Brooks was set to arrive soon - he and the girls had had an early dinner at the inn with his family. After that, his girls were heading over to the town square to meet up with their friends. Alex and Capri had been invited to join them, and were just itching to get there for what was apparently Two Moon Bay's social event of the season, the Blessings and Best Wishes festival.

Fortunately, this year, Christmas supper had no culinary disasters; the turkey cooked evenly to a golden brown, the girls' eggplant was, according to them, "like, really good!,"' and the creamed spinach was delightfully tasty. Everything else was pretty darned yummy, too, if I did say so myself. My double-dark chocolate layer cake was sinfully delicious, but even better were the little butter cookies Cal had brought from Abby's store. And Dixie's ambrosia — "Mama's secret recipe," made me think I'd died and gone to heaven. The only bad thing was that I ate so much dessert — so much *everything*, really, that I was worried I'd have to be transported by wheelbarrow into the kitchen to do the dishes. But, somehow, I was able to roll myself away from the table on my own.

With the fireplace roaring in the great room (think Capri), and Christmas tunes underlying the comfortable banter of my friends (courtesy of DJ Alex), I was thinking what a remarkable Christmas this was turning out to be. With the dishes put away, I was staring out the window toward the ocean, counting my blessings and feeling incredibly sated when the high I'd been on from all the butter and fat began to wane. Call it my overly-active imagination, but I could actually *feel* my arteries beginning to harden and my waistline expanding when the guilt set in. Tomorrow, I would have to pay for my gastronomic sins. I foresaw intervals and sprints and other torturous forms of exercise-atonement. It would not be pretty.

With more food left over than I knew what to do with, I crammed as much as possible into containers for my guests. There were plenty of meatless vestiges for the girls to eat tomorrow, and, unfortunately for my thighs, there were *plenty* of desserts. Although I felt a little guilty for giving away all but two pieces of each dessert, I rationalized that the girls really weren't that big on sweets anyway; they were more salty-and-savory gals. That meant that *I* would end up finishing *their* desserts, since I hated to see good food go to waste, and the vicious cycle would continue. As I sealed up the little plastic bags of temptation, I envisioned again those anguishing workouts. And a whole lot of kale.

The clicking, rhythmic sound of Rae-Rae's toenails on the hardwood startled me out of my thoughts. "Time for a bathroom break, guys?" I asked him and the lab, as she followed my boy into the room. Wagging her blonde tail in answer, Ruby gazed up at me with her warm loving eyes. "You are just the sweetest girl, aren't you, Rubes?" I said, indulging her with a little chin rub.

She was a keeper, that one, I realized, switching on the patio lights for them. And what a great companion for Rae-Rea, I observed, watching as she and Raegan bounded happily through the backyard, noses to the ground. Smiling contentedly, pleased that Raegan had a newfound friend, I checked on the pups. Their little rollie-pollie bodies looked plump and full as they snoozed together, cuddled up for warmth and security.

Assured that everyone was happy and accounted for, a sudden roar of laughter from the other room caught my attention. The others were well into a rousing game of *Taboo*. I strolled over to the table as Capri was attempting to give clues to her partner and new best friend, Cal.

"It's um, something we read about — and found — on the be — oh, wait, I can't say that word. And it, um, is really *valuable* . . ." she stammered, as Cal cried out, "Treasure! Buried treasure!"

Capri squealed with delight, leaping from the table. "Yes, *yes*! It *is* buried treasure!" she cried, throwing her arms around his neck. "You got it!" She was equal parts excited and surprised, I think, because she'd never *actually* given a clue that someone could guess, bless her heart. It was a big moment.

Cal laughed heartily. "Well, now, darlin', those were some good clues you were givin' me," he said, his eyes twinkling. "You made it easy for me to guess."

I smiled at him, thinking what a great guy Cal had turned out to be. Anyone who played *Taboo* with my daughter quickly realized that what she lacked in clue-giving abilities, she made up for in enthusiasm. Capri usually spent most of the time stammering over words that she "couldn't say," and inevitably ended up uttering the ones that would disqualify her team. Alex just *lived* for those moments. She'd click the buzzer repeatedly in her sister's face, declaring, "She said it! That's on the card — she's out!" with triumphant malignity.

As Capri continued to celebrate, she impetuously broke into some sort of crazy dance. We all burst into laughter as she suddenly became aware that we were staring at her with surprised fascination on our faces. She dissolved into giggles, amused by the fact that we were so intrigued by her.

Dixie took a sip of her wine, setting the glass daintily back on the table. She looked at me with curiosity in her gaze as she remarked casually, "Speakin' of buried treasure, sug, I heard y'all had quite an adventure last night."

"Uh," I started, a little surprised at first that Cal had told her of our 'secret.' But then, it quickly occurred to me that that was silly - they were a couple now, after all.

Before I had a chance to finish my response, Capri eagerly cut in, "That's right! We saw the treasure!" she enthused. "Well, not exactly the *treasure*, but the treasure *chest*! The kids who stole the shield from the inn dug it up. We buried it, though." She dropped her voice, leaning forward. "It's our secret. Like Mr. Cal said, 'some secrets are better left untold.'" She nodded wisely.

Dixie watched her with avid interest. "Well, I do believe you're right, there, sug," she agreed. "*And*, I think that is very wise — and admirable." She looked meaningfully at my daughter. "Don't worry - I won't tell a soul. I'll keep your secret, too."

The moment was interrupted by the sound of Raegan and Ruby tearing in through the open veranda, past the table, all the way to the front door.

Back from his bathroom break, my golden resumed his self-appointed role of butler and careened in happy, barking chaos toward the door. His protégé, Ruby, was hot on his heels.

Capri leaped from the table. "Mr. Brooks! Mr. Brooks!" she called out in greeting.

As Raegan accosted the entrance with his feet, followed by a generous licking of the glass, Ruby stood to the side, barking quietly, but clearly watching Raegan.

"Oh, Lord," I said to Cal and Dixie, "now there are two of them."

Cal chuckled in acknowledgement, as Capri slid in sock feet against the door. "Merry Christmas, Mr. Brooks!" she exclaimed, ushering him in.

Brooks beamed as he entered, returning Capri's greeting and waving to us all. His eyes held mine for a moment, and I felt a little shiver of delight. "Merry Christmas, Capri — and everyone!" he called, stopping at the entry bench to set down his keys and red scarf. It killed me that people wore scarves here, since it was, eternally, it seemed, eighty degrees, but I appreciated his fashion sentiment. I'm sure that once I was acclimated, I'd be wearing scarves, too.

I stood up to greet our newcomer. As we hugged hello, I felt tingly all over. "Merry Christmas," I said quietly in his ear, placing a kiss on his cheek. "Thank you for coming."

He grinned, those blue eyes holding me there for one long, heart-stopping instant. "Wouldn't miss it," he said. "There's nobody I'd rather spend Christmas with than you," he whispered. Then, as I was recovering from the mild heart attack his words had induced, he continued in a louder voice so everyone could hear, "These are for y'all; Mama's famous collard greens and my sister's peanut butter pie. Both are equally delicious, and fabulously unhealthy." He grinned. "And some home-made cookies and pie from yours truly."

As I set his mom and sister's dishes on the table, Capri and Alex relieved him of his desserts. "Wow, that's terrific," I told him. "Thank you so much. And, please thank your mother and sister for me."

He smiled, a sparkle in his eye. "Well, I thought maybe *you* could thank them — tonight — at the park." He watched my face, his gaze intense. I almost fell over, getting lost in the blue. "I mean," he added, misreading my reaction. "If you want to."

"I'd love to," I assured him, squeezing his hand.

Alex, digging into the box of cookies, rolled her eyes. "Ew, you guys — get a room."

Repressing a smirk, I slung an arm around her shoulders as she attempted to flee the table with her napkin of cookies. "Oh, I'm sorry," I said teasingly. "Are we making you *uncomfortable*?"

She smiled, giggling, as she wrestled away mid-bite. "Whatever," she declared dismissively, realizing she'd smiled — and giggled — in front of a parental unit *and* several other adults. That was in clear violation of teenage doctrine everywhere. She studied us warily, chewing. "I'm going to go video chat with Sami," she finally said in her indifferent tone, referring to one of her BFFs from home.

"Alright, hon," I told her, thinking that she was back to her normal too-cool-to-care self. Everything was right once again in the world. "Tell her to say 'hi' to her mom for me."

"Whatever," she replied from the entryway, not bothering to look over at me. I could *hear* the eye-roll in her voice.

As Alex flitted down the hall toward her bedroom, Capri sliced herself a generous piece of peanut butter pie. Maybe I'd been wrong about the girls and sweets, I thought shamefully, wondering if I could discreetly remove some of Cal and Dixie's desserts to add to the girls' stash. "Mmm, this looks so good, Mr. Brooks," Capri told him, nibbling a morsel from her fingertip as she closed the lid. Clasping her plate, she announced, "I'm going to go read and play with the puppies," she told us, heading into the great room.

"Ok," I answered. "But we'll leave in about half an hour." Bébé had given me strict instructions to get to the park before seven-thirty. Apparently, the festival officially kicked off then. I was about to ask Brooks what exactly the festival included – Bébé had been vague, declining to explain, but she'd made it clear that my presence was absolutely vital – when my phone began ringing from its place on the buffet. Hoping it was Rainie, I ran over to it. "Oh!" I exclaimed. "It's Britlee. Excuse me, everyone," I said. "I've got to take this."

Much to my relief, Brit and I had made up since the last time we'd talked; I just hated when things weren't right between us. I was just *dying* to tell her all about last night's adventure, but I kind of wanted to tell her in person. Grabbing the phone, I patted Raegan's head as I moved toward the veranda. "Hey, Brit!" I greeted her. "Merry Christmas!" I was so looking forward to talking to her, I felt almost giddy as I stared expectantly into the phone.

But instead of seeing my bestie's smiling face, Brit was turned away from the phone, yelling over her shoulder. "Caleb! I said get your behind over here and clear this table!" She shook her head in exasperation. Then, realizing I'd answered, Brit looked into the phone and beamed, her expression completely changing. "Well, hey, there, Riley *E*-lizabeth Larkin!" she cried. "Merry Christmas!"

I laughed, so happy to see her and hear her voice – even if she was yelling at her son. "Merry Christmas!" I replied, stepping onto the pool deck. The water glowed greenly-blue, casting the patio in an otherworldly hue. "How was your day?"

We traded stories, Brit regaling me with her always-entertaining recounting of her children's exploits, and me sharing the drama of the past few days with the stealing of the shield, the successful play, and catching the criminals. As much as I hated to do it, I felt it best to leave out the part about the re-burying of the treasure and my encounter with Temperance. I would save that for when we saw each other in person.

Britlee's voice grew indignant as she changed the subject. "Now, Riley *E*-lizabeth Larkin," she began, then paused, making sure I was paying attention. I straightened, feeling a lecture coming on. "I'm comin' to see you the last week of January." She gave me a peevish look. "Even though I *haven't* been invited." She folded her arms crossly.

Temporarily ignoring her attempt at self-pity, I gushed, "The last week of January! Brit, you're coming for my birthday?" My eyes grew misty. "You remembered."

She rolled her eyes, waving a Christmas-red set of fingernails at me. "Aw, honey, of course I remembered — I know you weren't wantin' to spend your fortieth birthday alone. And I'm not gonna let you." Her face softened into a smile. Then, remembering her earlier attempts to get attention, she reiterated, "*Even though* I haven't been formally invited, I thought I'd be a good friend and invite myself."

I laughed out loud. She really was too funny. "Brit," I said gently, indulging her mood. "If you remember, I gave you a *standing* 'you-are-welcome-at-any-time' invitation. *Any time*," I clarified. Then, awash with happiness, I declared, "Oh, I just can't *wait* to see you! I have so much to tell you," I raved. Then, realizing I'd opened a potential can of worms, I stopped, racking my brain for a cover story.

But Britlee smelled a rat. I swear she had some sort of sixth sense when it came to me and gossip. She could sniff out the juicy stuff like a bloodhound. "Oh? Like what?" Her eyes narrowed, probing into my soul. "What is it, Riley? Are you engaged? In a relationship? Did you get a job? Finish your book? What *is* it?" she cried, her voice becoming more impatient with each question.

Chuckling, I shook my head. "No — and yes — and no — and no." I smiled at her. "It's just," I began, then thought of a viable diversion that was actually true. "That's the weekend Reed's having his party upstate. You can be my date." Every year my foster-brother held a three-day affair at his lavish country manor in Ocala. It was a Scottish paradise that resembled an old castle, complete with a moat. Long story. Basically, my foster-brother celebrated his heritage like no other.

Rather than being thrilled, as I'd expected her to be, Brit's face was what you would call less-than enthused. She wrinkled her nose. "Isn't that the thing he does every year at Valentine's Day? When people shoot

Skeets and play polo and solve a murder mystery like a real-life, week-end-long game of *Clue*?"

I nodded enthusiastically. I personally *loved* that weekend, looked forward to it every year. "Yeah! That's the one. This year his wife insisted they do something different for Valentine's Day, though — I think they're going to Hawaii."

She scoffed. "Well, I don't blame her one bit. I'd be about tired of all that shootin' and horse-ridin' and skulkin' around a castle accusin' people of doin' somethin' they may or may not have done." She rolled her eyes. "I'd be about crazy from all that nonsense."

My face fell. "So you don't want to go?" I asked, hurt.

Her face brightened. "Oh, no, honey, I'm goin'," she assured me. "I'll solve the *fool* out of that game!"

I burst out laughing. Not minding that my friend had reduced Reed's painstakingly- planned weekend of fun into a few random acts of shooting, mystery-solving, and horseback-riding, I couldn't help but appreciate her humor.

Just then, Capri's voice interrupted our conversation. She burst through the veranda door, waving a book in the air. "Riley, come quick!" she exclaimed, scurrying onto the patio. "We were *wrong*! You've got to see this!"

Covering the phone, I shot her a look. "Capri, I'm on the phone," I said firmly. "I'll be with you in just a few minutes."

Britlee broke in, "That's ok, honey, I've got to get goin' myself," she told me. "I just wanted to call and wish you and the girls a Merry Christmas!" She raised her voice so Capri could hear. "I'll see you soon. And don't go thinkin' you're turnin' forty without me, honey! Love you, bah!" Making a kissing face, Britlee signed off.

Before I could reprimand her, Capri accosted me, her eyes alight. "I'm sorry for interrupting you, Riley, it's just . . ." She handed me the book she'd been brandishing like a mad woman. "We got it wrong."

I furrowed my brow. "Capri, what are you talking about, sweetie?" I asked gently. I had absolutely no idea what we could possibly have gotten wrong.

"The *treasure*," she replied, slightly impatient. "That chest we found
. . ." She paused, looking over her shoulder as Cal, Dixie, Brooks, and
Alex came outside, curious. I guess they'd heard her, too. "It was a *fake*.
A decoy. Temperance wrote about it in her journal."

I looked incredulously from Capri to Brooks, Cal, and Dixie, and
realized in a flash that they *knew*. I'd like to say that the Two Moon Bay
residents looked surprised, but they didn't. In fact, the only people who
appeared to be shocked were the girls and me. I gaped at my friends for
a moment, feeling somehow betrayed. But, then, I recognized just as
quickly that this was one of those secrets Cal Senior had been talking
about; if it isn't *your* secret, it isn't yours to tell. Now I got it. Sort of.

Cal explained patiently, "We didn't mean to *not* tell you, darlin'."
He searched my eyes. "We just needed you to figure it out on your own.
You — and the girls . . ." His voice faltered as he looked from me to Capri
and Alex, ". . . are a part of us now. This is our legend. *Our* secret."

I watched him, saw his mouth move, heard his words. They just
weren't getting through, though. Feeling overwhelmed, I shook my
head. "I've got to sit down," I murmured, throwing myself into a nearby
lounger.

Capri stepped toward me, and pointed to a page. "This explains it,"
she informed me, looking over her shoulder at Cal. "Blackheart's crew
sailed into the Bay that night to pick up the girls; he and Temperance
were planning to elope, and Destina was escaping her father and the
marriage he'd arranged for her."

Dixie piped up, "That's right, sug; their meetin' was no chance
encounter, as the Internet will have you believe. Temperance and
Blackheart had planned their meetin', had *planned* their getaway. They
even provided for the future by buryin' the real treasure — the ones from
both the *Doncella* and the *Bella Lucia* — in entirely different places on the
Bay."

I buried my face in my hands. This was too much.

Capri added, "Temperance wrote in her journal that they would return to the town at a later date to claim their treasures. But not even
Blackheart's crew knew where they were buried. Only the couple did."

Alex moved to the foot of my lounger. "You mean the chest we found had nothing in it? The *real* fortune — from two of the most valuable treasures we know of — are *both* buried somewhere else?"

Brooks stepped in. "You got it. Although Blackheart Bellacroix was known for keeping meticulous records of his ship's manifests, there's one thing he *didn't* write down. And Temperance, his love, didn't betray that one secret either, though her diary reveals that she knew where the treasures were buried."

I groaned, raising my head. "Ok," I said wearily. "I'll play. Then how do you know the 'real treasures,'" I said, using air quotes, "actually exist? And that they're *actually* buried somewhere in Two Moon Bay?"

Cal kneeled down before me. His blue eyes were twinkly and kind as he answered, "Because, darlin', Temperance and Blackheart both revealed half of the coordinates in their journals. The other half . . ." his voice trailed off as he shrugged. "The other half, only *they* knew. Their secret died with them."

I stared at him. "*Coordinates*?" I repeated, shaking my head. "Could this darned legend get any *more* complicated?" I muttered. This was way more than I'd bargained for. The whole thing was proving to be more than a *little* bit difficult to believe.

Cal nodded, easing the journal from my hands. Flipping some pages, he pointed. "See here? This is a silver candlestick, part of a pair. Inscribed on the bottom are the latitudinal coordinates where the treasure is buried. Temperance explained in her diary that the longitudinal ones were only known by her and her lover. She never even told her sister. Apparently that was a major sore spot between the two."

I closed my eyes, groaning. Oh, God, there was more. "Are you *kidding* me?" I asked Cal, holding his gaze. "I hate to ask, but what sister?" I glanced down at my watch, thinking that at this rate, the legend might not end until well after the festival was over.

Capri eagerly answered, "That's the best part, Riley - Temperance and Destina were *sisters!*" She watched my face as the news sunk in. "Destina's father was in love with Temperance's mother — who was one of their servants. He was deeply religious, and repented of his sins after his wife's maidservant became pregnant with Temperance."

"And," Dixie added, "to atone for his weakness, he named his baby 'Temperance' as a reminder to never again give in to his emotions. Although Temperance was raised by the Biscaynes to avoid scandal, Dario kept his daughters close by his side — and to one another. He vowed that no man would ever hurt them the way he had hurt his one true love. . . ." her voice faded as she lost herself in the romantic — and depressing — story.

Thankfully, no one said anything for a moment. That gave me a chance to absorb the crazy, convoluted tale. "Well," I finally said, "I guess it's true what they say: sometimes the truth really is better than fiction." I chuckled, appreciating it all. "Wow. It's like an eighteenth-century soap opera."

Cal's smile was knowing as he agreed, "Well, darlin' — I betchya didn't count on bein' part of a two-hundred-seventy-year-old pirate legend/ love story when you found this house on the Internet, now, didya?" he chuckled.

Dixie suddenly squealed in astonishment. "Oh, hey, y'all — we'd better get goin' — it's almost seven o'clock!" She looked at her delicate gold watch before grabbing Cal's hand. "We don't want to miss the festival!"

As the couple scurried back into the house, Capri retrieved Temperance's journal from my hands. Alex hopped up, thumbs whirring away on her phone. My teen was presumably ready to meet her friends. I marveled at how quickly they all leaped into the night's next activity. I was a little slower to react — I guess maybe it took me longer to process the intricacies of the legend than it did the others.

"Come on, Alex," Capri urged her sister. "We need to get the flyers before we go!" she proclaimed, hurrying inside.

Alex trailed after her, texting all the way.

"Oh, man - the flyers," I repeated, remembering with a flash that time was running out for me and the girls. I watched as everyone fled the pool area, wishing I could turn back time. Once New Year's came, everything would quickly change.

Brooks smiled down at me, offering his hand. "Penny for your thoughts?" he asked.

I placed my hand in his, wondering where to begin. "Oh, it's just," I started, pausing. "We decided to put up signs around town to see if Ruby belongs to anyone. The girls are hoping she's a stray, so they can keep her. It's gonna be hard enough to give away the pups in a few weeks, so we're hoping that at least Ruby can stay." My voice dropped off.

Though I hated to think about it, I figured that in less time than that, the girls would have to go back to North Carolina. As much as I wanted them to stay, they had lives there — along with friends and school. Going home was inevitable for them. And saying goodbye — again — was going to be even harder this time than it was before. Plus, there was the little matter of their parents. I would have to talk to them both soon, but had a feeling they wouldn't be as anxious for their daughters to return as I was to have them stay.

I searched Brooks' eyes, fumbling for the words. His gaze was kind as he smiled down at me, concern hiding behind his eyes. Somehow I figured he kind of knew without me saying anything. And that felt like enough.

Getting to my feet, I decided it was time to stop hiding behind my emotions. And uncertainty. "The truth is, Brooks . . ." I started, but then, gazing around at the ocean, and the backyard that suddenly looked like a *home*, like a real family lived there, I had to choke back sudden tears.

As the white-tipped waves shone in the gentle moonlight, I could have sworn that somewhere, on the distant breeze, I heard something. A sweet sad song, it sounded like, one that was familiar and true. A song of hope and longing — the song of a friend.

Meeting Brooks' eyes once more, I swayed on my feet, lost in the blue. "I'm just thinking," I told him firmly, my voice clear despite my tears, "that this is one Christmas I'm never going to forget."

Brooks squeezed my hands in response, saying everything that needed to be said without speaking a word. We walked toward the porch, lost in a comfortable silence.

As we mounted the steps, our hands clasped so it was impossible to tell one from the other, I was almost certain that as I closed the door and gazed back to the shore, I glimpsed the ethereal form of a dark-haired girl in a shimmery gown, gazing calmly back at me.

But this time, I could see her smiling.

If you enjoyed this book, please watch for the second installment in the *Two Moon Bay Mystery* series, *Chaos at Castle Buchanan*. Please leave your ratings online, and write me at alyssajohnsonauthor@gmail.com. I love to hear from you!

Acknowledgements

—◦—

- Rich McBride — thank you for being a trusted friend and first reader. I appreciate your input — and penchant for all things grammar!

- Rebecca Sue — I'm grateful for your inspiration, support, and friendship. Even if you are my much younger and better-looking sister!

- Deborah Thomas — the queen of all things witty and fun. I appreciate your willingness to edit with the eye of a professional and the heart of a friend.

- Jessica Cleland — thank you for another amazing cover!

- Mom and Dad — so many drafts, so many ideas, and you were always willing to listen. Thank you for all your support!

- Frankie — My most honest and supportive critic. I love you, babe.

- Readers — thank you for your support. Please connect with me on the Web; I love hearing your feedback, and appreciate your reviews!

Author Biography

 Alyssa Johnson is a lover of literature and enjoys sharing her favorite authors with her students. Johnson graduated from Clarkson University and now teaches English at a college near Myrtle Beach, South Carolina. When she isn't teaching, reading, or writing her charming romantic mysteries, Johnson is enjoying the beautiful vistas of North and South Carolina.

Johnson is the proud stepmom of six wonderful children, caretaker of three adorable rescue dogs, and wife of the love of her life, Frankie.

Made in the USA
Columbia, SC
10 November 2022

70848171R10136